THE HOME GAME

Martha Bolton

FaithHappenings Publishers

FaithHappenings Publishers
7061 S. University Blvd., Suite 307
Centennial, CO 80122

Cover Design ©2016 Curt Diepenhors
Book Layout ©2013 BookDesignTemplates.com

The Home Game / Martha Bolton. -- 1st ed.
ISBN (Softcover) 978-1-941555-11-8
This book was printed in the United States of America.

To order additional copies of this book, contact:
info@faithhappenings.com

FaithHappenings Publishers,
a division of FaithHappenings.com

ENDORSEMENTS

"A heartwarming depiction of Amish life, a woman's love for her man, and a man's love of baseball. Bolton hits it way out of the park!" —Beverly Lewis, author of *The Shunning*

"Love baseball? Love a good father-son story? Then you're going to love this fun and powerful novel by my good friend, Martha Bolton. After all, if an Amish man can run for president (as he did in her first novel, *Josiah for President*), then why can't one take on the professional sports world? *The Home Game* — it's got my vote!" —Mike Huckabee, Governor of Arkansas, 1996-2007, Presidential Candidate, Fox News Host

"My life was consumed by baseball. I played the game and then used that knowledge to parlay it into a business. I was surrounded by some of the greats of the game, and yet found I knew very little about the Amish connection to baseball until I met Martha Bolton and her book *The Home Game*. Learn what I learned." —Bill Hemrick, Co-Founder of Upper Deck Baseball Cards

"Twin boys in Martha Bolton's *The Home Game* grew up in the same Amish family, the same community, but are dramatically different. John loves farming, Levi loves baseball. John loves rules, Levi loves bending them. Bitter enemies, they go their separate ways and face temptations that cause them both to lose everything they once held dear. Full of amusing, poignant moments, *The Home Game* is a delightful Amish-style riff on the story of the Prodigal Son." —Suzanne Woods Fisher, bestselling author of *Anna's Crossing*

"With *The Home Game,* Martha returns to a rural Amish setting, and this time to a young Amish man's big dreams . . . It's all here; romance, intrigue, wonderful characters, and a spiritual underpinning that reflects not only true values and relationships, but the universal need to dream, and at times, dream really big! *The Home Game* is a thoroughly enjoyable read."
—Paul Miller

"Martha is an acclaimed comedy writer and author. However, her new venture of writing novels may be some of her best work. In my opinion, she is in the league of my favorite authors, John Grisham, and Clive Cussler." —Paul Bane, former senior pastor, New Hope Community Church, Brentwood, TN

"Martha Bolton keeps turning out creative, inspiring, entertaining, funny works of all sorts—scripts, books, plays. Here's her latest novel, *The Home Game.* I rest my case." —Gene Perret, four-time Emmy-award winning comedy writer and author

"Anything Martha Bolton writes, I read. Not just because she's hilarious, but because she spins a great yarn that takes me to better places than I'd hoped to visit, places that nourish my soul. You'll love this book. I sprained my wrist turning pages."
—Phil Callaway, best-selling author of *Laughing Matters* and host of Laugh Again radio.

"*The Home Game* is not only an excellent present-day telling of the Prodigal Son, but it is also a poignant love story with a nice folksy feel and a delightful touch of humor. If you enjoy Amish novels, romance, baseball, or just an occasional funny nugget tossed into the mix, you're going to love *The Home Game.*"
—Kathi Macias best-selling author of *Red Ink*

This book is dedicated to:

Mel and June Riegsecker
who started it all.

And to:
. . . anyone who has ever had a dream and swung for the
fences,
. . . who has found the courage to get back up after being
called out,
. . . and to all who opened their arms and welcomed them
home.

CHAPTER ONE

A fire was burning in Sugar Creek, Ohio. Not all of the flames were the visible kind, but they were growing in intensity and starting to spread. Before it was over they would have consumed, at least in the lives of those in our story, whatever was dried up, combustible, and in belated need of pruning and watering, leaving behind fields and relationships ready for new growth and hope.

On this particular day, the more noticeable smoke was seen around the business area. It would have been suspicious to anyone of a suspicious bent. The official word, however, according to the English newspapers, was that it had started from a stray spark from the blacksmith's shop. But there hadn't been a lick of wind that day, and everyone in this peaceful Amish community would vouch for Charley Miller. Charley was a blacksmith of the responsible sort, making sure whatever sparks flew off his anvil didn't drift any farther than he could account for.

No, the local Amish *knew* the origin of this blaze. The blame had to be laid at the doorstep of only one person. It had happened too many times before. These flames had to have been caused by the attractive but culinary-challenged Miss Hannah Weaver.

Hannah hadn't set the fire on purpose, of course. Most likely it had erupted naturally from the process of making donuts or deep-fried pies, which she sold—or tried to sell—at the Battered Donut Bakery and Café at the edge of town. Since the Battered Donut also happened to be downwind from Charley's blacksmith shop, one could understand the confusion.

But the Sugar Creek Amish community knew.

The Battered Donut Bakery and Café was a favorite gathering place for those in Sugar Creek and outlying areas, in spite of Hannah's regular kitchen mishaps. The Amish are a forgiving people, and more importantly, they knew enough to ask ahead of time which delicacies had been baked by Hannah and which had been baked by her sister, Ruth.

Hannah knew all too well that cooking and baking weren't her gifts, so there was no need in pretending otherwise. The poor girl kept trying, though, and this longsuffering community nobly looked the other way, which wasn't always easy to do with clouds of smoke billowing into the sky above the bakery, sometimes confusing poor Daniel Yoder, the local weather expert. More than once Daniel had mistaken the smoke from Hannah's deep-fried pies for an F-1 tornado fixing to bear down on their small community.

According to Hannah parents, Eli and Eunice Weaver, who owned the bakery, Hannah's problem was that she was too easily distracted. Once her mind drifted off, she tended to fry her deep-fried pies a little deeper than most, incinerating the little puff pastries like farm trash on a hot summer day.

Hannah often wondered if her great-great-grandparents had thought about the irony that the name they'd given their bakery would have one day. But the Battered Donut had been in business since 1895, long before Hannah was even born. How could they have known how fitting it would be over a hundred years later when their great-great-granddaughter worked there? Hannah usually laughed about it all, though.

"Oh, I batter 'em all right," Hannah would often say, only to be rebuffed by her sister.

"Coincidence, that's all it is," Ruth would respond, convinced the name had nothing to do with her sister's donuts. "It's just a coincidence, that's all."

Hannah and Ruth practically grew up in that bakery, spending every morning before school and most of their afternoons and Saturday mornings working there. They never worked on Sunday, of course. Still, it was a grueling schedule for the two young Amish girls. Their work day started at three o'clock in the morning, preparing the dough for all the donuts, apple fritters, and pies they were going to need once the community and tourists started stirring. When they were of school age, they did all of this before heading off to their one-room schoolhouse. Of course, it's a little easier to get up at three a.m. if you've turned in early the night before, which they always did.

But Hannah and Ruth were both beyond Amish school age now. At nineteen and twenty-one, eighth grade was far behind them. They had only their bakery and household chores to tend to, and those were hard enough.

On this particular day, Hannah Weaver had a bit more on her mind than babysitting donuts and fried pies, to be sure. There were the upcoming Amish softball tournaments and the much anticipated youth social gathering. The social gathering would be Hannah's chance to wear a certain mauve dress she was nearly finished sewing. And then there was handsome Levi Troyer, who was certain to attend both events.

Hannah's mind often wandered to Levi Troyer. Levi and all things baseball went together like homemade biscuits and honey, and Levi, by Hannah's standards, was even dreamier. Levi was fun, carefree, and spontaneous, and he could always make Hannah laugh. That's why Hannah was looking forward to the game and the social. Two occasions for plenty of fun and laughter. She figured Levi was looking forward to them too.

∂

Levi Troyer lived with his father, David, and twin brother, John, on their family farm. But he spent most of his time down at the baseball field that he'd made by clearing out a portion of their cornfield. Many of the Amish young people gathered at the ballfield at the end of a hard work week to play a little ball and socialize with each other.

Levi loved the sport. Everyone in the community knew it, and that was just one more thing Hannah admired about the young Amish man. For as long as she'd known Levi, which was ever since he and his family moved to Sugar Creek when the twins were ten years old and Hannah was nine, Levi had made it known exactly what he wanted to do with his life. He lived and breathed for the sport. It's all he thought about day and night. Where Hannah was easily distracted, Levi was steadfastly focused and dedicated to improving his game with every pitch he threw.

Hannah was attracted to Levi, but knowing he had this determined drive, she tried her best to guard her heart. *A man with that much passion for sports won't have much room left for courting,* she told herself. *That is, if Levi Troyer even has someone in mind to court!*

In her weaker moments, though, oh, how Hannah longed to be the object of Levi Troyer's heart! That's why she rushed through her chores every Saturday, so as soon as she was done, she could race to the baseball field and watch Levi play. Sometimes, she'd play, too, usually taking the first-base position in their softball games. Ruth teased her that she took first base just so she could be closer to the pitcher's mound where Levi always stood. But Hannah liked the action at first base, and she held the Sugar Creek record for most successful double plays.

Someday, Levi Troyer will want to spend his time with me away from the baseball field, Hannah told herself one day while waiting for the next batter to hit the ball and run in her direction on first. *He'll start thinking about marriage and raising a family, maybe becoming a farmer like his father. Why, I'd make a perfectly fine farmer's wife. I only have to convince Levi of that.*

Hannah's daydream was all too soon interrupted.

Whack!

The batted ball flew toward Hannah, snapping her back to the moment just in time to make the out. But as soon as the play was over, Hannah returned to her daydream of Levi, getting so lost in her thoughts that she missed the next play altogether.

"The ball, Hannah!" Ruth called to her. "Get the ball!

Hannah's record for double plays was surpassed only by her record of daydreams and missed opportunities because of them. It was a good thing for Hannah Weaver that no one kept score at these Amish games.

By the time Hannah was nineteen, several of her Amish friends had already married, and at least one of them was a mother. But Hannah was more than willing to wait on the man of her dreams. She wasn't interested in anyone else, even though a few of the young men had taken a fancy to her. But Hannah's blue eyes were set on Levi Troyer.

Oh, how do the women in the English world do it? How do they get their men to pay attention to them during baseball season?

Hannah had seen the sports magazines on the racks at some of the English stores, such as the local Walmart in Millersburg where she shopped every Saturday morning before going over to the baseball field later in the afternoon. According to the books and magazines there, which Hannah took a secret peak at whenever she could, sports were a big part of the English world. *So what's their secret? The women outside the Amish community must have figured out the secret to keeping a man's attention during baseball season. Surely!*

So what was it?

Hannah couldn't find her answer even in the magazines. But then, no man in the English world could possibly be as baseball-minded as Levi Troyer. That ball and bat (although most of the time he used an old fencepost to swing with) were all he thought about day and night, as far as Hannah could tell. Every time they had a conversation, it quickly turned to baseball.

English men can't possibly be like that! Hannah reasoned. *Sports wouldn't take up their whole lives, not when they can enjoy the company of their loving wife and children instead.*

Hannah's father, Eli, was well aware of Hannah's growing interest in Levi Troyer, and it concerned him.

"Don't waste your time on a fella who's determined to throw his life away on baseball," Eli often warned her.

"I like baseball, too, Father," Hannah countered. "A lot of the Amish young people play it."

"Yah, but you can't make a living with a ball and bat," Eli declared, ending the discussion.

But Hannah knew you could make a very nice living with a ball and bat in the English world. Levi had told her as much. In fact, if you're good enough, many ballplayers become millionaires. Hannah didn't want to correct her father, though. She didn't want to give the wrong impression about Levi either—that he was only interested in baseball because of the money. Levi just wanted to play. And as far as her ever being courted by Levi Troyer, she knew enough to wait until all baseball infatuation passed before taking that notion seriously. Besides, she and Levi still had to take their Amish baptismal vows before any discussion of courting could take place. That was the Amish way. All Hannah had to do, she figured, was wait until he matured a little more—or a lot, according to most folks in the community—and wait until she could win his undivided attention and his heart.

And if, for whatever reason, Levi decided not to take his vows, well, that would be the end of matter, at least as far as Hannah was concerned. There was no way she was ever going to leave her Amish community or her Amish faith. Not for love or money. Eli and Eunice Weaver had nothing to worry about on that end.

As for Levi Troyer's family? The flames of that fire were just getting started.

CHAPTER TWO

David Troyer had a nice spread in the Sugar Creek area, with plenty of land for both Levi and John to one day build houses for their own families.

For twins, Levi and John Troyer were quite different. Levi was dark-haired with a muscular build, stood about 5' 10" tall, and had a smile that exposed his playful, mischievous side. John was sandy-haired, a few inches taller than his brother, and possessed a focused, no-nonsense personality that oozed responsibility. Rarely did he laugh—even when he wanted to.

Anyone who got to know the twins with their polar-opposite personalities felt compassion for their father, David.

"Raising twin boys all alone is a special testing," David remembered Bishop Gingrich saying in his sermon one Sunday. It was a sermon about the various brothers in the Bible and what their journeys, together or apart, had entailed. "From Cain and Abel to Esau and Jacob to Joseph and his siblings—this brotherhood experience is a testing ground for many a parent," the bishop had said.

The sermon rang true to David, and obviously to John, who David could tell was paying rapt attention. Levi's mind, on the other hand, had no doubt drifted off to the ballfield.

David would be the first to admit that it hadn't been easy raising the boys on his own—or nearly on his own. From their births, David had to do the feeding, laundry, and cleaning. Once they grew to school age, he had to help them with their schoolwork, oversee their chores, and do everything else that goes along with childrearing. He did get help, though. You can't live among the Amish and not get help when you need it. The

Amish are known for their caring and supportive communities. Still, the majority of the caretaking fell to David, and he did his best to live up to his responsibility and keep some sense of order in his household. Sometimes that meant the one who was squealing the loudest got the bulk of his attention. As fair or as unfair as that might appear, it seemed to work for David, as it does for many parents.

Still, David had done his best, and for the most part, could be proud of his parenting. John, the firstborn, had turned out to be an exemplary son, doing whatever was asked of him, and often beyond.

And even with his mischievous side, Levi was still better, David figured, than a lot of young people he'd heard about. In both the English and Amish worlds, David knew of some who'd rebelled against the teaching of their parents, choosing to carve out their own paths, which sometimes took them through difficult troubles and trials that might otherwise have been avoided.

David's greatest goal was to raise his sons to put God first in their lives and to genuinely care about each other. Getting the boys to meet that goal had also been one of his greatest challenges.

Life hadn't been easy for David Troyer. The Amish community of Sugar Creek had first heard his story from Leah Gustafson, the midwife who helped deliver the twins up in Bird-in-Hand, Pennsylvania.

"That poor man was left with those babies to raise all by himself," Leah told her new neighbors after she'd moved to Sugar Creek ten years ago. "God knows best, but it just doesn't seem fair."

Leah's husband, Joseph, shushed her whenever she got to talking about the tragedy in that way. "We don't question God's will, Leah. Since the good Lord oversees all that happens in life, even the most difficult situations that we can't understand, then

He must have a plan for some kind of good to come out of David Troyer's situation, too."

But it had been twenty years now since the tragedy, and Leah was still waiting to see any good come from the death of Tess Troyer. That's one of the reasons she decided to help God out a little when she suggested her husband write to David and convince him to move his little family to the Sugar Creek area. "We love it here, David. Maybe you and the twins will too," Joseph wrote. "Why not try something new? Give yourself a change of scenery. The people are quite friendly here. It could be a good move for your boys. They grow up too fast, don't they? Well, you think about it. If you want to try it, we'll sure help you get settled in."

It took a while for Leah's plan to work, but eventually she and Joseph did manage to coax David away from all he'd known in Bird-in-Hand. David packed up his ten-year-old twins and headed down to Sugar Creek, Ohio. Just knowing he was going to be living near Leah and Joseph again filled David's heart with gladness. Leah had always been such a help to him with the twins. He didn't know how he'd have made it without them. However, the move also rekindled another memory in him— the night of the boys' birth.

&

Everything had been going along fine. The first baby, John, arrived with no problem at all. It wasn't until Levi began his journey down the birth canal that Leah became concerned.

"He's breach," Leah announced, trying desperately to reposition the second baby. But that baby wasn't about to be slowed from his mission. He seemed determined to get into this world on his own terms and within minutes of his brother.

David wiped the sweat from Tess's brow, while Leah took her pulse.

"We've got to get her to a hospital," she urged Joseph. "Run out to the phone box and call an ambulance."

Joseph nodded then ran outside and across the field to the community telephone, located in a wooden booth at the edge of their property. His hands shook as he dialed 9-1-1.

∼

Back at the house, David continued to swab Tess's forehead with a damp cloth. Beyond that and prayer, he felt utterly helpless. He wanted so much to ease Tess's pain, to somehow fight for her, breathe for her, but this was a journey that only her body could finish.

"You're going to be fine, Tess," he said, gently kissing her hand. "Help is on the way."

Tess smiled and gave a slight nod, although she barely had the strength to do either. Leah instructed her to try to get some rest in between the contractions, but with another baby on its way, there would be little rest for the pale and exhausted young mother. The birth pains continued full force. All they could do now was wait for the ambulance and pray.

"Just one more baby to go and it'll all be over," Leah said. "You'll be holding your precious babies before you know it. Don't give up, sweet Tess. You'll soon have two strong, healthy babies who are going to need their mamma."

Tess forced a smile then closed her eyes.

"I love you, Tess," David said. "God's not going to let anything happen to you. Twins, Tess. We're having twins! God is so good."

∼

It wasn't long after Joseph returned from making the call that they all heard the distant wail of an ambulance siren. That second baby must have heard it too, and decided the best thing for him to do was cooperate. Leah was finally able to move the baby into a different position, and within minutes Levi Troyer entered the world. Then, just as suddenly and as if on cue, John let out a squeal, drowning out Levi's cry.

"Look how happy he is now that his brother is finally here, too," David said, holding his firstborn in his arms.

Whatever the true reason behind John's wails, both boys were now in the world, and they were making sure everyone knew it.

Joseph helped out by taking a son in each arm and rocking them while Leah kept her attention on Tess, whose breathing grew increasingly more labored. Leah was seriously concerned. She couldn't ignore the tinge of blue in Tess's lips.

"Is that ambulance here yet?" she asked, her voice hinting at her panic.

Joseph looked out the window. "Oh, thank the Lord! It's coming up the driveway now."

"Get 'em in here," Leah cried.

❧

The EMTs rushed into the room with their medical equipment and stretcher in tow. They took Tess's vital signs, quickly started an IV drip, and hooked up the exhausted new mother to various monitors. David could tell by the look on their faces that something was going horribly wrong.

"Tess," David called to his wife, who drifted in and out of consciousness. "Hang on, Tess! You're going to be fine. You did it, honey. Do you hear our babies? Twin boys, Tess. They're beautiful. Just like you. Please, my love, keep fighting. You're going to make it. I love you, Tess. I love you!"

Tess turned her head, trying to look in David's direction, but her strength was spent.

"It's going to be okay, sweetheart," David said, squeezing her hand tenderly. "God gave us our family. He won't leave us now. He'll give us the strength to get through this."

David believed those words too. Believed them with all his heart. But sometimes the strength God gives us is the strength to let go.

Tess struggled to take a final breath, and then she was gone.

$\sim$

Leah and Joseph stayed with David the rest of the night to help care for the babies. David appreciated it, but it was hard to allow them, or *anyone* for that matter, to witness his raw grieving. David could do little to stop the floodgate of tears from bursting, or the onslaught of questions that overwhelmed his mind.

Why hadn't God intervened? David had promised Tess that everything was going to be all right. But now, *nothing* had gone right—not the way they'd planned for it to go anyway. If this was somehow in God's plan, what was the purpose? David saw none.

David's faith, though, had taught him to accept whatever happens as God's will. But how could something this tragic, this senseless, this painful be God's will? David questioned why God would give him two beautiful babies and then take his wife. How could this be a perfect plan? How could the same night hold so much joy and yet so much grief? What possible good could ever come of any of this?

$\sim$

The funeral wagon came by at dawn to take away Tess's body in preparation for the funeral services. David had stayed by Tess's bedside most of the night, weeping and praying that he'd awaken from this nightmare. But there would be no awakening. This was reality, and whether he wanted to or not, David finally reached a point of surrender. He knew he was powerless to turn back time on the heartbreaking event. Tess was gone. For whatever reason, God had allowed what had happened. The only thing left for David to do now was to trust that God wouldn't leave him alone in the aftermath of it.

There would be days, of course, when behind the smile and the façade, down deep where the hard truth lives, David felt a bit cheated. He'd so wanted Tess to be at his side so they could raise their sons together. There had been much excitement and anticipation for their child's birth. David had carved a cradle with his own hands from a tree grown on their farm, and Tess had made a baby quilt with a spot for the name to be sewn on once the baby arrived. How could he have known he was going to end up being the only parent to rock not one but two cradles? No, there was no way he could have known. Our life isn't a story that we read. It's a story that we write as we live it, one page at a time.

CHAPTER THREE

Ultimately David didn't blame God for the loss of his beloved Tess. He knew that death in childbirth, though rare, can occasionally occur even in the English world. Contrary to what some believe, the Amish aren't opposed to utilizing the services of doctors and hospitals, and most midwives wouldn't hesitate to ask for outside help in the event of an emergency. David also knew that when there is a complication in birth, it can sometimes take not only the life of the mother, but also the life of the child. So he counted his blessings every time that wave of grief dared to sweep over him, thanking God for his twin sons who were alive and thriving.

David didn't place any blame on Leah Gustafson either. Leah was a good friend and an experienced midwife, and he knew beyond any doubt that she'd done all she could to save Tess. As for the twins, the only thing they'd done in the situation was to be born. He certainly could place no blame there.

But David's heart broke for his sons, losing their mother in such a way. Before they could be held in her arms. Before they could feel her kiss on their cheek. Before they could lock in a memory of her face.

He felt especially bad for his youngest son. Levi was mere minutes behind John, but their births were very different. The little guy had to make the final part of his journey into the world without any help from his mother at all. She was simply too exhausted at that point, just minutes from death. Years later, David wondered if such an experience might somehow have marked Levi. Could that be why he'd always been so independent, not asking for help from anyone, even when he needed it?

Another person David didn't blame for Tess's death was himself. He knew he and Tess had done their best to have a healthy pregnancy. He'd seen to it that she ate well, got plenty of rest, and followed all the midwife's instructions.

As difficult as it was to accept, there wasn't anyone to blame. Tess's death was simply one of those unfortunate things that happen in life and make no sense on this side of heaven. All David could do was grieve what might have been, trust God, and go on with his life. And that's all he had time to do. He was too busy changing diapers and rocking babies to sleep.

"I no sooner get one to sleep when the other one wakes up," David told Joseph Gustafson one day.

"You should ask Leah and me to help you out more," Joseph urged.

David assured him he would happily start taking him up on that offer. With twin babies to take care of, he needed all the help he could get. For the most part, however, he wanted to do everything for those boys himself. It had been his parting promise to Tess, whispered into her unhearing ear just before the funeral wagon had taken her away, that he'd do whatever it took to care for their babies and see to it they grew up to be godly men.

David thanked Leah and Joseph for their kindness and help, not only with the birth of his babies but also for their pledge to help watch them as he began healing from the loss. Then he walked his friends to their buggy, said his goodbyes, and went about becoming the father those boys were going to need.

David Troyer had accepted his new normal. The words to one of his favorite old hymns gave him strength.

Farther along we'll know all about it
Farther along we'll understand why.
Cheer up, my brother, live in the sunshine.
We'll understand it all by and by.

David knew there was coming a day when all of his questions would finally be answered. Until then he would just have to trust God and keep putting one foot in front of the other.

CHAPTER FOUR

It wasn't so much Levi who seemed to mind always having his brother around. It was John, according to Levi's take on the situation. Most of the time Levi got the impression that John was more than a little perturbed that his twin had ever happened along in the first place. There had been only five minutes between their births, but the way Levi figured it, these days anyway, those were the best five minutes of John's life.

Then there was baseball. In their youth Levi actually enjoyed playing ball with his brother. But now John was too busy working around the farm to play much. *How can anyone be too busy for baseball?* Levi often wondered. But John had a reputation for going above and beyond in his work. Of course, the possibility that John busied himself on purpose in order to get out of playing baseball with Levi did cross Levi's mind more than once. John seemed to avoid those areas where Levi showed any hint of superiority. That's what Levi had noticed anyway.

☙

The Amish baseball field wasn't much more than a pad of dirt and grass at the edge of a cleared out cornfield. Levi had done the clearing himself and got a bit of chastising for it, as he recollected.

"That's not what the farm equipment is for," John had told him emphatically. But Levi paid his brother no mind. He'd trained himself to tune out John's petty judgments, especially where baseball was concerned.

When their regular baseball equipment wasn't available, the young people used whatever was around for the bases—often the shoes off their feet. Their "dugout," such as it was, was nothing more than a few old tree stumps. But Levi couldn't have been prouder of that baseball field.

Levi had also managed to get his hands on a few baseball bats, but he preferred using an old fencepost, which suited him just fine. He'd sanded it down a bit, but it still looked more like a fencepost than any baseball bat you'd ever seen. And he could sure swing it.

In later years they added a backstop and some benches so their friends and families could watch.

The players, even the girls, wore their typical Amish clothing for the games. There were no baseball uniforms to tell the teams apart or to distinguish one player from another. But then, other than in their Amish and Mennonite tournaments, these games weren't about competition. They were simply about having a little fun on a hot summer day.

"Keeping score," Bishop Gingrich would often say, "can be a temptation for the players to boast." For that reason these informal games were most often played without a scorekeeper. "Remove the competition and you remove the pride." Then the bishop would expand on the thought. "There are a lot of ways we keep score in life, and they can all be prideful."

Although he allowed the games, Bishop Gingrich had never been too keen on them—at least, according to John, who discussed the matter with him at length whenever he could. The bishop permitted the tournaments for recreation and fun, but he routinely cautioned the young people against spending too much time playing and not enough time completing their chores and studies—a sermon point that garnered the most nods from John.

‍ ॐ

John may not have attended many of the Amish ballgames, but he kept his share of scorecards. Mental ones, filed away neatly in his mind. He maintained a running tally of all the times he'd covered for Levi by doing his chores and helping him with answers on his schoolwork. John hadn't considered the fact that keeping such a list was probably evidence of his own shortcomings. But John's motives, according to John, were pure. He was simply trying to help his brother be more responsible. And perhaps there was some truth to that.

Levi did manage to get John out to the ballfield once in a while to actually play ball. Like the one day when they were both fourteen years old, and John hit a line drive past third base that knocked in two runners. John seemed thrilled with the sport then. He whooped and hollered as he ran to first base and then on to second. Then, when the leftfielder missed the ball and John ran on to third, his whole team cheered him on. But when John took off for home plate, the outfielder threw the ball to Levi, who in turn raced John to home, tagging him out just before he could touch the base.

"When are you going to grow up?" John snapped at Levi when they walked home together that day—although it wasn't exactly together. John kept his distance a good ten feet or so in front of Levi.

"It's just a game, John. Don't take it so seriously," Levi responded.

"*Me* take it seriously?" John's eyes widened and his face turned red. "You're the one who wastes the whole day playing it. There's more to life than baseball, you know. You should be spending your time learning how to run this farm. Someday we're going to have to run it all on our own, and where will you be then? Off hitting a ball and running around in a great big circle? Where's that going to get you? Right back where you started, that's where! And all the work will fall to me, just like it always does. Baseball hasn't taught you a thing about responsibility."

"Ah, but you're wrong, John. Baseball teaches me plenty about responsibility. I have to be responsible to touch the bases, yah?" Levi laughed, trying to get his dutiful brother to lighten up.

John smiled and nodded, grudgingly acquiescing the point. But then he looked at Levi squarely in the eye and said, "And not one of them counts if you miss home plate."

Levi figured it was the loss of that homerun that was really chafing John's hide, so he thought it best to drop the matter. John wasn't so quick to do the same, however, and continued his unwelcomed lecture.

"You can't feed a family with a ball and a fencepost, Levi," John said.

Levi laughed, determined not to let his brother get under his skin. "Haven't you noticed, John, that I don't have a family to be responsible to yet?"

"Is that so? Well, then, what are we?"

Levi saw where John was going with this, but he wasn't going to let him take him there. The guilt-inducing comments, which John was so good at, had grown beyond tiresome. Levi wanted to get back to the original topic and remind John that on this day they were both only fourteen, neither of them was courting anyone yet, they were a long way from inheriting the farm, and baseball was a lot of fun, so why were they even having such a silly discussion anyway? But saying all that would have led to an even longer discourse, Levi figured. All he wanted to do was play ball, either with or without his brother. There was plenty of time later for growing up and having a family, even running a farm, if that's what he decided to do with his life. But at fourteen, Levi Troyer was going to play ball!

"Play all the ball you want, Levi," John said. "But there's going to come a day . . . "

Levi could tell John was preparing to launch into "the topic" again, that "Great Day of Reckoning." As far as Levi could tell, it was John's favorite holiday. He seemed to look forward to it with as much anticipation as Christmas or Thanksgiving. John would evoke the Great Day of Reckoning into a discussion every chance he got. This was that day when everyone would give an account of what they'd done with their time here on earth. Levi wasn't sure how his actions so far were stacking up, but he figured John was keeping his own list of each of their deeds just in case God missed a few, as unlikely as that would be.

"On that day," John continued, "the good Lord isn't going to be in the mood to hear all your excuses, Levi. He's simply going to ask you what you did with what you'd been given. And then, my brother, what are you going to say?"

Levi stood proud. "Why, I'm going to say . . . I'm going to say, 'God, I took a fencepost carved from a tree You made, and I played a little ball with my friends. And we had a lot of fun, and people seemed to enjoy watching it." Levi grinned. "Oh, and 'I put up with my brother,' for which God will probably usher me right up to the front of the line. Now, please, John, lighten up!"

John didn't say anything else about the Day of Reckoning, or even baseball for that matter. It was a long walk home for that much silence to hang in the air, but neither of them offered to break through it. They kicked a few rocks out of their path, swatted away a couple of mosquitoes, and mumbled words under their breath about each other. But they didn't talk, not to each other anyway. And they didn't mend any fences either.

That was the last time John ever played baseball with his brother.

CHAPTER FIVE

Levi hadn't told Hannah about his dreams and aspirations. Not that he had any obligation to do that. They weren't courting, after all, but they did seem to enjoy each other's company, especially at their Amish gatherings. Levi had also taken notice of how often Hannah showed up to watch the baseball games. He loved it when she joined in on the fun, which she often did. He knew from their conversations that she preferred volleyball and croquet over baseball. She'd told him as much on several occasions. But she could hold her own out there on the baseball field, and even hit some of Levi's best underhand pitches and run fast enough to make it to second base most of the time.

From Levi's perspective, Hannah Weaver seemed to be the only girl in all of Tuscarawas County who might come close to supporting his love of the sport. Other girls, Levi figured, would most likely be like John, constantly reminding him of his duties around the farm. *That's not the kind of wife I want,* Levi often told himself. *I want a wife who'll ask me how far I hit the ball and whether or not I came up with any new pitches, not how much hay did I bale or did the cows get milked. And what if one day I decide the Amish way isn't even right for me? What if I want to try to go for a baseball career in the English world? I'm going to need someone by my side who will support me in that, aren't I?*

Levi knew his dream of becoming a professional baseball player had little chance of ever happening. *That's probably hard enough to do even in the English community,* he figured. *What major league ball team would ever take a chance on an Amish player straight off the farm, with no real experience in professional sports?*

Levi knew his future, just like John's, was already determined for him. He'd stay right there in Sugar Creek, Ohio, take his baptismal vows, and work the David Troyer family farm. That would please his father and fulfill his late mother's dream as well. And Levi was willing to live with that—as long as there were no other options.

Besides, Hannah Weaver would never leave all she knew to follow him into the English world. Levi was certain of that. Her family had their bakery and café, and they probably needed her to help out with the work there. Still, in Levi's imagination, where David's rules and John's jealousy couldn't penetrate, *anything* could happen.

CHAPTER SIX

Typically, Amish baseball is underhand slow pitch, although Levi liked to throw in a few fast pitches just to keep the game interesting. The talented young man seemed to relish showing off his impressive overhand fast pitch whenever he could. The display was only between Levi and the catcher, a position played most often by Charley, the blacksmith, while the other players were getting into their positions.

Charley was one of the rare few who could actually catch one of Levi's "special" pitches. Folks said it was all that working around those fire pits for so many years that toughened his hands for Levi's blazing pitches. Whatever it was, Charley could handle them.

At fifty years old, Charley was usually the oldest one on the baseball field. He liked getting out in the fresh air after working all week within the steamy confines of The Rusty Anvil, his blacksmith's shop.

A few of the Amish young people had attempted to hit Levi's special overhand pitches, his fastest ones, just to see if they could do it. Few had ever succeeded. They simply ended up slicing the air with their bat or standing there wondering if that *whoosh* they just heard had been the ball flying past them.

Levi Troyer was the most talked about baseball player in all of Sugar Creek. Many in the community would ask for a demonstration of his fastest pitches whenever out-of-town family or friends were visiting. Levi may have been a bit of a slacker as far as his brother and father were concerned, but he was no slacker when it came to baseball. That boy could play ball!

❧

Charley was a Mennonite who'd helped many of the Amish with their blacksmithing needs over the years. He'd become a good friend to the Troyer brothers, and to David as well, trying his best not to take any particular side when it came to the brothers, regardless of how many times one of them tried to coax him into it.

Charley would be the first to confess that he saw a little of his younger self in Levi, and now he was living out some of his own abandoned dreams through the young man's unyielding passion for the sport. Truth be told, most young people have daydreamed about standing in their position of choice and making that game-winning out, or hitting the home run when the bases are loaded, bringing in the winning points. So it was easy for Charley to identify with the talented Amish ballplayer and not judge him too harshly.

But Charley also understood where John was coming from. He knew what it was like to carry the demands of an entire operation on your shoulders. Charley had lost both his parents when he was seventeen, and he'd been fending for himself ever since. He knew how to work hard and the importance of carrying his own weight. John had legitimate points about Levi shirking his responsibilities, Charley figured. But he still didn't want to come between the brothers by offering much of an opinion either way. Charley just listened.

Knowing Charley was the boys' confidante, David often stopped by his shop to see what he could find out about how his sons were getting along. He always did it discreetly, of course. But usually Charley could figure out what he was really after. He could do the same with John too. As for Levi, he was easier to read than a billboard. He loved baseball and didn't care who knew it. He was easily distracted, and he readily admitted it. He was willing to play baseball with his brother any time he wanted, but he wasn't going to beg him. Nor was he going to let John stop him from playing it himself.

Charley knew the Troyer men as well as anyone. It was the trying to stay friends with each of them in the midst of all the confidences that was the tricky part. But then again, as a black-smith, he was quite used to putting out fires.

CHAPTER SEVEN

For Hannah, the baseball games were the perfect opportunity to spend time with Levi on a more social level. Problem was, all the other Amish girls appeared to have the same goal. At least, that's the way it seemed to Hannah. *Why, just look at how they all flock around him, like bees at a barbeque! It's most unbecoming.* Never mind that Hannah would like to be one of those bees. What really bothered her, though, was how the girls pretended they *weren't* doing what they clearly *were* doing—flirting with Levi.

"Oh, Levi, you are such a wonderful pitcher," one would say, almost gushing.

"Hey, Levi, did they ever find that ball you hit over the field and into the creek last week?"

Oh, I hope you didn't hurt yourself when you slid into third base, Levi."

"Levi, would you like some ice-cold lemonade?"

Hannah could see through every bit of it, but she refused to let all that gushing deter her from her own mission. She had a strong hunch that Levi had taken a special interest in her. He'd often glance her way throughout the games, and how could she not notice how often he stopped in at the Battered Donut whenever she was working. (When you're not used to repeat customers, you notice such things.)

For decades the Battered Donut had been a convenient stop for the locals in buggies and the tourists in automobiles, and on Hannah's days off, their business often doubled. That's why Levi's dedication to visiting the place whenever Hannah was working was the clearest indication of his possible love. That, and whenever there was a community picnic or other such gathering where food was served (which, to Hannah, seemed to describe *all* Amish gatherings), the first person, and sometimes the *only* person, who could be found requesting one of Hannah's infamous blackened pies was Levi Troyer.

On occasion John Troyer stopped by too. But he never offered to buy Hannah's baked goods, offering some excuse, such as being too full or borderline diabetic. Hannah didn't buy the diabetic excuse since she'd personally witnessed John eating enough of her sister's chess pie to run his blood sugar into the stratosphere had the diagnosis been an honest one.

She did take it upon herself, though, to ask John directly about something she'd been wondering about for a long time.

"Why don't you ever play baseball with us anymore, John?"

"Because there's work to be done," John said determinedly. "And besides, there isn't enough room on that baseball field for *two* Troyers."

"Sure, there is," Hannah said. "Look at all the Yoders and Millers out there. There's plenty of room for two Troyers. Besides, you're not the only Troyers in this county. Troyer is a very common name, as I'm sure you know."

John shook his head, ignoring Hannah's reasoning. "Believe me, my brother doesn't need one more voice cheering him on."

"He might need yours."

John considered it momentarily, but there was no changing his mind.

"Hannah, don't get me wrong. I miss the games, but I miss working with him on our farm even more. If Levi wants a brother, he knows where to find me." Then he thanked her for the donuts and left.

Ruth entered just then, having overheard only the tail end of the conversation. "What was that all about?" she asked. "Everything all right?"

"Sad," Hannah said, as she watched John get into his buggy and ride off. "Levi's down at the baseball field, and John's heading back to the farm. They're brothers. They both know where to find each other, but neither one is looking."

☙

Hannah knew Levi wasn't a bad kid. He simply had different priorities, and baseball was at the top of that list. And although Hannah's parents thought Levi Troyer was too full of dreams to ever make a good husband for their daughter, Hannah had a different opinion.

"Dreams are a good thing," Hannah would often say in Levi's defense. And she believed it. She had even named her horse Dreamer.

Hannah Weaver didn't like anyone being put down for having goals and ambitions. And she certainly didn't care much for the giving of nicknames. She knew all too well about such things. "The only Amish girl who can't cook" was just one of the nicknames she'd been trying to shake for years.

But Hannah and Levi had a lot more in common than wounding nicknames. They each had one of those "perfect" siblings. Like John, Hannah's sister, Ruth, cast a shadow of excellence and dedication over her sibling. Ruth had never had a turkey explode while baking or a batch of brownies adhere to the pan like mortar to a brick. Why, Ruth Weaver's wedding cakes were the talk of the town, and her pies and donuts caused many a tourist to fall happily off his or her diet. Living under that kind of pressure hadn't been easy for Hannah, even though she had no desire to compete in such a way. Ruth wasn't competitive either. She just happened to be a great cook.

As far as Hannah could tell, John Troyer was about as perfect as Ruth. But unlike Ruth, John seemed to enjoy lording his superiority over his brother. *When you feel like a failure already, it doesn't help to have a perfect sibling around for everyone to compare you to,* Hannah wrote in her journal one night.

Hannah wished she could try her hand at other ventures, perhaps making baskets, working at one of the English restaurants in the tourist area, or writing for *The Budget*, the Amish newspaper that delivered newsy updates to the Amish communities across America. She didn't have to follow in her parents' footsteps, or even her sister's. She could pursue her own path, couldn't she? Nothing wrong with that, right?

Still, what Hannah wanted most out of life was to marry Levi Troyer. She wrote *that* in her journal that night too. And underlined it. *That's the beauty of a journal,* Hannah thought. *You can write whatever you want to in it.*

CHAPTER EIGHT

Levi may have been a slacker on the family farm, but he excelled on the baseball field. He could easily outpitch, outhit, and outrun all the other young people. So it was no wonder Levi often heard John describe the sport as "a complete waste of a good day."

Eventually, John's indifference to baseball was fine with Levi. It meant his brother wouldn't be hanging around the field criticizing him and interfering with his efforts to become the best player in all of Tuscarawas County. Holmes County too. Maybe even the entire state of Ohio, for that matter. Who needs a black cloud hovering around and messing up a perfectly sunny day? Even if it doesn't rain on you, it's still there, making you wonder if you should call it a day and go on back home, or stay and endure it. And as far as Levi was concerned, John was as unpredictable and hovering as any dark cloud he'd ever seen.

John didn't see it that way at all. He figured every time he reminded Levi of his chores, he was helping his brother become a useful member of their Amish community. Even though he was only minutes older than Levi, he felt a certain responsibility to help ease some of the load on his father's shoulders, and keeping his boys in line was one of those responsibilities. There was a part of John that wished he could be more like Levi and forget about their farm duties and go down to that baseball field on Saturdays and play ball too. He enjoyed being out on those dusty diamonds and hanging out with his friends, and even though he couldn't pitch or hit like his brother, he was a better than average short stop. But like Ruth Weaver, who spent most of

her time in the bakery, he was duty-bound to help take care of
the family business first.

$\mathcal{O}$

David Troyer had commented on more than one occasion that
John should consider courting Ruth Weaver.

"I like her," John had replied. "Just don't know if she'd be
interested in courting me."

David frowned. "What makes you say that? You're a hard
worker, and dependable."

"Well, you know what they say—opposites attract. I'm afraid
the two of us would be too much alike. There wouldn't be any
sparks, you know?"

"Oh, I don't know about that. You should spend more time
with her and see if she might be the one God has for you. Sometimes having a lot in common can be a good thing."

John wasn't convinced. "When would we have any free time
for that? We both have our work."

"Well, you know what they say about all work and no play."

"What's that?"

"Makes an old man wait too long for grandchildren!" David
laughed. "The way you and your brother keep putting off marriage, I'm beginning to wonder if I'll ever have any."

"We're only twenty, Father."

"Joseph's son and daughter-in-law had two by then."

"I'll marry someone, in due time. And I give you my word,
I'll give Ruth Weaver proper consideration."

"A father can't ask for any more than that." David smiled.
"And I certainly wouldn't want to insert myself into these kinds
of life decisions."

"Of course not, Father."

"But she *is* very nice."

John couldn't deny that. "Yes, she is."

"And she's pretty."

"Yah, I've noticed that too."

"And she is one fine cook."

"Are you saying that because you like her cooking or because you want me to start dinner?"

"Maybe a little of both."

John smiled and nodded. "Meatloaf sound good?"

"It does. And John . . . "

"Yah?"

"Thanks for all you do for us. I don't know what I'd do without you."

"It's what I want to do, Father. But it feels good to be appreciated."

CHAPTER NINE

Levi Troyer's name was mentioned in *The Budget* on too many occasions to count. Most of the time it was by Amish who'd visited the area and were rightfully impressed with the talented young Amish boy.

"If you ever get down to Sugar Creek, you might want to catch one of their baseball games."

"There's a boy down there who can sure hit a ball! Levi Troyer is his name and, if you haven't seen him yet, you're surely missing something."

Levi tried his best not to let any of this praise go to his head. Besides, he was too busy trying to improve his game to stop and rest on his laurels. Levi's goal was not only to be the best baseball player in the Plain world, but also good enough to gain the notice of the professional baseball teams he'd heard so many tourists talking about. His commitment to all things baseball wasn't for prideful reasons, or to think for a minute that he'd ever have a shot at playing for one of those teams. After all, he was Amish. All he wanted to do was see how good he could get. That's why he'd sneak off to the baseball field hours ahead of his friends. *I'll do my chores tomorrow. I'll help John tomorrow. I'll make it up to him tomorrow.* That's what he told himself, over and over again, whether any of it was true or not.

CHAPTER TEN

Why Hannah was attracted to the more disobedient Troyer twin, she didn't know. She'd heard some of the unkind comments spoken against the twenty-year-old. Hannah was sure such words stung Levi, just like words that had been spoken behind her own back. It wasn't so much the assessments of her cooking; she'd gotten used to those by now. "Hannah clouds" was a term she'd coined herself every time she had to fan away the smoke that far too often hovered over the bakery. She'd heard, "Ruth is going to make someone a fine wife someday. But pity the poor man who has to eat Hannah's cooking," and "An Amish wife who can't cook? A man would be asking for a life of misery and buggy rides to the doctor."

No, she wasn't bothered by those remarks. The behind-the-back talk that *did* bother her, though, was when folks complained about her judgment in potential boyfriends, namely Levi Troyer. The way Hannah figured it, she and Levi were two misunderstood souls, both looking for a little respect and admiration.

Occasionally Hannah daydreamed about Levi leaving the community and asking her to go with him. In her daydream she always told him yes. Hannah figured daydreams were a safe place to do those kinds of things. In reality she knew that could never happen. She'd already promised her parents that she'd stay and honor her vow to God, no matter what Levi Troyer decided to do with his life. Oh, but she did so enjoy her daydreams!

That's the thing about temptation though. If you let it hang around too long in your mind, unpacking its baggage and making itself at home, you're asking for trouble. That's what Ruth had always told Hannah, warning her to push away such thoughts of Levi Troyer and the English world. "There are a lot of things you can't control in life, Hannah," Ruth told her sister. "But your mind certainly isn't one of them."

Hannah knew Ruth was right, and she tried her best to keep her thoughts of Levi well within the boundaries of her Amish faith. She truly did. No daydreams of marriage outside her church. And anyway, what if some of those judgments she'd heard about him were true?

"Levi Troyer is never going to amount to anything."

"He's just a dreamer."

"Good looks fade and muscles droop over time, and then what will a wife have left? A man who let his ambitions take him away from his faith."

Hannah's thoughts were interrupted by the aroma of fried pies burning on the stove. She snapped herself back to the moment and managed to save at least a few of them just in the nick of time. Well, the tops of them anyway. Hannah wiped her brow with her apron and breathed a sigh of relief that the situation hadn't been any worse. It would have been such a bother if the water wagon had to turn around and head back to the Battered Donut again. Even though, for them, it was a very familiar path.

CHAPTER ELEVEN

"You selling those apple fritters?" asked the short, burly man with more gold chains than Hannah had ever seen hanging around a person's neck, along with what Hannah figured was a New York accent.

"Yes," she said. "I made them just this morning."

"Can't get any fresher than that. Gimme a fritter and throw in a glazed one too. Doctor's orders." The man laughed.

Hannah joined him. "I'll bag them up for you right away, sir," she said, still chuckling.

Hannah couldn't have been more pleased. Only four apple fritters left on her tray. It was a new record for her. She'd made a half-dozen that morning, but now it looked like she wouldn't have to eat any more herself, as she'd been known to do in order to get the leftover count down to an acceptable level.

Hannah made small talk with the stranger as Ruth rang up his order.

"Where are you from, sir?" Hannah asked, thinking of his accent.

"Originally, New York. But I've been living in Vegas for the past fifteen years."

"Oh?" Ruth said. "And what brings you to Sugar Creek?"

"Well, I was up in Cincinnati on business, and, well, you see, my wife made me promise to drive down here before flying back to Vegas tomorrow. She wanted me to pick her up some of that Amish peanut butter."

"Yah, everyone loves our peanut butter," Hannah said, not surprised in the least.

"My wife puts it on everything."

"I call it *Amish salsa*," Hannah said, which made them all laugh. "So what do you do in Vegas?"

"I mostly try not to lose my money. I don't suppose you'd know about such things though. But now, if you were referring to my occupation, I scout out talent to manage."

"Music?" Ruth asked.

"Sports," the man said. "Namely, professional baseball. I doubt you know much about that world either, huh?"

"Oh, we play baseball," Hannah said. "Why, some of the youth are playing it right now in the field at the edge of town. If you have time, you should go watch."

"Hmm . . . " The man paused. "Old fashioned sandlot baseball, huh?"

"A cleared-out cornfield. At the edge of town. You can't miss it."

Ruth excused herself to go check on her cinnamon rolls.

"So what do you think?" Hannah asked. "Do you have time to stop by our ballfield?"

"Well, as much as I'd like to," the man said, glancing down at the time on his cell phone, "I really do need to get back on the road. Thanks for the invite though."

Hannah figured the stranger was politely turning her down, so she handed him his change and the donuts.

The man turned to leave then stopped and looked back. "But now, if there's someone worth seeing out there, I could make an exception. Any of the players good enough to warrant a change in my plans?"

"Maybe," Hannah said, smiling. "Why don't you stop by and see for yourself."

The man lifted an eyebrow. "That good, huh?"

"Oh, I'd say he's worth your time."

"The edge of town?"

"Just stay on this road. It'll be on your right. You can't miss it."

The man nodded and left. Hannah wondered if he'd even bother to stop by the game. She knew Levi would be there. Levi was always there this time of the day. But the man might have been leading her on, pacifying her hometown-hero pride, all the while having no intention of going to a leveled-out cornfield to check out some unknown Amish ballplayer. Still, she figured she'd done her part to further Levi's dream. She'd led the sports manager to him, and the man would know which player she was talking about once he saw him pitch. What happened after that was in God's hands . . . if God even liked baseball, which Hannah was pretty sure He did.

Ruth stepped back into the room, carrying a tray of hot baked cinnamon rolls. "So is he going to go watch the game?" she asked.

Suddenly reality hit Hannah. "Oh, Ruth, what have I done?"

"Sounds like you may have opened the door for Levi to get everything he's ever dreamed about."

"Exactly," Hannah said. "But it's in the English world. If Levi ends up there, where does that leave me?"

CHAPTER TWELVE

Over the years Phil "the Real Deal" Watson had seen it all. He'd sniffed out raw talent in some of the poorest neighborhoods in America. He'd been invited to the best colleges and universities to check out their best too. But an *Amish* baseball player? This was a first for the high-powered sports manager. Could it really be that he was about to discover untapped talent in this Plain community? The "cream of the crop" in the middle of the *real* crop? He doubted it, but Hannah had been nice enough to invite him to the game, so he figured he might as well show up. Besides, it would give him a good story to tell to the other sports managers over coffee. He was sure none of them had ever attended an authentic Amish baseball game.

Phil sat down on a grassy area by the makeshift ballfield. He was the only spectator, other than the young Amish who were awaiting their turn at bat. They didn't seem to mind the stranger being there. They were focused on the game. Phil wondered if they recognized the bag from the Battered Donut and figured it might have validated him in some way.

Phil wasn't sure which one of the players was the one the bakery girl had told him about. Then, figuring cream always rises to the top, he told himself he'd know him once he saw him play. *Or maybe the player's a girl. Good for the female baseball teams,* Phil thought.

Whoever it was, Phil doubted they'd be good enough for the farm leagues, but he figured he didn't have anything to lose by taking a look.

The fact that all the players were wearing Amish clothes and no one was wearing a number or name on their shirt didn't deter Phil in the least. *You can't hide true talent. Once I see him, and if he's good, I'll get a name, no question about it.*

Just then Levi stepped onto the mound.

"All right, kid. Let's see what you can do," Phil said under his breath.

⁊

Levi was in rare form that day. Every ball he pitched seemed to sail over the center of home plate with ease. His overhand fast balls, which he used only as practice pitches or to show off a bit, were as good as any professionally pitched balls Phil had ever seen. Excited, he clocked one of them at 92 mph!

"That can't be right," Phil mumbled to himself, rechecking the radar gun.

The next fastball came in at 94. That pitch, along with the Amish angle and Levi's rugged good looks, registered dollar signs in Phil's mind. This kid had success written all over him. Phil Watson had found his pot of gold.

Oh, the fans are going to love this!

There was work to do, of course. You don't find gold sitting in a box on the side of the road with a sign that says, "Take me." You have to mine it, chip away everything that isn't gold, and then and only then, take it to market.

The first thing Phil had to do was convince the Amish ballplayer to leave everything he'd ever known—his family and whatever other attachments the young man might have—and follow a dream that came with no guarantees. Phil was willing to take a chance on the kid, pour his resources into his training, and start a publicity campaign like none other. But only if it was for the long term. He wasn't looking for someone who'd do a season, get homesick, and want to return home. He had to have unflinching commitment. He wanted a career player, someone who had both the talent and the willingness to work hard. Whether or not this kid would be interested in such a deal, Phil didn't know. But he was determined to ask.

Phil watched for a while longer then looked up and saw Hannah walking across the field toward him.

"Well, was I right?" she asked when she got close enough for him to hear.

Phil nodded toward the pitcher's mound. "I assume that's the guy you told me to look at. Well, you're right. He's impressive. He got a name?"

"Levi. Levi Troyer. He's good, yah?"

"Oh, he's good, all right. He always pitch like that?"

"Well, he strikes out most of our players."

"I can see that."

"Did he show you his fast pitch?"

"Why do you think I'm interested?"

The inning was now over, and the outfield team came up to bat.

"Levi!" Hannah called out. Levi nodded, then made his way over to Hannah and the stranger.

"Looks like someone left their shoes at home," Phil said, looking down at Levi's bare feet.

"We needed 'em for the bases," Levi explained.

Phil laughed. "You're kidding me, right?"

Levi smiled and gave a slight shrug. "Hey, we've got a ball, a fencepost, and shoes for bases. What more do you need to play baseball?"

Phil laughed again and told Levi he'd like to talk to him after the game. Levi agreed then went up to bat.

"Can he hit as well as he pitches?" Phil asked Hannah.

"Even better."

The pitch was a little outside, but Levi took it and sent that ball sailing high into the air. It would have been an easy two-base hit had it not landed in foul territory.

"Just you wait," Hannah assured Phil.

Phil nodded, telling himself not to let his expectations get carried away. Finding an extraordinary pitcher, who's also an exceptional hitter, hidden away on an Amish farm was more than he could hope for. This was just one more oversell to add to his collection. Sure, the kid could pitch, but a double threat is a rare find, even in the English world.

The pitcher threw his second pitch.

"Ball!" the umpire called. "Two and O."

"Well, he's got a good eye, I'll give him that," Phil said.

Hannah smiled. "He knows what he likes."

Levi took position again. This time the opposing pitcher hurled that sphere right into the strike zone. Levi was ready for it. He connected and sent the ball soaring—over the shortstop, over the left fielder, and all the way to the line of cornstalks far beyond.

Phil watched as Levi easily rounded all the bases and ran in home, hardly even breaking a sweat.

"He can hit, yah?" Hannah asked.

Phil nodded. "Oh, yeah. He can hit. And run too."

Hannah smiled. "And just imagine how fast he'd be in shoes!"

CHAPTER THIRTEEN

L evi couldn't believe what he was hearing. The stranger, who'd waited through the entire game to talk to him, seemed to be offering him a shot at a professional baseball career.

"There are no guarantees, of course," Phil quickly clarified. "But I'd sure like to see if I can make it happen for you, kid."

Levi looked to Hannah for some assurance that he'd heard the man correctly.

Hannah was torn. She wanted to see Levi's dreams come true, but she didn't want him to leave and go live with the English. She swallowed, determined to do the right thing. "Well, Levi?" Hannah asked when he seemed unable to answer. "What do you think?"

"Are you serious?" Levi asked the man.

"You're good, kid. A little rough around the edges, but I see a lot of potential in you. Just tell me—you're allowed to play with a real bat and shoes, right?"

Levi laughed. "I can adapt."

"Now you understand this is pro-ball, right? You'll have to leave home and go into training. We'll see how that goes, and then take it from there. So what do you think? Is that something you'd be allowed to do?"

"Well, I haven't joined the church yet, so yah, I could. But I'd want to talk to my father first."

"Sure, sure. Is he here?"

"No, but we don't live very far from here."

"Great! I'll follow you."

Levi nodded. "Just bring your car around and meet me. I'll be the one in the black buggy."

Phil turned and looked at a row of about a dozen black buggies parked by the side of the ballfield. "They're *all* black, aren't they?"

Levi laughed. "We're allowed to have a sense of humor too, you know." Then he walked to his buggy and climbed in.

David was in the stable working when Levi and Phil arrived at the house. Levi led the way and opened the stable door.

"Father?" Levi called upon entering. "There's a man here who'd like to speak with you."

"Over here," David called out from one of the horse stalls.

Levi and Phil walked over and found David sweeping up.

"Father," Levi explained, "this is Phil Watson. He's from New York."

"Well, originally," Phil clarified. "Most recently, Las Vegas."

"That so?" David said. "So what can I help you with?"

Phil got right to the point. "Watched your son play ball today, sir. I scout out baseball talent, and I gotta tell you, I liked what I saw."

"Yah, he's a good ballplayer. But as you can see, I'm in the middle of cleaning out the stable, and I wouldn't mind at all if my son would help me out a bit."

"I'll be brief," Phil assured him. "Sir, I believe, with proper training, your boy might have a shot at making it to the majors one day."

David didn't want to seem insensitive, but he also didn't want the man wasting what was left of the sunlight. "The majors? You *are* aware that we're Amish, yah?"

"Yes, but please, hear me out. Sir, I've gotten my players on some of the best ball teams in the league. Your son could end

up making a lot of money. Enough to buy his own farm someday, if that's what he wants to do with it."

"We already have a farm, Mr. Watson. You're standing on
it. And my sons will inherit this land someday. What is baseball
going to teach him about running a farm? I'll tell you what—not
a thing! So now, if you're done, I'll bid you good day."

David continued cleaning the stable, thinking the stranger
had heard his words and taken his proper leave. But he hadn't.
Phil was well experienced in waiting out other people's re-
sistance. He wasn't going to be deterred that easily.

"Sir, if you'll just give me a moment more of your time . . ."
Phil ventured.

"Good day, I said," David repeated.

Levi stepped forward. "He says I've got talent, Father."

David wouldn't budge. "I've had my say on the matter, Levi.
Now, Mr. Watson, I implore you to leave so my sons and I can
get some *real* work done."

Phil wanted to continue his sales pitch, but he really did
need to get to the airport.

"Well, like I said, the kid has a real gift. This could be his
ticket to the good life. Fame, fortune, and beautiful fans. What
young man wouldn't want that?"

"*My son*, sir," David said. "We are content in the life we are
living. Now, if you don't mind . . ."

"I clocked his fast ball at ninety-two and ninety-four. That's
raw talent. With professional training, who knows how fast it
could get up to? Why, I could be looking at the next Babe Ruth."

"The candy bar?" Levi asked.

Phil chuckled. "Only the greatest ballplayer of all time, son."
Then, turning back to David, he continued. "Sir, what would
you say if I told you that I believe you could be sitting on a gold
mine?"

"I'd say we Amish don't wear a lot of gold. And we don't do a lot of sitting either. Thank you for your offer, but there's nothing more for us to discuss."

Phil sighed then took a business card from his pocket. "Well, then, would it be all right to leave you my card?"

David continued working. He had already had his say on the matter.

"I'll take your card, sir," Levi said.

Phil looked at David then back at Levi. "It's okay?"

Levi moved a few steps forward. "Like I said, I'm old enough to make my own decisions." Levi took the man's card from his hand.

"Well, I sure would like to give you a shot at it. Would you like that, son?"

David stopped his work and looked sternly at the man. "I'm giving him a shot at far more than anything your world has to offer. And, sir . . . he is *not* your son!"

"Uh, well, yeah, okay, then . . . " Phil shrugged. "You two go ahead and talk it over."

"When do you need my answer?" Levi asked.

"Well, spring training starts soon, and I'd sure like to get you started in the minors this go-around. So the sooner you let me know, the better. My number's on the card there. Got a way to reach me?"

Levi nodded. "We have a community phone box out in the field."

"A community phone box? I love it! Well, you think about it. If you say yes, I'll book your flight and send a car around for you."

Levi assured Phil that he'd let him know as soon as he could. Then, at last, Phil left. As soon as the stable door closed behind him, David let loose.

"What's there to think about, Levi? You're a farmer—just like me and your brother are farmers, and your mother's parents were farmers, and their parents before them."

"Am I not free to choose my own path?"

"Of course, you are. But, son . . . you don't know the temptations that come with that world. You heard him yourself—fame, fortune, and beautiful fans. Where is God's will in any of that?"

"I'm not after any of those things, Father. I just love baseball. And you heard him yourself. I'm good at it."

"We are Amish, Levi. We lead a separated life."

"Maybe the English world isn't as full of temptation as you fear, Father."

David shook his head. "You have to trust me on this."

"I trust that you've taught me to make good decisions. I haven't always, but I feel good about this one."

"Sounds like you've made up your mind."

"Not yet. But I am seriously considering it."

"I should have put my foot down on all this baseball playing years ago," David muttered. "Levi, it's time to put down that ball and bat and take care of your responsibilities here on this farm. This farm has fed you all these years. Now you need to put something back into it."

"Give me responsibilities I care about, Father. Then see how well I do."

"And exactly what is baseball going to teach you about life?"

"If I were to do this and started making money, I'd send some of it home to you. I give you my word."

"We don't need your money, Levi. We need your help and your sweat. An Amish man has no place in professional sports."

"Then maybe the Amish life isn't for me anymore."

Unbidden tears stung David's eyes. "Levi, you don't know what you're saying. What has that man been putting into your head?"

"He hasn't put anything into my head that wasn't already there. Baseball is what I was born to do."

CHAPTER FOURTEEN

John overheard most of the conversation between David, Levi, and the stranger. He couldn't help it. The three men were talking loudly, and sound travels easily in these quiet farm communities. The fact that John was outside and standing with his head tilted toward the slight crack in the stable door seemed to help a bit too. The only thing John hadn't overheard in the conversation was any discussion of how his brother was going to pay for his dream-chasing plan. The Troyer family wasn't rich, but David had planned well. There was plenty of money to be accessed if any of the trio had a pressing need. But John was concerned that Levi, charmer that he was, could persuade their father to give him money, which didn't sit well with John at all. The money was for all of them, and only accessible in a dire emergency. In John's mind, Levi's baseball dreams were as far from an emergency as one could get.

What John didn't know was that Phil would take care of everything if Levi chose to take him up on his offer. All Levi had to do was show up by the start of training camp. Phil had even promised to cover his flight to Las Vegas. As for the rest of his needs, John figured Levi was somehow just expecting it all to fall into place. So why was he feeling so upset at the thought of Levi leaving home? If it wasn't out of concern for his brother's well-being, like David's motive for his son, then what was it that really bothered him?

The possibility that it could all be legit, that's what. *What if someday Levi really does make it in professional baseball? What if he becomes the best pitcher the English world has ever seen and makes millions of dollars and has lots of girls wanting his attention?* That was a scenario John's own insecurity couldn't bear. He vowed to himself right then and there that he'd do whatever he could to stop that stranger's offer from ever happening. It was up to him to protect his brother from such excesses and enticements. It was the brotherly thing to do.

~

Phil may have exited the stable, but he hadn't left the area. He figured he still had a few minutes before he had to leave to catch his plane, so he sat down on a bale of hay to eavesdrop a bit on Levi and David's discussion, too. John noticed him and quickly hid behind the buggy where Phil couldn't see him. Both of the men could now clearly hear David and Levi's "private" conversation, totally unseen by one another from their individual vantage points.

"Enough of this talk," David said. "That man gave you his card. You're going to trust him with your soul, too?"

"It is quite well with my soul, Father."

"Have you even prayed about this, son?"

"Prayer is for more important things. God doesn't care about baseball."

"He cares about His children who play it, and the place they give it in their lives."

"Father, I just want to play ball. That's all I've ever wanted to do."

David shook his head, once again fighting an onslaught of bitter tears. He was on the verge of losing his son, not so much to baseball, but to the English world. "How many years have I prayed that you'd outgrow this misplaced passion of yours!"

"No one outgrows baseball, Father."

Levi hadn't meant any disrespect to his father. He loved David, but he loved baseball too.

"Father, if I do choose to go, you won't need to worry about me. I can handle it."

"Son, you may think I don't know much about baseball, but what I do know about it is this. No one knows how they're going to hit the ball until they see the pitch. Not even you, Levi."

CHAPTER FIFTEEN

Whether he intended it or not, Levi had started a train in motion, one that would be difficult to stop. Never before had he openly defied his father as he'd done in front of Phil Watson. Oh, he'd done it secretly plenty of times. Every time he headed off for the ballfield instead of plowing the fields with John was an act of defiance, as were the times he didn't chop the firewood because he had to practice his overhand pitches or swing.

But this was different. This was face to face, will to unyielding will, a father's good judgment slamming head on into a son's determination to make his own journey in life. No matter how you slice it, it was defiance, pure and simple. To Levi, though, he was just pursuing the chance to play ball.

❧

David sighed deeply then left the stable, walking right past John, unseen in the shadows. He did notice Phil, however, and was understandably upset that the man was still hanging around. David didn't mince his words. "Sir, I've asked you to get off my property. The next time I do it, I will not be doing it alone."

Phil nodded, shrugged his shoulders in surrender, and thanked him for his time. Then he walked to his black Mercedes and got in.

David felt in his heart that he'd done the right thing. He felt duty-bound to protect his inexperienced and overly trusting son from the temptations of the English world. But Levi was just as determined to take the man up on his offer.

Levi had heard Phil's voice and rushed out of the stable, hoping the sports manager was still there. But Phil's car was already turning out of their driveway and heading down the road. Levi chased after him for a while, waving his arms and yelling for him to stop, though he knew the man couldn't hear him. He ran until Phil's car was out of sight, then the disappointed Amish ballplayer sat down by the side of the road to catch his breath.

No one passed the entire time Levi sat there. It wasn't normally a busy road but one of those pristine backroads you see in Amish country. A road you can turn onto and feel as though you're stepping back in time, back before all the so-called progress moved into the English world and changed the landscape forever. Tourists often take these backroads on their visits to Holmes and Tuscarawas counties. Levi had heard them say how wonderful it would be to live in such tranquility as the Amish. But on this day he saw none of that tranquility. His chance of a lifetime had just driven off, and he was left with a father he'd offended, a brother who'd no doubt celebrate Levi's missed opportunity, and a tattered old ball and splintery fencepost waiting for him down at a leveled-out cornfield. Levi assured his conscience that he'd apologize to his father later. *After I make it big, I'll buy my father a bigger farm, a new buggy, anything he wants. That'll change his attitude about baseball . . . and me. Then, we'll see who the slacker is!*

After catching his breath, Levi walked back to the house. By the time he reached the front porch steps, he could tell David and John had already turned in for the night. No candles burned anywhere else in the house. Levi was relieved that he wouldn't have to face them before morning. He hadn't gotten his thoughts together yet, and he figured it was better not to engage in any more hard discussions until he did.

Levi decided he might as well turn in early too. He walked to his room and had every intention of praying about his situation before going to sleep, as his father had suggested. Instead he found himself gathering some clothes together. Then he reached up to a shelf and took down a hidden jar of money. He twisted off the lid and poured the contents onto his bed, on top of the quilt his grandmother had sewn for him. He counted it out—bills first, then coins. It wasn't much, but he ended up tallying over a hundred dollars, money he'd saved from helping Charley with some horseshoeing. It would have been more if Levi had shown up more often, but baseball took precedence over just about everything in Levi's world, including earning a little spending money. Still, he figured what he had was more than enough to help get him along on his journey.

He quickly stuffed the money into his pocket and his clothes into an old suitcase. Then he took Phil Watson's business card out of his pocket and studied it. He'd never seen a card that fancy before.

"Phil Watson," he read aloud. "Fulfilling dreams, one future major leaguer at a time."

Levi, clutching the card in his hand, prepared to go outside to the phone box and make a call. But when he looked up, he saw John standing in the doorway.

"So you're really doing this, are you?" John asked.

"I have to, John."

"Have to? That's what you always tell yourself, isn't it? That you have no choice. Gives you an excuse to do whatever you want, yah?"

"I'm not a farmer, John. Maybe you are, but I'm not. This life holds nothing for me."

"Is it the life that holds nothing for you, Levi, or the work?"

"You don't think baseball's work? Pushing yourself to hit harder, run faster, and pitch straighter than you did the day before?"

"It doesn't compare to guiding a team of horses while they plow a field so I can plant food for us to eat. And what has all of your so-called 'hard work' ever gotten you, huh? A visit from a stranger full of himself and empty promises. I heard you in the stable. It got pretty loud."

"Well, what if he can do what he says?"

"Turn you into a ballplayer for the English? You're Amish, Levi. Or have you forgotten that?"

"I haven't taken my vows yet."

"And what about everyone and everything you're leaving behind? Or won't you even look back?"

"Looking back only gives you a crick in the neck."

"Well, think long and hard about that man's offer. Because it'd be such a bother to get all my things moved into your room, only to have you change your mind later."

"Don't worry, John. If I go, I'm not coming back 'til I can buy all of us a bigger farm and house."

John laughed. "And who'd take care of it? The same guy who walked out on his responsibilities for this one?"

Levi didn't answer. He knew John was simply luring him in, and he didn't want to leave home on the heels of another verbal altercation. So he let John's comments hang in the air. Still, he'd hoped John could have told him a proper good-bye, or wished him well on the possibility of fulfilling his dream one day. But John didn't say another word—and neither did Levi.

☙

Levi walked over to the community phone box that stood at the edge of the field and dialed the number that was embossed on Phil's card.

"Mr. Watson?" Levi said when a man answered.

"Speaking."

"This is Levi Troyer. The Amish ball player. You left my house a little bit ago."

"Sure, sure. Got some questions for me, Levi?"

"Yah, one." He paused. "Can you come back and pick me up?"

"You serious?" Phil said, practically slamming on the brakes.

"Serious and packed."

"What about your father?"

"I'm old enough to sign anything you want me to. So can you come back and get me?"

"I can turn around right now. But I have to be sure you know what you're committing to. I'm in the business of making professional baseball players, not flying twenty-year-olds for a weekend in Vegas. I've got to know you're going to stick with this."

"I give you my word, sir."

"Can I trust that?"

"Mr. Watson, I love baseball. It's all I've ever wanted to do. I'm not going to throw this opportunity away."

"It'll mean leaving all you know. You won't be in Kansas anymore."

"I realize that. And this is Ohio," Levi said, correcting Phil's error.

"Uh, yeah, I know. It's a line from a movie . . . Never mind. I forgot, you didn't grow up watching movies and TV, did you? Well then, I guess you've never flown either, huh?"

"No, sir," Levi admitted.

"Well, this is your new life, and you're going to have to get used to it. All right, look . . . this is what we'll do. Rather than turn around and come get you right now, I'll book you a flight for Friday morning and send a car around to pick you up. That way you'll have a little more time to say your goodbyes and all. If you change your mind in the meantime, just let me know. How does that sound?"

"Fine, sir. But I don't think I'll change my mind."

"Well, now, you do know I can't guarantee you'll make it to the pros."

"I realize that."

"But I will make you this promise, kid. If you board that plane on Friday, I'll do whatever I can to make it happen for you. So I hope you'll be on that flight."

Levi didn't hesitate. "I will, sir. I just want to play baseball."

◈

Phil ended the call, ecstatic. He wasn't sure how Levi had talked his father into it, but he wasn't going to worry about it. *That's on the kid*, he figured. It was Phil Watson's job to find the talent and then manage them. How they worked the particulars out with their families was their job.

Once he learned the wheels were in motion on Levi's end, it didn't take Phil long to start calling some of his friends in the baseball world.

"I'm telling you, Jimmy," he said, speaking into his hands-free cellphone as he drove to the airport, "this kid's the best pitcher I've seen in a long time. NASA couldn't beat his precision."

"But he's Amish," Jimmy said. "They don't play, do they?"

"They do. Just not professionally. Too much temptation, I guess."

"Pro ball is a temptation? Who would've thought, huh? So you gonna sign him?"

"Oh, yeah, I'll get him. You know me, Jimmy. I get what I want, and right now I want that Amish pitcher!"

Phil made a few more phone calls, letting his friends know about his discovery and asking them to come down to the upcoming practices and watch his boy play. Most were open to the idea, probably out of curiosity more than anything, he figured. It's not every day an Amish baseball player finds his way onto a minor league baseball team. *I don't know how it's going to turn out*, Phil thought, *but something tells me it's going to be an interesting baseball season!*

CHAPTER SIXTEEN

John was unusually quiet at breakfast the next morning. The day before he'd covered for his brother's chores again, and once again, Levi hadn't even acknowledged his efforts or thanked him. As the fresh eggs and hickory-smoked bacon were passed among them, John didn't mention the bales of hay he'd so often loaded by himself, or the chickens he'd fed, or the cows that were milked, most all of which had been done while Levi was down at the ballfield, impressing strangers with his fast ball. John didn't speak a single word about any of it. But inside he was seething. Levi had left him with all the work *again.* Only this time he really was *leaving* him. To play ball in the English world! As far as John knew, his thoughtless brother hadn't even officially told their father yet. That brother of his, that self-focused, slacker brother of his, was long overdue for his comeuppance. *Someday it's going to come!*

After the breakfast dishes were put away and after David had left the room, John finally spoke. "Have you told him?"

"I'm writing him a letter. He can read it after I'm gone."

"That's so like you," John said, disgust registering in his voice. "Taking the easy way out."

"He'll only try to talk me out of it, and this is something I have to do."

"He's just looking out for you, you know, because we both know you don't do a very good job of looking out for yourself."

For once Levi agreed with his brother. "Maybe I need more practice. Being out there on my own, where no one's around to take up my slack. Succeed or fail, it's all up to me."

"Well, just make sure whatever you're chasing in their world is worth what you're losing in ours."

Levi wanted to answer. Wanted to assure John that he wasn't losing anything. That David was still his father and John was still his brother no matter where his journey took him. Even Hannah was still the only girl he'd ever love. Nothing at all was going to change any of that. But deep down he knew the truth. Just about everything in their lives was on the verge of changing. And they all knew it.

CHAPTER SEVENTEEN

David caught up with his old friend Joseph down at the fishing hole. He knew Joseph would be there, getting in an early day of fishing. When Joseph saw him walking toward him, he gave a welcoming wave.

"David," he called, "how are things going with you, my friend?"

"Could be better," David answered without going into details.

"You need to fish more. Whenever my day's heading in a wrong direction, I can come out here, spend some time with God, and before I know it, I've got a fresh perspective on it all."

"And you've probably caught yourself some dinner, too, yah?" David laughed.

Joseph shrugged. "Not always. But Leah's hoping I catch a big one today. So what's on your mind, my friend?"

"It's Levi," David said, sitting down on a large rock. "All he wants to do is play baseball. The kid doesn't seem to want any part of farming."

"Well, what is he now? Twenty?"

"I know, I know—plenty old enough to be making his own decisions. But I fear he's about to make another poor one."

"How so?"

"Well, a fella stopped by our house yesterday. Said he'd gone out to the ballfield and watched the young people playing ball."

"Yah? An Amish fella?"

David shook his head. "A sports manager from Las Vegas. He said he thought, with the right training, Levi could be playing professional baseball someday. Said he'd like to manage him."

"Well, he's right about one thing. Levi *is* good. But what about his Amish vows? Is he getting any closer to taking them?"

"He says he's still not ready."

"But he hasn't shut the door?"

David shook his head. "No. And I pray for him every day concerning that. Nothing would please me more than if Levi were to follow in his brother's footsteps and join the church. But it has to be his decision, and that's never going to happen as long as baseball is number one in his life."

"So has Levi given the man his answer?"

"I don't think so . . . which surprises me. You know how impulsive the boy can be."

"Well, we both know how much Levi loves baseball, but I doubt if he'd walk away from everything he's got here."

"I didn't used to think so either," David said. "But it would appear he's leaning in that direction. I could sure use some advice right about now."

"My advice? Be patient, my friend. When Levi grows up—whenever that is—I'm sure he'll take his vows and marry some pretty Amish girl and give you lots and lots of grandbabies."

"Oh, how I hope and pray you're right." David sighed. "But I'm not so convinced of that anymore."

❧

That night David found himself missing Tess more than he had in a long while. His mind raced with so many thoughts, and though he'd prayed many prayers over his distracted boy, it seemed lately that God wasn't listening. David knew better, but that's what it felt like to him. What made it even worse was recalling the fact that he'd been the first person to toss a baseball in young Levi's direction. It was an action he used to remember fondly, but now he was regretting it more and more with each passing day.

CHAPTER EIGHTEEN

It was almost closing time for the Battered Donut. Hannah wiped off the counters and was removing her apron when she heard the customer bell ring. She looked up and saw Levi Troyer walk in.

Hannah quickly straightened her bonnet. "Oh, I'm so sorry, Levi. We've already put everything away for the day."

"You don't have a single donut left for me?" he asked, pouting his bottom lip just a bit for sympathy.

"Well, that depends," Hannah said, playing along. "Are you going to eat it or use it for batting practice?"

He flashed the smile that made her knees wobbly. "Now, you listen here, sweet Hannah. If we were ever to start, well, you know, courting, I'd have to insist you stop talking that way about yourself and your cooking."

"Ever to start courting, huh?" Hannah said, blushing just a bit. "Why, Levi Troyer, you don't have room in your life for courting. Especially now that your dreams might soon come true."

"You heard about the man?"

"You mean the sports manager who came through town yesterday and saw you play?"

"How'd you know about that already?"

"Oh, I have my ways.

"You know, for a community without television, news sure travels fast around here."

"Well, to be perfectly honest, I may have been the one who told him about you. He stopped in here for a donut yesterday, and, well, when he told me what he did for a living . . . "

"*You* sent him to the game?"

"He was going to drive right past the field on his way out of town anyway. I didn't want him to miss it, that's all. So he was impressed, huh?"

"Enough to stop by our house afterwards and talk to my dad."

"And?"

"He wants to fly me out to Las Vegas for training camp."

Hannah tried to ignore the sinking feeling that threatened to overwhelm her. She swallowed, hoping she sounded more positive than she felt. "Training camp? You must be so excited. Wait . . . You mean you'd have to leave here? That's . . . that's what I was afraid of."

"Well, yah," Levi said. "He can't very well bring the team here, you know."

"But . . . *Las Vegas?* I don't know much about it, but I'm sure it's nothing like Sugar Creek. There probably isn't a single covered bridge anywhere."

She took a deep breath. "What . . . what'd you tell him?"

"I said I'd think about it. And even though Father thinks otherwise, I'm praying about it. Well, kind of praying. After the fact, I guess, since I already told the man yes. And I'm packed."

"Packed?" Hannah's blue eyes widened with surprise. "When do you leave?"

"Friday. He's sending a car around to drive me to the airport."

"So that's it? You're really going? You're leaving your farm . . . and Sugar Creek? Just like that?"

"Hannah, you know baseball's always been my dream. The way I see it, I'd just be trading one field for another one, yah?"

Hannah lowered her head. Levi raised his hand to her chin and tenderly lifted it back up.

"Hey, I'll never forget that you're the one who told him about me."

"Thanks," Hannah said, her heart sinking. "But I . . . I didn't think it would really happen . . . at least not so fast."

"Well, he told me if I change my mind to just let him know. So nothing's set in stone until I get on that airplane. Until then I can keep thinking about it."

"Well, thinking is good, yah. Like when you think about doing something you shouldn't do, and you talk yourself out of it. But if you're thinking about something you shouldn't do, and all that thinking talks you into doing it, then maybe you shouldn't have been thinking so much about it in the first place. Don't you think?"

Levi scratched his head, trying to decipher what Hannah had just said. "No wonder you have a hard time following recipes."

They both laughed then Levi touched her hand. "Hannah, I don't know if any of this is going to happen, and I don't even have any right to ask, but . . . if it does and I do get to go, would you . . . would you wait for me?"

Hannah knew her answer, but she wasn't sure she should let Levi know it. She'd heard people say that men appreciate their wives more if they've had to compete a little for them.

"Well," she said, "you might be gone a long time. And you know I could never leave my Amish faith, so moving to the English world is not even an option for me."

"Aw, don't worry. I'll probably fail at this too, and they'll just end up sending me back home anyway."

"You? Fail at baseball?" Hannah rolled her eyes. "That's never going to happen."

"So you don't think I'm a slacker like everyone else says?"

Hannah smiled tenderly at Levi. "When I look at you, Levi Troyer, I see someone who knows exactly what his gifts are and is determined to use them. If that makes you a slacker in their eyes, then so be it. You just have different gifts, that's all, and people don't quite know what to do with them."

Levi wanted to kiss her right then and there. But it wasn't the right place or time. Not for their first kiss. But he did touch his fingers to her cheek. "Thank you, Hannah."

"For what?"

"Believing in me . . . even though I don't know why you do."

"I believe in you because I choose to."

CHAPTER NINETEEN

Unaware that Levi had already made up his mind, David continued to try to win him over. "You're already involved in our Amish tournaments and doing very well," he pointed out as they cleared off the dining table after supper the night before Levi was scheduled to leave. "You're coaching the Amish and Mennonite teams. How much more baseball do you need?"

"This is professional ball, Father. Do you have any idea what that man offered me?"

"It is no life for a boy of Amish upbringing."

"You've raised me to know right from wrong," Levi said.

"And you've always followed my advice, yah? The rules?"

"Father, how can I get into trouble playing baseball?"

David wasn't getting anywhere, but he wasn't about to give up. "Your family is here, Levi," he pleaded. "Who do you know in that world?"

"I know Phil. He seems like an honest man, yah?"

"He's a fast talker. Fast talkers slip in what you don't want right in the middle of a mouthful of promises. You'd be easy prey for someone like that."

"He believes in my talent, Father. That's something I don't get a lot of around here. Besides, I doubt if I'm the only Amish player he's going after."

"Oh, I'm pretty sure you are."

"No, I think there's a whole bunch of us. He said he's going to put me on a farm team. So he must have a lot of farmers going to training camp."

David shook his head and resisted the urge to laugh at his son's naiveté. This matter was just too serious. "Son, that world is going to eat you up and spit you out."

"I have the freedom to choose my own path, yah?"

David sighed. "Yes, and you may live to regret such freedom."

"Or it could be the best decision I ever make. I've been reading about these English teams, how much money the players can make. Who knows? Maybe I'll even play for the Yankees someday."

"The *Yankees*? That's your life's goal?"

"Shoot, I'd be happy with the Dodgers. Or even the Red Sox."

David wanted to say more, but he held his tongue. There was no point mowing over the same hayfield twice. It was obvious that Levi's mind was made up. All that was left for Levi to do was make it official.

"I already called him, Father," Levi said as if reading his father's mind. "I'm leaving in the morning."

Pain twisted David's heart, but he forced himself to speak in a calm tone. "I see."

"Phil's sending a car around for me at nine tomorrow morning."

"When were you going to tell me?"

"I didn't want you to talk me out of it. I have to do this. I can't turn my back on what could be the greatest opportunity of my life."

"That's what I've always feared."

Levi frowned. "Feared what, Father?"

"That it would be far easier for you to turn your back on your family than to stay."

CHAPTER TWENTY

Levi looked out of the window and held his breath as the aircraft zoomed down the runway. Although he'd seen plenty of airplanes as they flew over the skies of Ohio, this was his first time to be on one, and it was exhilarating.

Adventurous, free-spirited Levi Troyer didn't want to think about everything the flight attendant was warning the passengers about, even though she did it with a great deal of calming humor.

"For those of you who have never flown before, I just want to say that, no, the wings do not flap when we take off."

Levi laughed along with the other passengers. Then, as the airplane lifted off, he watched out of his window as the skyline of Cincinnati shrank smaller and smaller beneath him.

Then, later in the flight, when the plane took an unexpected dip, even the pilot got in on the fun.

"Sorry about that, folks. When did they put a speed bump over Albuquerque?"

The levity among the flight staff seemed to ease his fears and took Levi's mind off being some 38,000 feet above the ground. He didn't quite understand why the pilot felt he had to tell everyone that fact, but he tried not to think about it. Levi figured it would hurt just as badly to fall from 1,000 feet as from 38,000, so he leaned his chair back (easing him backward all of two inches) and decided to make the best of it. He'd trust that the pilot knew what he was doing, and he'd enjoy this new adventure.

❧

Levi was plenty hungry when the flight attendants announced they would begin serving lunch, even though a turkey sandwich on a bun, a small bag of pretzels, and a few celery sticks were a far cry from the food Levi had been used to eating in his Amish community. But he was too hungry to complain.

"If you'll look out the windows on the left side of the plane," the pilot said as the airplane neared its final destination, "you'll see the Grand Canyon. If it's on the right side of the plane, then I'm not as good a pilot as I think I am."

Levi laughed again. *This new world is quite the friendly place,* he thought to himself. *What's my father so afraid of?*

As the aircraft made its final descent into the Las Vegas airport, the pilot announced, "We should be on the ground in twenty minutes. Sooner if you all lean forward."

A few passengers tried doing it for fun, but it didn't seem to help. After the plane landed safely, Levi gathered his belongings and walked through the tunnel into the airport, where Phil was waiting to meet him, just as he'd promised.

"How was the flight?" Phil asked.

"Well, it was an adventure."

"Your first of many, I'm sure. Come on, we'll get you settled into your hotel room, and then we'll all go out to dinner tonight so you can meet some of the team."

"I'll look forward to that. We can all share farming stories. They're all farmers, right?"

"What?" Phil asked, doubting that he'd heard him correctly.

Levi dropped the matter. There were too many other things to occupy his mind. He was in Las Vegas! He could hear the machines clanging right there in the airport. The people sitting in front of the machines seemed excited, so Levi assumed they were all winning a lot of money.

As Phil led him toward baggage claim, Levi asked about the noisy machines. "What exactly does a slot machine do? Are these people all winners?"

Phil swallowed a smirk. "A slot machine is not a baseball, and that's all you need to know for now. Stay away from them, kid."

Later, as they drove to his hotel, Levi read some of the signs that flashed along the way.

"What's poker?" he asked.

"An estate sale you didn't plan to have. Don't even think about it. Listen, kid, all I want you to do is eat, drink, and sleep baseball. You stay as far away from these places as you can."

Levi's curiosity led him to ask plenty of other questions, and Phil answered them as best he could. But it was obvious this big city was overwhelming for this young Amish man. And though he may have hit town with only baseball on his mind, it was clearly going to be just a matter of time before some of these other interests started pushing their way in.

CHAPTER TWENTY-ONE

The other players on the Desert Rats farm team weren't sure what to make of the Amish pitcher when they saw him walk into the locker room wearing his regular Amish garb. Levi didn't see any reason to buy other clothes since he had a perfectly good pair of pocket-less pants and a shirt to wear—several changes of them, as a matter of fact.

"Gotta save money for a car," he told Phil when he offered to buy him some athletic wear. But Levi wasn't interested in being more indebted to Phil Watson than he already was. His Amish clothes would do just fine.

"Thanks for the offer, but you already gave me five thousand dollars. After the first and last on my apartment and some groceries, that'll leave me twenty-five hundred for a car to get me to and from practices. I can't let you keep giving me money like this."

"Oh, it's a loan," Phil assured him. "I'm banking on your talent hitting the jackpot, kid."

Levi was ready for that. But first he was itching to drive, and however he could make that happen was fine with him. Phil had promised to take him to a car lot before ball practice that coming weekend, and Levi couldn't wait. He was already picturing himself in one of those fancy BMWs he'd seen parked at some of the hotels in Las Vegas. Or maybe the car he'd seen only once in his life driving through Sugar Creek, but he still remembered its name—Lamborghini. He wasn't sure he knew how to spell the name correctly, but he sure remembered what that car looked like. Levi knew if he wanted a real chance of buying a car like that someday, he was going to have to hang onto every dime. "If my Amish clothes were good enough for the ballfields back home, then they're good enough for the ones in Las Vegas."

❧

Even though the weekend didn't get there soon enough for Levi, it finally did arrive. Phil slapped his hand across Levi's shoulders as they stood on the lot of Honest Ed's Used Cars and Trucks.

"Well, which one do you like, kid?" Phil asked.

Levi could hardly believe it. There he was, standing in front of the statue of Honest Ed himself, holding his brand new driver's license and a wad of cash that was more than enough to buy one of Ed's pre-owned vehicles right there on the spot.

Levi saw a man approaching, so he figured it might be Honest Ed in the flesh. He'd seen his ads all over town, and he recognized his big toothy grin and the flashy way he dressed. He was fanning himself with money spread out in his hand like a deck of cards.

"Ah, I love the smell of greenbacks in the morning. Howdy!" Honest Ed held out his hand to shake Levi's hand. "What can I do for you, young man? You in the market for a car?"

"Yes, sir, I am."

"Well, you've come to the right place. We've got compacts, mid size, full-size, convertibles, and, oh, *yeaaah*, we've got trucks, baby! And we've got more in the back that we'll take off the blocks for you. But first, let me ask you a few questions. Cash or financing?"

"Cash."

"Price range?"

"Twenty-five hundred dollars, tops."

"Married? Kids?"

"No. And no," Levi said, realizing Ed wouldn't have known his marital status by his clean-shaven face, as they would have back home in Amish country.

In light of his answer, Ed quickly led Levi away from the family vans near the office and walked him over to the sportier cars that were parked facing the road.

"Family cars sell the best, but these beauties are the ones that'll get a man to pull in off the street," he said, flashing a grin with teeth whiter than an Ohio snowdrift.

One shiny red pick-up truck caught Levi's eye. It had barely a scratch on her. "How does that one run?"

"Ain't she a beauty? Just 200,000 miles on her. Barely broken in. And I put in a new transmission myself . . . Well, new to her. Got it off a sedan that got swept away in a Florida hurricane. But why fuss over a little rust? I've got rust in every joint of my body. Hasn't slowed me down any!" He laughed. "Come on to my office. We'll sign the paperwork, give that sweet truck a jump start, and you'll be on your way."

"Is it guaranteed?" Levi asked.

Honest Ed stared at him blankly. "To do what?" he asked. "Obviously, kid, you don't know Honest Ed's motto. 'If I sold it, I'll tow it.' Doesn't get any better than that. That's how we keep our rock-bottom prices. But don't you worry any. She's a fine truck. I don't sell junk." Ed moved a bit to the right to turn their attention away from the tow truck bringing one of Ed's "fine" trucks back to the lot.

Phil looked intensely at Honest Ed, trying to read his face, which wasn't easy to do, considering the flashing lights on his tie. "You sure there are no problems with that red truck?"

"Well, now, there aren't any guarantees, but she'll run. I'll fire her up and let you hear the purr of that engine yourselves."

Phil and Levi waited while Honest Ed climbed into the truck and turned the key in the ignition. Nothing happened.

"She's been sitting awhile," he explained, then he turned the key again. And again. "I'll grab some jumper cables. Sometimes they just need a little help. It'll only take a minute."

Sure enough, with a fresh jump to the battery, that truck started right up. And then she died once more.

"She's just holding back, waiting for the right time to show off her power," Ed said in her defense.

"Maybe we oughta look at one of those other ones," Phil said, pointing down the row.

Ed pretended not to hear him and tried the ignition once more. This time she held her charge.

Levi was sold. He handed the man his cash, signed the new registration, and that shiny red truck with 200,000 miles on her "and hardly a scratch" (outside of the missing front bumper) now officially belonged to a young Amish man who was about to get one of the biggest lessons of the English world: There will always be people who are more than willing to take your money.

But Honest Ed was as honest as he needed to be for this fresh-off-the-farm ball player who was getting his first taste of independence. That shiny red truck was running, and Levi Troyer couldn't have been happier. Phil congratulated him and then went on home.

☙

When Levi drove off the car lot that night in his very own red truck, all he could think about was his future. *I'm going places!* He was feeling good and hitting all the green lights too. *If only John could see me now. Or Hannah. This is how I've always dreamed my life could be. John can keep the horse and buggy. I'll take a red truck any day.*

Levi pushed down on the accelerator just enough to hear the engine roar. Then he revved it, just like he'd seen some of the tourists do in their Amish community. Levi remembered his father getting upset at such thoughtlessness, but now Levi was finding out for himself the enticement of doing such a pointless act. The only problem was, that shiny red truck didn't want its gas pedal to be floored. With all the miles she had on her, she was plumb tuckered out. The poor truck sputtered and died again right there in the middle of the intersection. Going places? Now having lost both his cash and his trust, Levi Troyer wasn't going anywhere. At least not without Ed's trusty tow truck.

Levi turned the key in the ignition a few more times, then faced a harsh reality—he wasn't in Sugar Creek anymore. Levi Troyer, the young Amish man who knew exactly what he wanted out of life had just been taken. It wouldn't be the last time.

CHAPTER TWENTY-TWO

Phil arranged for the truck to be towed to a repair shop, and Levi ended up paying almost as much for the repairs as he'd paid for that "fine" truck in the first place. Phil advanced the money to him, and Levi's tab to Phil was growing by the day. But Phil knew the kid was good for it. Levi Troyer was headed straight to the top, but he was going to have to work for it.

"Here's your schedule, kid." Phil handed Levi the practice and game schedule then waited while Levi looked it over.

"Wow," Levi said, both excited and wary. "When do we rest?"

"Rest?" Phil laughed. "You're a country boy, raised around blacksmiths your whole life. You should know better than anyone that you've got to strike while the iron is hot."

Levi figured Phil was right. But that iron was going to stay hot for a while yet. Tonight he had other things on his mind. After thanking Phil for helping with the repairs, Levi climbed into his truck and hit the road. He drove around town half the night, looking at the sights and lights of Las Vegas and enjoying his new wheels and newfound freedom. Coming from a community without a lot of lights competing with the stars for attention, Levi was in awe of the Vegas night scene. Intrigued by all the casinos lined up one right after another, he began to get the notion that Las Vegas was a place that made millionaires. He'd never seen anything like it. No wonder his curiosity to learn more about this fast-track to riches was mounting a full-scale assault on his better judgment.

Guess it wouldn't hurt to see what it's all about, he thought as he parked in front of one of the smaller casinos. Even before he walked in, he could hear the sound of the slot machines, bells clanging as they announced that someone had just hit the jackpot.

Levi stood and watched over the shoulder of one man who kept feeding the machine his dollar bills without so much as a moment's hesitation. Levi waited until he had a good idea of how the game was played, then he took the seat next to the man and started feeding another machine a little of his own hard-earned cash. Well, not quite "earned" yet, since he was still operating on Phil's paycheck advances.

I'll just play for a little while, he promised himself. That plan would've worked too, but he hit a small jackpot with his fifth dollar bill, and that boosted his confidence to keep on trying for more.

"You're playing for free now," the man next to him coaxed.

Levi figured the man knew what he was talking about, so another dollar went in. It wasn't long before one of the casino barmaids approached Levi with a tray of cocktails and offered him one. At first he waved her off, but with her broad smile and persistent generosity, he decided he'd take her up on the offer. Maybe a drink would make him feel a little more comfortable in this glitzy town. But one drink led to the next . . . and another one.

Levi also continued to feed the machine everything he had on him, including any jackpot he'd won.

"You know, that's why they call it a one-armed bandit," a lady on the other side of him said. "It'll take whatever you're willing to give it."

And Levi was giving it plenty.

He stayed and ended up drinking another cocktail. They were free, and they were helping him forget about all the trouble he'd had with his fine red truck, the money he'd already lost at the machines, and how lonely he was for his home . . . and Hannah.

Success, with no one to enjoy it with, sure doesn't feel like success, he said to himself. And the wooziness he felt right about then also made him wonder if maybe all that free alcohol wasn't really free at all.

CHAPTER TWENTY-THREE

S o you're Amish, huh?" one of the other players in the locker room asked when Levi showed up on their first day of practice still wearing his Amish clothes. Levi wondered why the players were staring, so he decided to tell them a little more about himself to put them at ease.

"I grew up on an Amish farm. But baseball's my life now, and I've got to tell you, I'm thrilled to be playing on a farm team. Where are all your farms located?"

Everyone in the locker room stopped what they were doing and looked at him, then erupted in laughter.

"No farm here," said Allen, a sandy-haired player who stood taller than the others. "City boy through and through."

"We've never had an Amish ballplayer on our team before," someone named Ben said. "Do you even know how to play?"

"A little."

"Don't let him fool you," Phil interjected. "I don't know what they were feeding him on his family farm, but that boy can sure pitch a ball, I'll tell you that."

"Yeah, but can he hit and throw?" asked Mark Johnson, one of the other players, who just so happened to pitch a pretty good fast ball himself.

"He's good enough to give you a run for your money, Johnson," Phil said. "Clocked him at ninety-four, straight over home plate."

The other fellas razzed Mark about how this new kid on the diamond was going to replace him one day as their team pitcher.

"We'll see about that," Johnson said confidently. "Upstarts have come through here before, but look who's still the king of the mound." Not to mention that several times he'd gotten close to being picked up by the majors. Mark Johnson was no slouch. And he had a point. He was still standing after others had come and gone. But this farm team had never encountered anyone like Levi Troyer before. The whole league hadn't, for that matter. This Amish kid from an Ohio farm was about to show them all exactly how much he knew about baseball.

❧

Coach "Big Jim" Kelly stopped by to officially welcome the team. He didn't mince words. "I'm Coach Kelly. Do what I say, and we'll get along fine. Don't give me everything you've got, and I'll be your worst nightmare. Every run, every hit, every game counts. I do *not* tolerate slackers. Your best better show up every time you step onto that field, or I'll put you on the first flight home to your mommas. We didn't pick you to help us lose. We're here to win. If that's not your game plan, we're not your team. Do you hear me?"

Marco Diego spoke up. "Loud and clear, Coach."

Levi wasn't sure about Coach Kelly. There wasn't anything he could put his finger on, but he just didn't like him. Maybe it was Kelly's perfectionism that reminded him of John. That's all Levi needed—someone else riding his tail. He thought he'd left all that behind.

Noticing Levi wasn't paying attention, the coach walked over and stood right in front of him. "Did I make myself clear?" he asked.

"Yes, sir."

"Well, now that we all understand each other, welcome aboard. See you out on the field, men."

❧

"Sentimental fella, huh?" Levi said after Coach Kelly left the room.

"No," Marco said. "But I didn't come here to lose either."

Levi had heard that the team catcher, Marco Diego, was originally from Cuba. Levi had read about Cuba in his school work, but he'd never met anyone who was actually from there. Talking to Marco about it was going to have to wait until another time, though. They were due out on the field for practice, and Levi didn't want to get on Coach Kelly's bad side this early in the game. There was plenty of time for that later.

CHAPTER TWENTY-FOUR

Levi knew he should have listened to Phil and stayed away from downtown, but he was over twenty-one now, and all those bright lights and the song of the slots were calling him. And how could a place that generous with its own money be bad? Besides he'd just gotten paid, and from what those signs were flashing, he could double or even triple his money. What harm was there in that?

It didn't take Levi nearly as much time as he'd figured to go through his entire paycheck. It was time to leave. He wasn't sure how he was going to pay his rent, buy gas for his car, or eat, but it was a problem Phil didn't need to hear anything about. Levi would just have to figure it out on his own. After all, Phil had warned him to stay away from that place.

But that's when Levi found out just how friendly some people in the casino could be.

"Hey, kid," the man in the expensive Italian suit said. "I couldn't help notice you lost quite a bit back there. Down on your luck, huh?"

"Yeah. I'll make up for it next time."

"Why wait?" The man handed him a metal card. "Here . . . take this."

"What is it?"

Ignoring Levi's question, the man said, "Name's Vinny. Vinny Delmonico. Have yourself a good time and charge it all to me. A little loan, that's all."

"But I don't even know you," Levi protested.

"That's okay. I know you. I'm a friend of Phil Watson. Known him for years. Saw you at your ball practice today."

"You did?"

"Phil's told me about you. Amish, right?"

"So that was you? In that big black car?"

The man nodded. "Yeah. I don't usually get out. Phil just comes to the car . . . and we talk. He's got a card too. So, yeah, we had a little business to . . . discuss."

"Were those your friends with you? Those two big guys?"

"Yeah . . . sure. They go with me on all my calls. My . . . accountants. So, like I said, any friend of Phil is a friend of mine. I'll tell him I saw you."

"No," Levi said quickly. "Why don't we keep this just between the two of us?"

"Sure, kid. I understand. It'll be our secret."

Levi thanked Vinny for his generosity. After Vinny left, Levi walked back to the cashier's booth and tested the card.

"Two hundred dollars, please," he said.

The cashier read the name on the card and counted out the cash. *That was easy.* Then he made a promise to himself. *As soon as I win my paycheck back, I'm paying Vinny right away and then staying away from this place, just like Phil said.*

Another promise Levi Troyer wouldn't keep.

CHAPTER TWENTY-FIVE

John stopped in at the Battered Donut for a dozen glazed. "That ought to last you and your father quite a while, huh?" Ruth asked.

"Maybe until supper." John laughed.

Ruth boxed up the donuts then handed them to John.

"How's your father doing, John?"

"I worry about him" He sighed and shook his head. "That's why I've been doing most of the farm work, and I do the books and horse auctions too."

"You've always been a blessing to him. You're a good person, John."

John lifted his eyebrows in surprise. "I don't think anyone's ever said that to me before. They'll tell me I'm a hard worker or dedicated or responsible. But they never just say 'good.'"

"Well, you are."

"Thank you, Ruth. That means a lot to me."

Hannah entered with a tray of fresh apple fritters and placed them on the counter.

"Ah, Hannah, I thought you were working over at the Shake and Skate."

"Part-time. But I still help out here whenever I can."

"And we need her," Ruth said. "We've been getting a whole bunch of new customers. Isn't that always the way? As soon as word got out that Hannah wasn't working here as much, business doubled."

Hannah blushed. It felt good to be needed. But it also felt good to be exploring new opportunities. After enough culinary mishaps, Hannah's parents had finally acquiesced and given her freedom to try different jobs. They knew their youngest daughter had many talents—hidden talents, buried inside of her. Deep inside. They just needed to be uncovered and given the freedom to grow and develop to their fullest potential.

That Hannah Weaver was a special girl indeed.

CHAPTER TWENTY-SIX

S teeee-rike!" the umpire yelled after the batter swung wide and missed Levi's near-perfect pitch.

"O and two," he said and then settled back down behind the catcher and awaited Levi's next display of pure power.

The local fans cheered on the Amish ballplayer, who was only one strike away from pitching his first no-hitter in the farm league. Coach Kelly had let Levi pitch these last couple of games so the team and fans could see what he could do. And Levi was wowing them. As for Mark Johnson? Well, he'd seen just about all he could stand.

"The next game's mine, right, Coach?" Johnson asked.

Coach Kelly nodded. "Yeah, yeah. I'll put you in. Just trying to let the kid get his feet wet."

Johnson watched as Levi threw his next pitch straight as an arrow right into the strike zone. The batter went for it, but he was too late. That ball was snug inside the catcher's mitt before the batter ever finished his swing.

"Strike three!" the umpire called out.

The Desert Rats erupted into cheers and lifted the Amish player onto their shoulders. Levi wasn't used to such a display of exuberance. All he'd done was pitch a no-hitter, something he'd done plenty of times back home in Sugar Creek. What was everyone getting so excited about?

Another thing Levi wasn't used to was getting a bucket of ice dumped on his head. It took him by surprise when it happened, and he almost turned around and decked the guy who'd done it. But then he realized it had been done in good fun. And since he'd taken plenty of swims in icy water "just for fun" during the winter months growing up in Tuscarawas County, he let the matter go. Besides, it felt good under the blazing Las Vegas sun.

Levi's good sportsmanship paid off when his farm team invited him to join them to celebrate their victory at the Dugout Bar that night. Even Mark Johnson encouraged him to join them. Mark was envious, to be sure, but he wasn't stupid. Their team had won, thanks in no small part to their new pitcher. And a win for the team is a win for all.

≈

Other than stopping in at a couple of casinos, Levi had never been to a full-fledged bar, so initially he balked at the invitation.

"Come on," Mark pressed.

"Uh, well, uh . . . sure, I guess I can meet you over there," Levi said, feeling a little uneasy at the thought of drinking right out in public. Oh, he'd done it behind the barn a few times before David caught him. But John had taken the blame. John also caught him a few more times after that. Or maybe a dozen times. But barroom drinking was a whole different matter.

"You've got to come," the other players coaxed. "We wouldn't have won without you."

Levi decided he was up for trying anything he could in order to fit in. The team was finally starting to accept him, and more than anything, Levi wanted to be "one of the team." He was tired of standing out for his Amish ways and faith. He wanted to blend in with the English, and he figured publicly abandoning some of the strict Amish principles he'd been raised on was the quickest way to do that. They weren't really his principles anyway. They were simply how he'd been brought up. But now he was free to decide for himself, to do his own exploring, and to live however he wanted. *Nothing wrong with that*, he thought.

CHAPTER TWENTY-SEVEN

John stood at the doorway of Levi's old bedroom and looked around.

"It's still not right," he said out loud, assessing his new placement of the furniture.

"I want to be able to see the fields from the window when I lie down in bed."

Poor John. Levi had been gone for months now, but John had been working all morning, rearranging the furniture for the umpteenth time and finally getting all his things moved into Levi's vacated room. Levi's bedroom had the best view of the farmland. "He never even appreciated it," John muttered under his breath. "If he had, he'd have spent more time here, instead of always running off to the ballfield."

Now that his brother was gone, though, John figured it was only right that he should move into that room and enjoy its spectacular view. He was sure to enjoy the fall months most. John loved it when the trees turned such vibrant colors. Harvest had always been his favorite time of year, a time when everyone would reap what they'd sowed.

But fall was still months away, and he had to get through summer first. With no air-conditioning in the house, he was feeling the heat.

John hung his Amish clothes on the wall hooks, dusted off the hand-carved furniture, put his shoes in order, and set his kerosene lamp in the perfect position, right next to the Holy Bible, King James Version, and his personal copy of the *Ordnung*, given to him by Bishop Gingrich himself. Next to that he placed his well-worn book of Amish hymns. Levi may have been the ballplayer in the family, but it was John who knew how to cover all the bases when it came to his soul.

Another touch that made the room his was the strategic placement of various scripture plaques, which he hung up on the walls. Wall hangings of this sort were allowed in their Plain Amish homes. One read:

"Pride goeth before destruction, and an haughty spirit before a fall." The plaque noted that those words could be found in Proverbs 16:18.

Next to that plaque hung another one. "So then every one of us shall give account of himself to God. Romans 14:12" John had personally underlined the words "every one" with a Sharpie pen. Even though the words "every one" included John, anyone who knew the family dynamics knew exactly who those messages were being aimed at—his brother, Levi. But John considered his placement of those plaques to be an honorable gesture. They were his way of convicting Levi and helping him turn his life around. That is, if his brother ever came home to see them. But Levi was too busy making a name for himself in the English world. And down deep, John did miss him. He had a strong sense of family. Even with all their disagreements, Levi was still his brother. As long as Levi did things his way, carried his own weight, and never failed, John would always love him.

⁓

John was delighted with his new room. The only downside was that his joy was over-shadowed by David's relentless grieving. From this new vantage point, John was in a better position to hear his father crying out to God every night and praying for divine protection over Levi. John heard his own name mentioned too, in prayers of thanksgiving for "the son who's never caused me a day of grief." But the bulk of David's prayers, and his most earnest ones, were spent on Levi.

Whether his brother was there or gone, poor John Troyer, the hard-working, dependable twin, just couldn't win.

CHAPTER TWENTY-EIGHT

Eli and Eunice Weaver prayed their daughters would grow up to be strong women who'd one day meet and marry the man God had for them. Eli didn't figure Levi Troyer was in the running for that for either one of his daughters.

"Why don't you set your eyes on John Troyer?" Eli suggested to Hannah one night after supper when she happened to share a little too much interest in the undependable Troyer twin, Levi. "John seems to be reliable, diligent, and he's got a good head on his shoulders. And he's honest too. If you want to marry a Troyer, John would be my pick for you."

"Well, John is nice . . . and quite kind-hearted," Hannah admitted. "He stops in every Saturday to buy bread and donuts to take to the elderly. But he'd be my pick for Ruth. They'd be perfect together. They're two of a kind."

"Exactly. They don't need each other. You *need* someone like John, Hannah. He'd help fill in some of the areas that you are . . . well, uh . . ."

"Lacking?" Hannah smiled. "I am a complete person, father."

"I don't mean it that way. But surely you know that opposites do that for each other."

"Yes, I've heard that opposites sometimes attract. But I've also heard that it can be a good thing to have a lot in common with your spouse. I think Levi and I are very much alike."

"You are *not* irresponsible, Hannah. You may lack certain . . . skills, but you're dependable, highly intelligent, and a lady of fine character. Even when you fall off the horse, so to speak, you're not afraid to get right back up there on it."

"Levi's the same way, Father."

"Yah, he gets right back up and heads out to the ballfield—or Las Vegas," Eli said. "You're wasting your time waiting for him."

"But I'm still free to make my own choice in the matter, yah?"

Eli sighed. "Yah. But if you ever want my blessing, you'll need to reconsider that choice."

৵

"Well, I like Levi," Ruth spoke up in his defense when the matter came up yet again over dinner the following day. "He's always polite whenever he stops by the bakery. And I say if Hannah has found a man that likes her cooking, well, he's as good as caught. You know what they say, 'The shortest way to a man's heart is through his stomach.'"

"So stomach cramps after eating one of my cinnamon rolls is as good as an 'I love you' shouted from the rooftop?"

"Okay, not usually," Eunice said, laughing. "But if he comes back for seconds, maybe."

"Well, Levi is always coming back, so I'm thinking that's a good sign.

"You like him a lot, yah?"

"I do, Mother."

"Well, he comes from a good family, I'll give him that. But he needs to get more serious about what's important in life," Eli said.

"And to Levi, that's baseball," Hannah said.

"And where does faith and family fit in?" Eli asked.

"Can he not have it all, Father?"

CHAPTER TWENTY-NINE

Levi was ten minutes late to practice the next morning, and Coach Kelly didn't hesitate to call him on it as soon as he walked out onto the ballfield.

"Troyer! You think you're the first full-of-himself upstart to come through here? Well, you're not. Guys like you are a dime a dozen, and there's no room on this team for a prima donna."

"Sorry, Coach," Levi said. "It won't happen again."

"Oh, it won't, I promise you that!" Coach Kelly leaned closer. "Listen to me. If you have any thoughts of making it into the majors, this is where you prove yourself. Not just whether or not you can play, but whether you have what it takes for the limelight. Fail to take this seriously, and there's not a pro-team in any league that'll look at you. You hearing me, Troyer?"

"I overslept, that's all, Coach. I said it won't happen again."

"Overslept? Oh, I'm sorry. What time would you like us to start practice to make it more convenient for you?"

"I wouldn't expect you to do that, sir."

"No, seriously, if the time I set doesn't work for you, tell me what time would."

Levi didn't really think he was serious, but he went for it, flashing a boyish grin. "Noon?"

Coach Kelly laughed politely then changed his expression and shouted, "No! I'm not going to do that. We're a *team*, Troyer. We do things for the good of the team, not just *one* player. You don't make the rules here. Do I make myself clear?"

"A team. Yes, sir. I understand."

"You mess this up, and it's all on you."

"I know that, sir."

"Do you, Troyer? 'Cause I don't think you do. Look, you may have been a star on your home team, but that doesn't mean you can cut it here."

అ

Coach Kelly wasn't convinced that his newest player really knew much about teamwork, but he let the matter go . . . for the time being, at least. It would come up again, of course. And every time it did, the relationship between Levi and Coach Kelly became a little more strained.

Levi never did figure out why the coach got so worked up over ten lousy minutes. That was the same quality he detested in his brother. That black-and-white, follow-all-the rules, no-nonsense attitude of John's. Hadn't he left that back on the farm in Sugar Creek? It was only *ten* minutes. It wasn't like he missed the whole practice time. And it wasn't like he'd do it at a real game. But the coach had called him out on it in front of the whole team. Levi figured he had only two options on how to respond—either take it or leave it. He wasn't about to go back home and face John after messing this up, so he took it.

CHAPTER THIRTY

It didn't take long for the major league scouts to start taking notice of the Amish ballplayer. Levi was still wet behind the ears and had a long way to go before he could ever be considered for the big time. But they were watching. Phil kept a close eye on his prodigy too. He was grooming Levi to someday land a lucrative, life-changing deal for both of them. *If they want my Amish ballplayer, he's going to cost them,* Phil pledged to himself. And if Phil kept any promises at all, they were the ones he made to himself.

"If your ballplayer keeps pitching like that, we'll ante up someday," a scout for the Cardinals assured Phil.

Phil laughed. "My friend, you haven't seen half what my boy can do!"

సౌ

Levi had developed his own string of signature pitches, each with nicknames that he or Hannah had given them. First was the Hay Roller, a trick pitch coming in low and slow. Hi-ho Silo was his high and just-a-hair inside but still within the strike zone pitch. His Log-Splitter Ball was known to fly straight down the line then drop in hard and fast over home plate, like an ax dropping in on firewood. But his favorite and most feared pitch of all was the Troyer Tornado. This signature pitch was a mix between the English Fast Ball and the Curve Ball, only it was faster and had a twisting motion unlike anything professional baseball had ever seen before. And just like a real tornado, all it left behind was a whole lot of destruction.

On the minor league fields, Levi was doing more than just fitting in. He was gaining respect, peaking professional interest, and gathering a treasure trove of fans. It seemed this Troyer twin had finally found his place, but it wasn't in the Amish world. It was in a world he'd dreamed about ever since he picked up his first fencepost and slammed it against a ball. No one could hold him back now. No one—except, of course, Levi Troyer himself. But after his years of dedication to the sport and all his hard work to get to this place, why would he ever do a thing like that?

CHAPTER THIRTY-ONE

Levi was late to practice again, and Coach Kelly laid into him with yet another tirade. After the coach was through, he gave a similar warning to the rest of the team.

"Now if the rest of you have any ideas of setting your own rules around here, let me tell you just how replaceable you are. We don't have to put you in the line-up. You can warm the bench all season long if that's what you want. And believe me, if you have any hopes of impressing a major league team, this is the place and the time you're gonna have to prove yourself. I've been coaching a long time, and I'll tell you this—these major league teams are bidding on major league players! You've got to act like one long before you are one. They want to see it's in you. And they want to know you're a team man. It's not 'me,' it's 'we.' It's not 'I,' it's 'us.' If that stabs your overblown ego, too bad! Once you sign your name on that dotted line and the majors pay you the kind of money they're going to pay you, they're gonna want every bead of sweat your body can muster up, and they're not going to put up with any "my way or the highway" spoiled brats, I'll tell you that. So you might as well start getting used to being a team player and giving it your hundred percent now. That goes double for you, Troyer."

With that, Coach Kelly stormed out of the room.

❧

After practice that day, Marco took Levi aside.

"You okay, *mi amigo?*" he asked.

Levi shrugged. "Hey, that's not the first time I've been preached to."

"Well, if you think *he's* hard to please, just wait 'til the fans start turning on you."

"So I've heard."

"One minute they love you, the next minute they're ready to run you off the field."

"You ever have any second thoughts?"

"No way, man," Marco said. "Baseball's in my blood. I've loved this game since I was a young boy in Cuba."

"So when did you come to America?"

"When I was twelve. My uncle came first—on a refugee boat. Years later, when my mother told him I was a pretty good ballplayer, he made me a promise. He said if I stayed in school, did my homework, and stayed out of trouble, he'd do whatever he could to get me to the States so I could be seen by the scouts."

"And he kept his word?"

"We both did. How 'bout you? What's your story? Amish means a big family, right?"

"Just my brother and me. We're twins."

"Twins? So you're close, huh?"

Levi shook his head. "About as far apart as two people can get."

"He play any sports?"

"John? No." Levi laughed. "Thinks all this is a waste of my time."

"I have a sister like that."

"How'd you handle it?"

"Promised her I'd buy her a car when I make it big. That sure hushed her up."

Levi gathered up his gear and put it in his bag. "Well, I've got to tell you, you're one good catcher."

"You don't make it easy. That Troyer Tornado just about burns a hole in my mitt."

"I'll try to go easier on you."

"No, no. I want to win more than I want to have feeling in my fingers." Marco laughed. "I'm just glad you're on our side. So how do you think the draft picks are going to turn out this go-'round?"

"Beats me," Levi said. "I've never done this before."

"Yeah, me either. Maybe we'll go to the same team."

"If we even get picked."

"Oh, you'll get picked, man," Marco said. "There's no doubt in my mind."

"Thanks. I sure hope you're right."

"So, tell me, what do you think of Las Vegas so far?"

"Well, it's *nothing* like Sugar Creek, that's for sure. Sugar Creek is mostly farmland. But we get a lot of tourists, so there are plenty of hotels and restaurants. And lots of shopping. But it's different than here. Way different."

"You have tourists? A farming community?"

"It's a peaceful place. Rolling green hills that go on for miles. People come from all over, looking to slow down. Sugar Creek can help them do that."

"Sounds wonderful. So why'd you want to leave?"

"I wanted to see what I was missing, I guess. And play ball, of course. Oh, and I wanted a car. We Amish don't have cars."

"We never had a car either. My mother and I walked everywhere. But I used to dream about what was out there, beyond our shores. I knew there had to be more. Never imagined all of this, though."

"Kind of takes your breath away, huh?"

"When I first got here, my uncle warned me. He said freedom can bring both good and bad. Use your arm for baseball and your brain for everything else, he told me."

"Sounds like something my father would say."

"Good advice."

"Arm for baseball and brain for everything else," Levi repeated. "I'm going to remember that."

☙

On his way home that afternoon, Levi passed by a flower shop and decided there was something he needed to do.

"Can I help you?" the clerk asked.

"Yah . . . er, yes. I'd like to send a dozen roses to someone."

"Very well. And who will they be going to?"

"Hannah Weaver of Sugar Creek, Ohio. But send them to The Battered Donut Bakery and Café. I don't have an address."

"That's okay. I can look it up. Now, what color would you like?"

Levi looked around. The reds were rich and vibrant. But it was the yellow ones that caught his eye and reminded him of Hannah.

"I'll go with yellow."

"Beautiful choice. And what do you want to say on the card?"

"Say, 'I love you, Hannah Weaver. You're the only one I've ever loved. Just like these flowers, you are the sunshine of my life. I'm lost without you. I can't wait to get married someday and have lots and lots of children.' How's that?"

The clerk held up the two-inch square card.

"Too long?" Levi asked.

The clerk nodded.

"How about 'I love you and I miss you.'"

"That I have room for. And it really does say it all. She'll have them by three o'clock today, sir."

Levi thanked the clerk and got back into his car. He was feeling pretty good—about himself, about Hannah and their future together, and about life in general. Someday they would all be together. In the meantime, *play ball!*

CHAPTER THIRTY-TWO

On her way home from the bakery, Hannah stopped in to see Charley. Though the blacksmith wasn't Amish, Charley was a good friend to almost everyone in the community, shoeing their horses and repairing a lot of their farm equipment. He was also known for being level-headed and offering good advice free of charge. And he was one of the few who saw the good in Levi. Hannah needed to talk to someone who wouldn't judge him. She also needed some advice on what to do about other jobs she might like to try in the community.

"What if I was never intended to be a baker?" she asked.

"Do you think God would have placed you in a baker's family if He didn't think you could learn?"

She shrugged. "I just think I might want to try something different, that's all. We all know cooking is *not* my gift."

"Well, what kind of things are you interested in?"

"Oh, all kinds of things," Hannah said, but then couldn't think of a single one.

"Can you weave baskets?" Charley asked, after giving her plenty of space to offer her own idea.

"I made one once. It wasn't much of a basket, but it did make a good fire. That's why I'm here, Charley. I need direction."

"Well, the best advice I can give you is to find work that you love to do, and then it won't feel like you're working at all. For me, it's blacksmithing. I like taking a rigid piece of iron, putting it into the fire, and then shaping it this way and that, so it can become something useful. There's no feeling like it in the world."

"Have you ever had a piece that didn't want to be bent?"

"Oh, sure. Some pieces take a little more fire than others. But eventually they go the way I need them to. And when I'm done, I have something useful, and in some instances, a piece of art."

"Can a girl be a blacksmith?"

Charley thought for a moment. "Don't see why not. And we all know you're already used to working around fires."

Hannah laughed. "And dough that I have to hammer into shape. Hmm . . . Might just be the perfect job for me."

"But now, I'll be honest with you," Charley said, "you do get pretty dirty doing this job."

"I've never been afraid of dirt. You've seen me out on the ballfield, right?"

"Good point. All right then, blacksmithing is one choice. What other things do you like to do?"

"Well, I like to write and read."

"Ever think about working at *The Budget*?"

"Doing what?"

"Writing. You could help organize the letters from the Amish communities across the country."

"Are they needing help?"

"Don't know. Why don't you stop by there and see?"

"Yah, maybe I will. If the Shake and Skate doesn't work out. Levi always said you've got to find whatever it is that you were born to do, and then go do it."

"He's doing that, isn't he?" Charley said. "So what do you hear from our old friend these days?"

"Well, in his letters, which aren't nearly as regular as I'd like them to be—although he did send me flowers . . . " Her voice trailed off, and she sighed lovingly. Then, snapping herself back to the moment at hand, she said, "He says things are going well."

Charley nodded. "Good. Well, tell him we all miss him, and we're praying for him. Will you do that, Hannah?"

"I will, Charley."

"And don't tell any of our other ballplayers I said this, but our games aren't nearly as much fun without Levi playing in them."

"I know what you mean. I should write *that* in *The Budget.* Maybe he'll read it and come home."

Charley laughed. "That might be a good plan."

"If Levi even reads *The Budget* anymore."

"Oh, he could be having it mailed to him, so he can keep up with everyone's news," Charley suggested. "Who knows? He may know more about what's going on here in Sugar Creek than any of us do."

CHAPTER THIRTY-THREE

Levi Troyer was the talk of minor league baseball, and his impressive stats were continuing to draw the attention of the major leagues. Phil "The Real Deal" Watson couldn't have been happier.

"I knew you had it in you, kid," Phil said when he stopped by the minor league locker room after the game.

"If I'd known you were here, I would've played even better," Levi told him.

"Better? How? Strike out the umpire too?"

Phil wasn't in any hurry, so he sat down on the bench and shared what was on his mind.

"I'm starting to get calls, kid."

"Yeah?"

"Serious ones. From some of the major league teams."

"That so?"

"Oh, yeah."

"Think I'll get an offer?"

Phil's voice took on an extra note of seriousness. "Oh, you're gonna get plenty. The problem will be deciding which one to take."

"So how do I decide?"

Phil smiled. "Count the zeroes, baby. Just count the zeroes!"

Levi nodded, and then Phil suggested they drive downtown to celebrate.

"I thought you told me to stay away from that place," Levi said.

"Well, I think news like this calls for some kind of toast, don't you?"

෨

Levi didn't overdrink that night. Maybe he was trying to convince Phil that he had nothing to worry about. If that was his
goal, he accomplished it. Phil was relieved to know his Amish
player was getting along rather well in his new surroundings.
The prominent sports manager was on the verge of landing a
lucrative deal for his star player, and he didn't want anything
interfering with that. Thankfully, Levi Troyer had followed
Phil's advice and avoided any kind of drinking or gambling
problem. Phil Watson couldn't have been happier.

He also couldn't have been more wrong.

CHAPTER THIRTY-FOUR

Phil suggested Levi meet him at the Dugout Bar. Marco said he might head over there later, and Phil couldn't wait to tell Levi the news. Three major league baseball teams had made offers for the Amish ballplayer: the Cleveland Indians, the Las Vegas Vipers, and the Boston Red Sox.

"You're kidding me, right?" Levi asked, stunned when he heard the news.

"Didn't I tell you, kid? You've always been major league material. I saw it out there in that cornfield. You just needed a little refining, that's all. So which way are you leaning?"

"Well, if I have a choice, I think I'll pass on the Red Sox. Nothing against the team. I'm just afraid my father would never get over me wearing red socks." Levi smiled then asked, "Nothing from the Yankees yet, huh?"

"Haven't heard from them. But that's not to say they won't step up to the plate."

"I don't know why, but I've always dreamed of playing for the Yankees."

"Just about every new ballplayer wants to play for the Yankees. But they're American League. Pitchers don't hit. It'd be a shame to waste your batting talent. Same with the Kansas City Royals and the Minnesota Twins. So what do you think, kid? Who's it going to be?"

"Well, the Minnesota Twins might be kind of interesting."

"Yeah, the PR firm would have a field day with that, huh?"

"But if I pick Vegas, I wouldn't have to move again. I've gotten kind of used to it here."

"The Vipers are a good team. They haven't won a World Series yet, so they could use you. And they're National League, so you can show off your hitting skills too. Marco's going with them."

"Yeah, I heard. That'd be good to know someone on the team."

"But I wouldn't pass so fast on the Indians," Phil cautioned. "They're American League, so you couldn't hit, but they'd be close to Sugar Creek."

"That'd never work. My brother would think I'm flaunting my success in his face."

"What does he want you to do? Hide your gift under a rock?"

"Not every day," Levi laughed, only half-joking.

"Well, he wouldn't even know, would he? They don't watch TV or follow professional sports, right?"

"No. But he'd know. Somehow, someway, he'd know."

"You can't let that hold you back."

Levi nodded. "Yah, I know. Just don't need to make things any worse than they already are."

"Well, we'll talk to them all and see who offers us the best deal. In the meantime," Phil said, raising his glass in a toast, "here's to the future best major league ballplayer!"

Levi lifted his glass too. All of his hard work and perseverance on those dusty diamonds of home was finally about to pay off.

CHAPTER THIRTY-FIVE

This is Tammy Logan. I'm here with baseball sensation Levi Troyer," the pretty and petite sports reporter said into the camera. "Levi, word has it you've caught the attention of several professional baseball teams. So which one are we going to see you playing for?"

"Well, Tammy, I've been doing a lot of thinking, and a lot of talking with my manager, Phil Watson. I think we've decided on the Las Vegas Vipers."

"Really? Well, they could certainly use you."

"To tell you the truth, I'm just glad someone's interested in me. As you know, this is my first year in English—er, non-Amish baseball, so it's all happening pretty fast for me."

"Oh, I'm sure there are a lot of people interested in you, Levi. Starting with your swarm of female fans."

Levi blushed. Tammy asked a few more questions then gave her congratulations and her signature sign-off to the television audience. When it was a wrap, she was in no hurry to leave.

"If no one was interested in you, I would've been."

Levi's heart was pounding double-time. He wasn't sure if it was because Tammy was strikingly beautiful, or if his commitment to Hannah was trying to knock some sense into him.

"Want to get a drink together?" she asked.

Who'd turn down a night on the town with Tammy Logan?

"Uh, well, sure, I guess." *It's just a drink.*

"Got a favorite place?"

"A bunch of us usually go down to the Dugout. It's pretty close."

"Or we could go to Antonio's. A little more intimate," she offered.

Levi felt a lump in his throat. He wanted to leave, knew he should, but Tammy was waiting for an answer. *Is this some of that temptation my father warned me about?* He thought about his beautiful Hannah waiting for him back home. He thought about her the whole time Tammy was running her fingers through his hair and down his neck. Finally, he pulled away. "I'm sorry, Tammy. But I have a girl back home." Once he'd spoken the words, he breathed a sigh of relief.

"Got anybody here?" Tammy asked.

Levi gulped.

"You know what they say—what happens in Vegas, stays in Vegas," she said.

"Tammy, believe me, you're a beautiful girl. But I don't want to do anything that could hurt Hannah. We're going to marry one day."

Tammy backed away. "So you're engaged?"

"Not yet. Not officially. But sort of. It's complicated. She's determined to stay Amish, so before we could marry, I'd have to quit professional baseball and join the Amish church."

"If she loved you, she'd join you in your world, wouldn't she?"

"If that's what she wants to do. And if I loved her more than baseball, I'd be willing to . . . I don't know. We're still working out the details."

CHAPTER THIRTY-SIX

For whatever reason, the Yankees never made an offer for Levi Troyer. Phil didn't miss a beat worrying about it, though. His prodigy had three solid offers, and he, being the skilled negotiator that he was, kept upping the ante on each of the team owners and general managers. Only one accepted all of his demands—the Las Vegas Vipers. Levi signed a lucrative three-year contract with them, making more money than he'd ever dreamed of. He couldn't wait to step onto that major league ballfield and show the world what he could do. He also secretly dreamed of pitching a no-hitter against the Yankees someday as payback for passing on him. *That'll teach 'em!*

On a team full of big-name major leaguers, Levi spent the first part of his first season riding the pine. Everyone told him he had to pay his dues. But once they started putting him in the game, there was no stopping that Troyer boy.

Levi's first chance to pitch came at the expense of Barry Bayfield, the Viper's veteran pitcher who was having one of the worst days of his pitching career. But his loss would be gain for Levi who was eager and more than ready for his turn on the mound. Coach Larry Brenner had given Bayfield plenty of chances to improve his pitching, but the team was down by three. Bayfield had already walked three in the last two innings alone. The team couldn't afford any more. It was the top of the ninth, and the Vipers had to hold them if they wanted any chance of winning. Brenner took the risk on the Amish pitcher, hoping he could do one of his three-up, three-down strike-outs that everyone had heard so much about. Then it'd be the Vipers turn at bat. Maybe they could catch up and win.

"Okay, Troyer, this is it," Coach Brenner said. "You ready to get out there and show 'em what you can do?"

Levi's heart raced in his chest. "I was born for this moment, sir."

"You really believe that?"

"I do, sir."

"Then get out there and prove it to these major league fans."

ॐ

The sportscaster had to check his notes to put a name with the player who'd just stepped onto the mound. "Well, folks . . . looks like it's Levi Troyer on the bump in the top of the final inning. We've all been hearing about this Amish pitcher. Now we're finally gonna get to see what he's made of."

The enthusiastic fans cheered as Levi took position and stretched his neck to the left and then to the right. He socked the ball into his mitt a few times, and then he leaned back and lobbed that ball to Marco.

"Ball!" the umpire shouted.

So much for impressing the fans. Levi's first major league pitch was high and outside. Not the major league pitching debut he was hoping for.

His next pitch wasn't any better.

"Ball two."

The fickle fans groaned. A few shouted for the return of the veteran pitcher. Levi shook it off. He could do this. He *knew* he could. But his next pitch was just as uninspiring.

"Ball!" the umpire called again.

The count was now three and O. *Focus,* Levi told himself, trying to soothe his anxious nerves. *You can do this! It's no different than when you were back on the farm . . . except for the thousands of people in the stadium watching and millions more on TV.*

Levi could feel the beads of sweat forming on his forehead. He took his position again and shook off his first signal from

Marco. Marco gave him several more, and Levi finally nodded on one of them. He cocked his head to one side, closed his eyes briefly, then opened them and flung that ball toward home plate with Mach-force. This time it went straight down the line, and the batter swung at it.

"Steeee-rike!" the umpire shouted.

The fans in the stands went wild. They were finally getting a first glimpse of what this Amish boy could do. Levi went on to strike out the player, making the opposing team's first out.

He struck out the next batter too. Two outs, one more to go. Levi hurled three Troyer Tornados straight over the plate.

"Strike one!"

"Strike two!"

"Strike three! He's outta there!"

With three outs, it was now the Vipers' turn at bat. Marco hit a line drive to left field, yielding him a double. The next two batters got a single each, lining up the ducks on the pond for Levi's turn at bat.

"Well, folks, we're gonna see if this Amish pitcher can hit too," the sportscaster said. "If he's as good as they say he is, it'll be the Vipers on the board with four more to take the lead and win this thing."

Levi tapped his bat a few times on home plate then took position. His eyes narrowed as he waited for the ball to leave the pitcher's hand.

"Get ready, folks. He's swinging for the fences," the sportscaster said.

The pitch was good and Levi connected, sending that ball flying like a rocket, deep into centerfield. For a moment the outfielder wasn't sure where it had landed and rolled.

"Somebody draw him a map!" The sportscaster laughed. "He's trying to find the ball, and Troyer's already halfway around the bases. One, two, three, and . . . four! They've all made it home, folks. Troyer has done it for the Vipers! Seventeen—you're going to want to remember that number, sports fans. It belongs to Levi Troyer who just scored the Grand Salami for the Las Vegas Vipers. Amish or not, *that* is how you play baseball."

CHAPTER THIRTY-SEVEN

Hannah could hardly keep from squealing right then and there in the middle of the magazine aisle at Walmart. She would have done it too, but she was reasonably certain such behavior would have been frowned upon by both the English and Amish worlds. But there it was, right in front of her. She might have missed it had she not turned her head in that direction as she walked down the magazine aisle for no particular reason— no particular reason at all.

"Levi Troyer Pitches First Game for the Vegas Vipers"

There it was, right on the cover of *Sports Time* magazine. Hannah couldn't believe her eyes.

Levi did it! He really did it! He made it to a major league team!

Hannah took a quick look around, and then, realizing she was the only one in the aisle, she picked up the magazine and turned to the story on page 34. She tried reading it as quickly as she could, knowing full well that her mother and father and sister, who were shopping elsewhere in the store, could easily walk around the corner at any moment and catch her a good eight aisles over from the paper goods aisle, which was where she was *supposed* to be, getting napkins and paper towels for the bakery. Instead she was there, reading about Levi Troyer right in the middle of Walmart.

But Hannah was a fast reader and was halfway through the article before she heard her family in the aisle next to her. She wasn't sure what they were talking about, but she recognized their voices. She slammed the magazine shut and quickly placed it back on the shelf. But then another thought came into her mind.

I wonder if Levi is collecting these articles. Maybe I should make an album for him. One of those really nice English albums with the plastic sleeves. It'll be my secret gift for him. Not that I'd be looking at the photographs in an idolizing way. Good gracious, no! I'd simply be putting them into the sleeves for safekeeping. Then, when he returns home, whenever that is, I can surprise him with what I've done.

It all sounded so perfectly honorable. Of course, she'd have to secretly buy the album and the magazines at the store, sneak them into her room, and keep it all hidden in her closet. And she'd have to work on it by candlelight in the secrecy of her room. But it was perfectly honorable.

Hannah quickly tucked the magazine under some cloth that she'd picked out to purchase, chose an album and tucked it in there too, then pushed her basket to the next aisle.

"So that's where you are," Hannah said when she saw her family.

"Are you ready to go?" Eunice asked.

"Sure. I'll go on ahead and make my purchases then meet you outside at the buggy stall."

Her father nodded his permission. "We just have a few more things to pick up and we'll be along shortly."

Hannah pushed her cart to the front, breathing a sigh of relief. She paid for her items then walked to their buggy and waited inside it, keeping a lookout for her parents and Ruth as she finished the article. Then she closed the magazine and again hid it within her purchases. She didn't like sneaking around like this. It didn't feel right. But she knew Levi would be so overjoyed when she gave him that album. *Oh, why can't my parents just be happy for him?*

CHAPTER THIRTY-EIGHT

It was only a hairline fracture, requiring Hannah's arm to be in a cast and sling for only six weeks. But the incident was the talk of the entire community. No one had ever seen someone do a somersault on rollerblades like that before, while somehow managing to maintain control of her tray of food the entire time.

Hannah was glad the break wasn't worse than it was, and she also took the close call as a warning that she should probably leave the Shake and Skate and look for another line of work. She thought about going over to *The Budget*, as Charley had suggested, but then she saw a "Help Wanted" sign in the window of the Poofy Poodle Dog Grooming shop.

She applied and got the job, but one of the poodles staying overnight in the facility somehow got loose and got into her shoofly pie from her leftover lunch bag, and according to the video on the security cameras, the chewing lasted half the night.

Hannah started looking for another job immediately.

❧

Hannah wished she could be more like Levi, knowing exactly what she wanted to do with her life. But it had always been elusive to her. According to her own self-doubts, she couldn't cook (and there was indeed some evidence to that), she couldn't sew (and there was some evidence to that as well), and even though she'd always thought of herself as a good skater, there she was with a hairline fracture proving otherwise.

So how does anybody know what they're supposed to do with their life? Hannah wondered. *Father says I'm smart, so I could be a school teacher. But that job at our one-room schoolhouse is already covered.*

Hannah found herself between a rock and a hard place—the rock being her supportive family, and the hard place being the very real fact that even if she had the job of her dreams, whatever that was, what she wanted most of all out of life was to be Levi Troyer's wife.

CHAPTER THIRTY-NINE

Levi didn't recognize the phone number on his caller ID. "Hello?" he said into his cell.

"Hey, how's it going, Tornado?" the voice said. "Vinny. Vinny Delmonico."

"Vinny! Sorry, I didn't recognize the phone number. Did you change it?"

"I have a lot of numbers," Vinny said. "So I see you've been having yourself a good time."

"Yeah, I was going to talk to you about that. I'm going to pay you back. Real soon. *Real* soon, Vinny."

"Oh, I know you're good for it, kid."

"What am I up to now? Two thousand? Three?"

"Over ten grand. That's with interest, of course. But it's all good. It's all good, right, Tornado?"

"Yeah, yeah. Everything's going great."

"That's what I like to hear. Reassures me that I'll get my money back. Sure would be a shame if something were to happen to that pitching arm of yours. Know what I mean, Tornado?"

"Oh, don't you worry, Vinny," Levi said. "I take real good care of it." Then Levi realized what Vinny had really meant.

"I'm not saying you have to worry," the man continued. "But things just happen around here. Nobody's fault. They just happen."

Levi tried to swallow the lump in his throat. But it wouldn't budge.

"So the casino treating you good?" Vinny asked. "They bringing enough drinks around?"

"Oh, yeah. I don't have to ask for anything."

"Good, good. Well, get yourself some of those shrimp cocktails too."

"Can't. The team doctor wants me to watch my cholesterol."

"Well, you tell him Vinny said it's okay."

Levi laughed, unsure whether Vinny was serious or not. "And don't worry, Vinny, I'll have the money for you real soon."

"I know you will, kid," Vinny said before hanging up. "Otherwise, you just might find yourself swimming with the fishes."

Levi told himself that it was just Vinny's sense of humor, that he hadn't meant that literally. But his bill to Vinny Delmonico *was* mounting up. And whether anyone at home believed it or not, there were some things Levi didn't want to learn the hard way.

CHAPTER FORTY

W e need to hire a driver, John," David said when he came into the house from a hard day's work in the field.

"We going somewhere, Father?"

"Yah. On a trip. To Cincinnati."

"Cincinnati? What's in Cincinnati?" John asked, figuring he already knew the answer.

"Your brother. We're going this weekend. I heard he'll be playing there. I'd like to see how he's getting along."

"If he needed something, he'd have written. Going up there's a waste of time and money."

"We sold two horses at the auction last week and got a good price for them, yah?"

"A thousand each," John admitted. "But we have other places for that money to go. Besides, I thought we could go fishing Saturday. We haven't fished together in a while."

"We can fish anytime. I'll hire a driver myself if you'd rather I go alone."

"You're not going alone, Father," John insisted. "What kind of a son would I be if I didn't go with you?"

"You are an obedient son, John. Helpful and detailed. You fix everything that needs fixing around here, the furrows in your garden are exactly eighteen inches apart, and you do the shopping and most of the cooking and cleaning."

"Oh, please, tell me I'm not that boring!" John pleaded.

David shook his head and chuckled. "If only your brother had half your fine qualities. So we'll go then? I want to see my son, John."

"You have two sons, Father."

129

"And one of them will be in Cincinnati this weekend."

"One who hasn't shown an ounce of gratitude for all you've done for him . . . or what I've sacrificed for him. But I'll hire us a driver."

"Thank you."

"Now get some rest. I worry about you, Father."

"And I am worried about your brother, as I'm sure you are too. I feel in my heart that we need to do this."

David turned to leave, but stopped when John called out to him. "Father, who worries about me?"

David fixed his eyes on his eldest son. "You, John? No one ever has to worry about you. You're as sure and steady as a summer rain. See you in the morning, son."

David walked out of the room to turn in for the night. John, on the other hand, was wide awake with a bevy of emotions running through him. When he was sure David was out of earshot, some of his frustration spilled out in words spoken under his breath. "Of course you'll go to Cincinnati, Father. And I'll take you there. Because if anyone needs anything at any time, there's always John. But when John needs a little individual attention, a little praise, there's always . . . *him.*"

CHAPTER FORTY-ONE

L evi Troyer had made quite an impression on major league baseball. At game after game after game, Levi was the media darling. Ever since the Amish pitcher had joined the Vegas Vipers, fans and players alike wanted to see what this rising star pitcher could do. And with his Troyer Tornado coming in at over 102 mph now, Levi was more than ready to show them.

"Steeee-rike!" the umpire called out.

"He's painting the corners, folks," sportscaster Will Grayson said. "That's what he's doing—painting the corners. We've got us an Amish Rembrandt on our hands."

It was the bottom of the sixth inning, and no one had gotten a hit off the handsome Vipers' pitcher yet. Could Levi go the whole game again? The crowd cheered him on. If he could do it, it would be his second no-hitter in the major leagues.

Levi shook off Marco's first signal then gave a slight nod at the one that followed. Thrusting his arm back, Troyer leaned forward and hurled that ball towards home plate. Officials clocked it at 99 mph. It was perfect and menacing. There was nothing the batter could do but swing at it and hope for a connection. The poor guy tried his best, but he wasn't quick enough.

"Strike three!" the umpire hollered.

The crowd went wild. The Amish pitcher, who may have been a novelty when he first joined the major leagues, was now commanding everyone's attention. It wasn't a fluke or a lucky pitch every now and then. This Amish boy could play ball!

"Top of the seventh, Vipers at bat," Will Grayson announced, as the teams changed positions.

The first two Viper hitters took a single base each, and then it was Levi's turn at bat. The pitch was high and inside. A little too inside.

"Ball!" the umpire called.

"Troyer got himself a little chin music there," Will said.

The next pitch wasn't much better.

"Ball two!" the umpire said as the player on second base stole his way to third.

The score was eight to zero. The Vipers were in a good position. But with one teammate on first and another in the hot corner, Levi had the chance to raise it another three points. The Vipers could take this match-up in a resounding shutout.

This time the pitch to Levi flew right toward the strike zone. Even with its speed, Levi watched that ball with the keen eye of a tiger, waiting for its prey. Watched it spin closer and closer. And then, when it got into range, he pounced on it, swinging that bat like he'd swung so many fenceposts back in Sugar Creek. He sent that ball right back to the opposition, rocketing high over right field. The right fielder chased after it, but by the time he caught up to that ball and hurled it back into the infield, all three of those Vipers had made it safely around the bases and were home.

"Eleven to zero, Vipers!" Will shouted. "It's all over now but the shouting, boys and girls. The Vipers are on their way to another shut-out victory, thanks to ol' Number 17. What did they feed that boy on that Amish farm?"

The Vipers managed to get in two more runs that same inning, and by the end of the game, they'd won it fifteen to zero. Levi had his second major league no-hitter under his belt.

"I've been covering baseball for three decades, folks," Will said. "And I'm telling you, you're watching baseball history in the making. Number 17 is heading straight to the top. Trust me on this one, fans, this is one baseball card you're going to want to collect."

CHAPTER FORTY-TWO

John walked into the bakery and looked around for Ruth. She wasn't anywhere in sight—only Hannah, who smiled and greeted him.

"Good morning, John."

"Good morning, Hannah."

"Your usual?"

"I have a usual?"

Hannah grinned. "Yah. Anything my sister has cooked."

John lifted an eyebrow, as if surprised. "Am I really that obvious?"

"Well, you certainly aren't the only one who orders that. But the others don't do it with their necks strained toward the kitchen to see if she's here."

"My morning stretches, Hannah. That's all."

Hannah smiled and nodded, unconvinced.

John continued. "Exercise is very important to me, Hannah. I could drop to the floor and do twenty push-ups right now if you need more proof."

Hannah laughed out loud. "That's okay, John. There's something contradictory about someone doing push-ups in a donut shop. What do they call that? An oxymoron?"

"I beg your pardon," John said, a bit taken aback by the term. "Surely you'll recall that I completed the eighth grade, our final grade of school, with honors."

"Yah, you were a year ahead of me and a very good student. But I don't recall any honors being given out."

"It was a private ceremony. At our house."

"Levi never mentioned it."

"He didn't attend . . . of course. Or Father."

"I know you were a good student, John, whether you've ever gotten any recognition for that or not." She smiled and handed him his donut.

"Not that I want to brag," John said. "But I took my education quite seriously."

Hannah wasn't about to let John leave without asking the question that had been troubling her. "Still no word from your brother?"

John shook his head. "No, nothing. Nothing at all. My father and I have left him in God's hands."

"Yah. I haven't heard much lately either. That's all we can do, I guess—leave it all with God." Hannah wiped down the counter. "But, John . . . " Hannah hesitated a moment before going on. "Did you know he's playing for the Las Vegas Vipers now?"

John took a bite of his donut. "Yah, I heard as much. How did you hear?"

"I read the headline on a sports magazine while shopping at Walmart," Hannah said.

"Yah, me too. I was just walking down the aisle and happened to glance over in that direction. I didn't open it, of course."

"Of course not. Not approved reading."

John swallowed. "Too much vanity and excess."

"And all the pictures of those football cheerleaders . . . who could use a good Amish apron to cover up, if you ask me."

"I didn't notice," John said, taking another bite. "And I especially didn't read the part where they talked about all the money my brother is making just to pitch a ball."

"I didn't read about that either. Was that six million for three years?"

"Something like that—if you can even believe it. Sometimes the news gets things wrong, you know. And I suppose you read about him buying a Lamborghini?"

"Is that a cheese?"

John waved his hand in the air dismissively. "A car. A cheese. As if I care."

"And this week I didn't read about the Vipers being favored for the playoffs either," Hannah said.

"I must have missed that."

"The article continued on page forty-two," Hannah said. "Well, anyway, after you read everything you didn't read, aren't you just a little bit proud of your brother?"

"Those are the heroes of the English world, Hannah," John snapped. "We have our own standard for what makes a man great, and I assure you it's not swinging a bat."

"Levi's a good man, John. He's made some mistakes—as have I. None of us are perfect. But I can assure you it means everything to me to have my family and friends give me a second, third, and who knows how many 'do overs.' When people believe in you, no matter how many times you mess up, it makes you want to succeed."

"Well, let me just say that it's equally rewarding when the person who's gone the extra mile, taking up the slack for someone else's shortcomings, gets a little appreciation for the good they do too."

Hannah's heart leaped with excitement. "Oh, John, you're so right! And it would mean so much to Levi if you told him that."

The veins on John's neck began to bulge. "Levi?! I was referring to me!" John protested. "Miss Hannah, would you please tell me what possible good my brother is doing with his life right now?"

"Well, from what I've been reading—uh, I mean, haven't been reading—a lot of young people consider Levi a hero."

"Real heroes do not leave their family behind to do their work for them while they go off and play baseball. By the way, my father and I will be going to see him in Cincinnati this weekend. Whatever good that's going to do."

"Oh, please tell him I said hello."

"Of course. If he even has time to see us."

John was so bothered by Hannah's unyielding defense of his brother that he walked out without even waiting around to see Ruth, who walked in from the kitchen just as the front door closed behind him.

"What's he so upset about?" Ruth asked.

Hannah shrugged her shoulders. "I don't know. But if he ever cuts himself, he's going to bleed green with envy!"

CHAPTER FORTY-THREE

Levi looked up and thought he saw his father in the stands directly above the dugout. He stood tall, and it was hard to miss the silhouette of that Amish hat, an unusual sight among the face-painted, banner-waving, horn-tooting crowd that showed up at most professional ballgames. The figure stayed and watched for a while as Levi struck out two batters in a row. But the man in the hat didn't react with the crowd. He didn't cheer or yell out Levi's name. He simply stood there and watched.

Levi had already determined that if it was indeed his father, he was going to run and throw his arms around him as soon as his team came up to bat—even if he had to climb the fence to do it. He wasn't going to care one bit if Security tried to stop him. *He's my father, and I've missed him. And I sure don't care who knows it.* Levi's heart swelled at the very notion that his dad might've taken a bus or a transport van all the way to Cincinnati to see him. *Did John come along, too?* Levi wondered. *Shoot, I'd even hug John if it's them!*

But when Levi turned and looked again in the direction of the silhouette, the figure was gone. He scanned the area above the dugout, but there was no sign of the man with the Amish hat. Disappointed, Levi continued with the game.

The next player up at bat hit a pop fly toward left field, which was easily caught by the short stop. Three outs, bottom of the fifth. Levi and the Vipers headed into the dugout.

While Levi awaited his turn at bat, he continued to search the stands.

"What's wrong?" Marco asked.

"I thought I saw someone I recognized up there."

"Who?"

"My father."

Marco nodded. "I've seen my mother too. Then I remember she's back in Cuba. They have a word for that. It's something like 'wishful sightings.' It happens when someone dies and your heart wants to see them again so badly that your brain makes it happen. Or makes you *think* it happened."

"No," Levi said. "It wasn't a wishful sighting. It was him. I'm convinced of it."

Levi got word to the security guards to see if they could find him, and they tried their best. But there was no longer any sign of the mysterious Amish figure. Levi was so distraught he could hardly keep his mind on the game.

"Why would he leave, Marco? He stood and watched me for a while, but then he was gone. If it was my father, why would he leave?"

Marco tried to understand. If Levi's father had really come to the game, then why *did* he leave without even talking to him? It made no sense.

At last Marco gave the only answer he knew. "Maybe that was all his heart needed to see, my friend."

CHAPTER FORTY-FOUR

David and John had indeed been at the game, but John managed to convince David in a change of plans.

"Look, at the end of the game, Levi's going to be surrounded by reporters and fans. He won't have any time for us. Besides, we'd only embarrass him. This is his world now, Father. Surely you see that."

David sighed. "Perhaps you're right. I've seen what I came to see. Your brother is well and appears quite content."

The cheers and the organ music rang in their ears as they made their way toward the exit, where they met their driver who would take them back to Sugar Creek. By the time Levi had the security guards look for them, they were gone. But there was no doubt about it—a lot more time and prayer was going to be needed for this Troyer boy to ever want to return home.

～

On the way home to Sugar Creek, David wondered if he'd done the right thing by leaving. "I should at least have stayed and talked with him," he told John.

"Father, Levi's made his choice, and as disappointing as it is for you, he didn't choose our way of life. I know it's hard to hear, but it's the truth. He would have been uncomfortable with us there. We shouldn't have gone. I tried to tell you, Father. He hardly ever mentions his Amish heritage in his interviews anymore."

"How do you know that?"

John hesitated, stumbling over his words. "Well, I . . . uh, well, I've talked with some of the English tourists. And sometimes I might read a headline or two at the stores. Look, it doesn't matter. Levi's leading a different life now. He wants no part of us. You have to accept the fact that he might never come back."

"There's always hope."

"You need to let him go. He no longer wants to be Amish."

David's countenance fell. "John, if what you say is true, it would have broken your mother's heart."

❦

John's words were difficult to hear, to be sure, but knowing the hard truth helped David find the courage to do as John had suggested. Day by day, somehow, someway, David had to let Levi go.

There was only one problem with that scenario. What John was telling David *wasn't* true—not a word of it. Levi had never backed away from telling reporters or his friends about his Amish roots, or crediting David with the fine job he'd done as a single father raising twin boys.

John was rewriting Levi's story faster than Levi could live it. Adding a little here, taking away a little there, convoluting everything he'd read. But what choice did John have, at least as far as he was concerned? He could sense the fire of his father's judgment against Levi's choices beginning to burn out. John had to do whatever he could to stoke those flames again—for the sake of their father, of course. John wasn't about to let his brother hurt David anymore.

❦

The discussion continued when they got back to Sugar Creek.

"Levi's always put baseball first," John said. "Even before you, Father. And frankly, it's been more peaceful with him out of the house."

"John! I will not allow you to speak of your brother in such a way again."

"All I'm saying is, you shouldn't worry so much about him. You don't need that kind of stress. I'm still here. No matter what, I'll always be by your side."

John waited for David to speak, to offer him a dose of his own coveted validation. It took a few moments, but finally he did.

"You've always been a faithful son, John. But I have to believe that one day God will bring Levi home again so my family may be complete. It is my greatest hope."

It wasn't exactly the validation John was seeking or the long overdue correction of his brother he'd been waiting for. But for now, it would have to do.

"Well, if and when Levi does come home," John said, "after all he's done to hurt you, I want you to know that I will not welcome him back."

"John, he's still your brother—and my son."

"And he doesn't want to be either."

John walked to his room without saying another word. It was clear there was no changing his father's mind on the matter.

CHAPTER FORTY-FIVE

The mail truck ran a bit early the next morning, and as usual, John was the first one to hurry out and get whatever had been delivered. He thumbed through the various envelopes on his way back to the house, stopping at a certain one then tucking it into his coat.

Satisfied, he sat down on the porch, picked up his ledger, and went to work. Over the years, John had taken on more and more of the day-to-day operations of the farm. It made sense since John was doing most of the shopping for supplies and such. But the weight of all that responsibility was growing heavier than the prestige of it, and it was wearing on him.

David spotted John on the porch and figured he'd bring him a glass of lemonade.

"You busy, John?" David asked, sitting down in his rocker.

"Just going over these figures. Here's the mail." John handed David all but the one letter that was in his coat.

David thumbed through the envelopes in his hand, clearly disappointed. "You taking any of the horses over to the auction this week?"

"Yah. Gonna try to sell a couple of them."

"You're doing a good job running our auctions, John. I know it used to be Levi's job, but as you say, he might not be coming home for a while."

"I was doing most of his jobs even when he was here, Father."

John was busy trying to decipher figures, and David's chatter frustrated him. "I'm trying to do the books here, Father, and these numbers won't add themselves. Can we talk later?"

"Sure, sure." David sighed. "I just want to say I appreciate all you do around here."

John wanted to feel pleased that his father had noticed his many efforts—compliments were few and far between—but at the moment he was too overwhelmed for any of it to sink in.

"I'll be in to fix lunch in a bit," he said.

"I'll fix it today," David offered. "You've done enough."

David went back into the house, and John tried to return to his bookkeeping, but he could no longer concentrate. It wasn't what David had said. No, the words felt good to hear. But there was something in his tone that troubled him.

CHAPTER FORTY-SIX

Ruth hadn't been snooping when she came upon it. Goodness, no! It was an innocent encounter. With the weather being unusually cold that night in Sugar Creek and all the other quilts in the house already spoken for, Ruth was sure her sister wouldn't mind if she borrowed the quilt she had tucked away in her closet. As far as Ruth knew, that quilt had been hidden there ever since Hannah's not-so-perfect attempt at quilting. Ruth remembered it well. It's not customary for a member of the Amish community to be shunned from attending a quilting circle, although it wasn't an official exclusion coming down from the bishop or anything like that. It was more for Hannah's own good. Much like her cooking, the sweet girl tended to get distracted with a sewing needle too. Hannah had pricked her fingers enough to have made a donation to the Red Cross. And on two separate occasions, she accidentally stitched the quilt to her apron.

That very quilt was the one Ruth was after on this cold night. That poor, uneven, puckered-in-all-the-wrong-places quilt that had been offered at numerous Amish and Mennonite quilt auctions. Only one bidder had ever dared to utter an offer on such a sad bed covering. That was quite an embarrassing day for Hannah too, especially since it was Levi who'd placed the bid. But Hannah told Ruth she wasn't about to let the love of her life take that sad quilt home. Hannah ended up using her own money to outbid Levi at every auction where it was featured, making Ruth wonder exactly how much money her sister had put in that quilt by now.

Ruth tugged at the quilt in the closet, promising herself she'd give it a good shaking out before placing it on the bed. There was no telling what kind of eight-legged creatures might have curled up in there looking for a warm night's sleep.

But when Ruth gave her sister's quilt the final yank, it wasn't a daddy longlegs that jumped out, or even a dreaded brown recluse. It was Hannah's secret album that she'd been making for Levi. In the stillness of the night, it hit the floor with a thud. Ruth froze in her tracks long enough to make sure Hannah was still asleep and nobody else in the house had stirred. When she was certain it was safe, she picked up the curious album and took it, along with the quilt, back to her room. She spread the quilt out across her bed, and there, by the light of her kerosene lantern, she prepared to take a peek—just one quick peek—at her sister's private album.

Ruth had seen such albums in some of the English shops around town. But what was her sister doing with one? And such a fancy one at that.

For the record, Ruth didn't open it without a quick and sincere prayer of repentance. She knew she was breaking every rule of sisterhood to poke her nose where it didn't belong. She also knew there was a reason Hannah hid that album in her closet. It was because she shouldn't have been keeping such a thing in the first place. The Amish don't have their photographs taken, so what was her sister doing with a *photo* album?

Ruth raised the lantern closer so she could open the album and see exactly what was inside. When she flipped over the cover, she got her answer. There he was—Levi Troyer, looking as handsome as ever in his baseball uniform. Ruth's heart raced. She knew if her parents caught her going through her sister's private things, she'd be in trouble. She also knew Hannah could be in trouble, and certainly wouldn't be happy with her either.

But Ruth couldn't keep her curiosity in check. She turned page after page, justifying her actions to herself. *What if there's something in here that reveals a dangerous condition of Hannah's heart? Surely it would be my sisterly duty to talk to Hannah about whatever I find, and help bring her back to her senses. What kind of sister would I be if I didn't look through the whole thing?*

So that's what Ruth did. She looked through the entire album, every plastic page and its contents. There were dozens of newspaper and magazine clippings with headlines admiring Levi for his pitching, or his batting, or yet another homerun. One article talked about him being named MVP. Ruth wasn't sure what MVP meant, but she figured it was simply more praise to add to the pile. She found at least a dozen magazine covers with Levi's face taking up the whole page. And, oh, he was handsome, to be sure! But had Levi Troyer forgotten all his Amish upbringing? It certainly appeared so. But then, Ruth thought, how could anyone stay humble having all that attention heaped upon them? Mostly Ruth wondered what effect all of this was having on her sister's heart.

Not only was Hannah's album filled with photos and interviews of Levi, but it also held the letters he'd written to Hannah. She'd saved every one.

So that's why Hannah always gets the mail before me!

There weren't as many letters as Ruth would have expected, and only one or two in recent months. But there were enough to help Ruth understand why her sister would have waited all this time for Levi Troyer to return and marry her one day. *I could never do that,* Ruth thought. *Especially if the boy stops writing.*

Ruth didn't read the letters, of course. She had to maintain some boundaries. Besides that, she thought she heard someone walking down the hallway. Quickly she tucked the album under her pillow, blew out the flame on her kerosene lamp, and lay back on her pillow.

Probably just the wind, she figured when the sound subsided. Still, Hannah wondered how she was going to get the quilt *and* the album back into Hannah's closet before her sister woke up in the morning. She also wondered whether or not she should talk to her sister about what she'd found. *What if Levi never returns to Sugar Creek? Hannah's only setting herself up for heartache.* But the real reason she wanted to talk to Hannah about the album was to discuss Levi's amazing career.

Levi Troyer, the Amish boy who couldn't manage to keep his focus on anything other than baseball, had fulfilled his dream. His tenacity had paid off. He was a full-fledged hero in the English sports world. And if the photos were any indication, he was a very, very happy man.

When all was quiet again, Ruth tiptoed back down to Hannah's closet and replaced the quilt and album, leaving them just as she'd found them. But she still couldn't sleep a wink the rest of the night. She tossed and turned and turned and tossed. Ruth was finding out what just about every parent, bishop, pastor, priest, and counselor the world over already knew—it's hard to fall asleep with a head full of other people's secrets.

CHAPTER FORTY-SEVEN

Hannah was still looking for a job well-suited to her personality and gifts. She tried babysitting next. It was decent money, but on the first day of her employ, while she was watching the five youngsters, ages five to eleven, who were playing outside, she lay down on the hammock and closed her eyes for only a second—or so she thought. But that second turned into a ten-minute nap. Hannah was in the middle of a glorious dream about Levi when a young voice interrupted the moment.

"Hey, aren't you supposed to be watching us?" the eleven-year-old boy said.

Startled, Hannah snapped herself awake, almost tipping over the hammock and knocking herself to the ground. She steadied the webbed bed then climbed out of it.

"The children!" she gasped. She looked around the area, even across the field, but none of the younger kids were anywhere in sight.

"Oh, glory be!" she cried. "I've lost them!"

Then she heard giggles coming from the tree branches above her. Hannah looked up and saw eight little legs dangling down.

She divided the eight by two and came up with four. Counting the eldest, it was the exact number of children she'd started the day with. Five. "All present and accounted for." She sighed in relief.

When the parents of the youngsters returned home later that day, Hannah confessed the incident, then gave her notice. She wouldn't be available to watch them anymore. But the couple was understanding and forgave her. Still, Hannah held herself to a higher standard—especially where children were concerned.

She immediately began her search for another job.

Hannah had always enjoyed writing, so she finally followed Charley's advice and applied for a job at *The Budget*, the newspaper that serves the Amish and Mennonite communities across America. After seeing a sample of a few of Hannah's poems and other writings, and taking into consideration that her family was well known in the Sugar Creek area, *The Budget* hired her to write newsy copy on the happenings in and around Sugar Creek, Ohio.

It's only writing, she said to herself. *How hard can it be?*

All went well at Hannah's new job—for the first month, anyway. But soon Hannah's distraction began to show up in different ways. One newsy article caused the biggest stir. What Hannah was supposed to have written was: "All of us in Sugar Creek are looking forward to the upcoming youth social, which will be held at the Yoder barn again this year. Andrew Yoder says he thinks he should be recovered from his heart attack in time to host the event. In other news, Lottie Miller delivered her fifth baby. Both are doing fine."

But Hannah was in a rush that morning and had several other things on her mind. This is the copy she wrote instead: "All of us in Sugar Creek are looking forward to the upcoming youth social, which will be held at the Miller barn. Lottie Miller is recovering nicely from her heart attack, and Andrew Yoder says giving birth to his fifth baby shouldn't keep him from the event."

Hannah didn't notice the mistake until the paper was already printed and mailed off. The regular editor, who had to leave early that day for a family emergency, had left Hannah in charge of both writing and proofing the copy. Hannah was more than embarrassed when letters started pouring into *The Budget's* office, wondering if Lottie's heart attack might have been caused by the news of Andrew Yoder's "most unusual condition."

The editor graciously allowed Hannah to write a correction in the very next issue. It cleared up the matter as far as Andrew Yoder being "with child," but Hannah feared her days at The Budget might be limited. Hannah's boss laughed about the whole incident and assured Hannah she wasn't in any trouble whatsoever, since the subscribers had gotten a good laugh out of the mix-up. Still, Hannah thought perhaps she should once again look for another type of employment. *It's probably best for all concerned,* she told herself.

CHAPTER FORTY-EIGHT

David Troyer almost didn't see the sports magazine on the shelf at Walmart that day. Several times he averted his glance from that direction as he looked for the box of envelopes he needed. But that cover photo of a player standing in front of a baseball stadium was a striking pose and almost impossible to ignore.

Besides that, it was *his son.*

"Levi?" David said under his breath. Then, looking around to make sure no one was in the aisle with him, he picked up the magazine. David hadn't seen Levi in over two years, not counting Cincinnati, which hadn't included a conversation and therefore didn't count at all. Even the obligatory Christmas and birthday cards had tapered off. David excused Levi's indifference to keeping in touch, figuring he was simply trying to find his way in life. But he never stopped thinking about him and praying for him.

He thumbed through the magazine, searching for the piece about Levi. On the way, a page featuring cheerleaders appeared. David closed the magazine as quickly as he could.

"Well, *they're* certainly not Amish," he said, as he reached up to put the magazine back on the shelf. But before he could release the magazine from the grip of his fingers, he looked down the aisle and saw Bishop Gingrich walking toward him.

"Out shopping, are you, David?" the bishop said as he approached.

"Yah. Just picking up a few things."

"I see." The bishop glanced in the direction of the sports magazine then back at David. "A few things, huh?"

"Yah, a few things," David said, discreetly releasing his fingers from the magazine.

The bishop nodded, satisfied. "Saw John out in the field earlier this week, harvesting your corn. Get a good crop this year?"

"Oh, very good. I don't know what I'd do without John. He sure is a help to me."

"And Levi? Heard anything from him lately?"

"No, not in a while. Still chasing that dream of his, I suppose."

"Well, we'll continue to pray for him, that God will lead him home one day. You know what the Good Book says: 'Train up a child in the way that he should go . . .'"

David finished the scripture. "And when he is old, he will not depart from it."

The bishop nodded. "Keep trusting, David."

"Oh, I am, Bishop. Nothing would give me greater pleasure than for Levi to return to his Amish ways and to us."

"Well, God wouldn't have taken their mother home if He didn't think you could handle raising your sons. All your hard work will not return to you void. That's a promise, David."

David thanked the bishop for his encouraging words and for his prayers. It felt good to have shared his concern. And he wanted to trust God. He truly did. But after all this time, it was getting harder and harder to see the day coming when Levi would return home. And from the image on that cover of what was now a popular, self-assured major league baseball player, his son wasn't anywhere near *wanting* to come home. That truth was painfully obvious. As far as David could tell, his youngest son's life was turning out just the way Levi had always dreamed it would. Fame, fortune, beautiful fans . . . and baseball.

How does a father compete with all that?

CHAPTER FORTY-NINE

John showed up right on time at widow Waneta Swartzentruber's house. The Swartzentruber Amish are the most conservative of the Old Order Amish, forsaking not only the use of electricity, but usually indoor plumbing too. They have dirt driveways and tin roofs on their houses. Anything fancier than that would be considered worldly. Even the bright orange triangle on the back of most Amish buggies is considered too fancy to the Swartzentrubers. Most will opt for just a few pieces of reflective tape.

Waneta was eighty-three years old and couldn't see that well anymore. But she had the eyes of an eagle every Saturday when it came to seeing John's buggy coming up her driveway.

Waneta thought the world of John Troyer. For years he'd been delivering fresh produce and eggs from their farm, as well as dry goods from the general store and fresh-baked breads and such from the Battered Donut.

What Waneta enjoyed most, though, even more than the food, was talking to John, who never seemed to be in any hurry at all. Unlike some folks who do their good deed and rush away to get back to their own lives, John took time for Waneta, and she appreciated it.

"Hello, Waneta," John said when he reached her front porch where she now stood eagerly at the open door.

"Good morning, John. Well, did you bring 'em?"

"Always do," John answered.

"Chocolate glazed?"

"A dozen of them. Ruth just finished frosting them for you."

"Well, come on in then. Let's have us some!"

Waneta and John sat at the table and enjoyed coffee and donuts and lively conversation. John loved it when Waneta talked about the old days in Sugar Creek, sharing stories she recalled about the many interesting and remarkable people she'd known.

John wondered aloud if his life would seem interesting to anyone after he was gone.

"Of course it will," Waneta assured him. "It all depends on who's doing the storytelling, doesn't it? Because this is what I remember about John Troyer. He was that handsome young prince who courageously drove his carriage through a blizzard one night to save the beautiful princess who was trapped in her home with no chocolate donuts in any of her cupboards, and was quite possibly on the verge of starvation. But despite the storm and the blustering wind, and perhaps a dragon or two—or they might have been a couple of foxes—he made it through without losing a single crumb. And the beautiful young princess lived happily ever after—even though she gained a few pounds—all thanks to this handsome hero. That's the John I remember. So what do you think?"

John allowed himself a slight smile. "Well, I do recall it snowing a few times when I've come out here. Don't know if it could be called a blizzard though."

"When you're hungry for chocolate donuts, it's a blizzard," Waneta said with a laugh.

"I suppose you're right," John said, playing along.

"I remember something else about you, John."

"What's that?"

"I remember watching you and your brother always playing together. Why, the two of you were inseparable. Wherever Levi was, you had to be. And wherever you were, he had to be."

John was saddened by the distant memory. "That was a long time ago, Waneta."

"What happened, John? Why aren't the two of you close anymore?"

"Guess we just grew up and grew apart. Well, one of us grew up anyway."

"But you still love him, don't you?"

"Of course I do. He's my brother. I'd love to be working the farm alongside him right now. But he's got his baseball. That's all he thinks about these days."

"I remember when you used to play baseball too."

"Life's not just about baseball, Waneta. Life is also about work. Hard work."

"I know." Waneta nodded and smiled. "But never forget, John, it's about chocolate donuts too."

CHAPTER FIFTY

Levi hoped none of the other ballplayers had noticed his hands shaking that day in the dugout. Up until then, he'd been able to control the involuntary tremors. But it had been a while since his last drink, and his growing dependence on alcohol was getting harder and harder to conceal.

The Vipers were in the batting position, and there was one more hitter ahead of Levi. Number 17 knew he had to get control of himself.

The next batter stepped up to the plate and hit a line drive to third. The third baseman scooped it up and threw it to first, but the runner slid in under the catch.

"Safe!" the umpire called.

The runner on second base decided to play it safe and remain right where he was.

It was Levi's turn now. He walked up to the plate, wrapped his hands around the bat, just as he had done so many times to the fenceposts back home, and prepared himself for whatever pitch might come his way. The pressure was on. It was the bottom of the ninth, and the Vipers were still down three.

The sportscaster covered the action from the press box. "With two players on base, Number 17 needs a homerun to tie it up for the Vipers. Score is ten to seven. With two outs against them, it's up to Levi Troyer now, folks."

Levi squeezed his hands a little tighter around the bat, but the shaking wouldn't let up. Anyone paying attention would have seen that something was going on with the Amish ballplayer. But the fans and the coach were just waiting for him to win the game for them.

The first pitch was hurled toward him, but Levi backed away from it. It didn't look good enough to take.

"Strike!" the umpire called out.

Levi gave a look of disagreement to the umpire but remained silent. The pitcher sent the next ball flying right over home plate. Levi realized the worth of the pitch too late and swung, slicing through nothing but air.

"Strike two!"

Levi tried to calm his nerves by telling himself the sooner he got this game over with, the sooner he could get a drink. But the seconds dragged on.

The next pitch looked good enough, so Levi took it. This time he laced that ball as hard as he could, launching it all the way to the stands.

"No doubt about it," the sports announcer said. "That baby's gone downtown!"

The crowd cheered as Levi dropped the bat and ran to first, then second, third, and all the way to home, bringing in the other runners in the process.

"He's done it, ladies and gentlemen," the announcer said. "It's a home run for Levi Troyer. The Vipers have tied it up, ten to ten. This game isn't over yet, folks."

The spectators were on their feet, screaming with delight. The game went into an extra inning to break the tie, and though the Vipers lost in the end, Levi Troyer had kept his reputation as the Vipers' "final-inning deliverer" intact . . . and his growing problem safe in the shadows.

If any of Levi's teammates had noticed his hand tremors during the game, they didn't say a word about it, to him or anyone else. Levi was grateful for that. Coach Brenner had made it clear multiple times how he felt about substance abuse of any kind. It could be used as grounds against him for a breach of contract and immediate dismissal. Besides, Levi told himself the uncontrollable shakes could be a symptom of any number of medical conditions. Alcoholism was only one, and if Levi Troyer was certain of anything, he was certain of this—he was still in control.

CHAPTER FIFTY-ONE

David was reasonably certain that after the barn and beer incident, along with the good talking-to that followed, Levi had stayed away from drinking. *It was just the one time,* David told himself. *Everyone makes mistakes.* And he'd been clear when he said, "If I ever catch you behind that barn drinking anything stronger than sweet tea or lemonade, I'll take away that ballfield for good."

And he meant it. But David wasn't aware of how many times John had found empties hidden in the bushes down at the ballfield, or all the times Levi had come in late smelling of something a lot stronger than Amish lemonade.

John wanted to tell their father about the other incidences, but he knew the young people would be upset if David went through on his threat and closed down the ballfield. And even if he did tell his father, David probably would have asked why he hadn't told him about it sooner. So John kept his brother's secrets.

And that was one of the things John resented about Levi most. As far as John could tell, that was when Levi began to pull away from him. John knew too much. Even though John had taken the blame for Levi in the beer incident, the only one David knew about, and John had yet to betray that confidence or any other, he felt he'd lost something. Nobody had ever told him that sometimes there's a price to pay for being the holder of someone's secrets.

CHAPTER FIFTY-TWO

Phil Watson had hinted at the topic of Levi's drinking only once, but Levi didn't want to hear it. He made it abundantly clear to Phil and anyone who broached the subject that he was over twenty-one now, and his life was his own. He also made it clear that anyone who interfered with that notion would be kept out of his inner circle. An ample amount of prestige was to be had from being in Levi Troyer's inner circle, so Phil didn't broach the subject anymore. He didn't want to risk losing his star player one day. That's why, when situations came up, Phil covered for him. Like John did. Time and time again. Whenever Levi called Phil to pick him up from a local bar, Phil was there.

"I can hold my liquor as good as anyone," Phil's prodigy would slur each time Phil helped him into his car. Phil knew these encounters weren't the time for a head-to-head conversation—especially when one of those heads was pretty fuzzy. He usually let Levi sleep all the way home, only waking him up when they arrived. Then he'd help him into his house.

"Thanks, man," Levi would say—his signature send-off. "You're a real friend."

Phil often wondered if a real friend would help him in bigger ways than simply giving him a lift home and promising not to say anything to the coach. Perhaps he should suggest counseling or group meetings. Even have a head-to-head talk. But a ride was all Phil Watson seemed able to do to help the Amish boy who Phil had promised he'd look after. But Phil was a busy man. There were deals to close, stats to go over, and other play-

ers demanding his attention. And that's not even counting a little time for his own personal life. A sports manager of Phil
Watson's reputation certainly didn't have the time to keep
wasting on these late-night calls from an Amish ballplayer
who'd gotten himself in over his head in a strange new world
and couldn't seem to find his way back.

But this Amish ballplayer was Phil's pot of gold, and if there
was one thing Phil Watson couldn't walk away from, it was
gold.

CHAPTER FIFTY-THREE

Levi had become the life of the party at all the after-game get-togethers. A "fun" drunk, if there is such a thing, Levi would buy drinks for the entire bar. "It's no fun drinking alone," he'd say. But then he'd wake up the next morning, not remembering a thing that had been so much "fun" the night before. All he felt was misery.

When Levi first started drinking, all it took was a can or two to give him quite a buzz. But now it was requiring more and more drinks to get that same feeling. He was on a daily rollercoaster ride that was getting less and less thrilling by the bottle. He'd lost interest in participating in any team celebration, signing autographs, or even giving TV interviews. All he wanted to do was sit on a barstool and drink until he was somewhere else in his mind—anywhere but Vegas, where it was becoming increasingly more difficult to keep from falling off the pedestal the media and his team had set him on.

Somehow, though, he never missed a game. He may have been buzzed or hungover, but he always showed up in time for that first pitch. He missed a few of the opening introductions, which some in the press mistook for a "star tactic" in order to up his negotiating power. But even then, he still showed up. Being on time for practice, however, was a different matter altogether.

Though he was offered them from some less than scrupulous outsiders, something inside of Levi resisted the temptation to try performance-enhancing drugs. He prided himself in his natural talent and wasn't about to let a drug steal the credit for what he'd accomplished. Even so, Levi couldn't see how much the alcohol had taken over his life, what it was subtly stealing from him, and how difficult a guest it was going to be to one day kick out the door.

CHAPTER FIFTY-FOUR

Hannah waited to hear the sound of her father's snoring down the hall. She knew it wouldn't be long before her mother blew out the flame on the kerosene lamp and drifted off to sleep herself. Then Hannah could go into her closet and look through her album again, and bring it up to date with whatever new photos and articles she'd collected that week.

Personally Hannah didn't see anything wrong with keeping that album about Levi Troyer. The fact that she was sneaking into her closet and looking at the photos of Levi in the shadows of the kerosene lamp while listening intently for any footsteps down the hall, and the fact that she was now reading each article for the twentieth time, wishing with all her heart that Levi was back home in Sugar Creek, was all beside the point. Sometimes guilt just shows up all on its own, whether it's justified or not. Hannah didn't want her parents to be disappointed in her, though. So right or wrong, justified or not, she kept her secret from them. Besides, she was pretty sure that if it did happen to be wrong, she'd be forgiven once she repented, destroyed the album, and vowed to turn away from her wayward ways, which she certainly would if it ever came to that. That may have been a convoluted way of looking at the situation, but she meant it with all her heart.

In the meantime Levi was as close to her as that filled-to-the-brim album. And Hannah was oh, so thrilled for him. He'd done it! That elusive dream of being a professional ballplayer landed right in his mitt. Hannah's heart danced at the thought. And then, just as quickly, her heart sank. *What if, with all that fame and glory, Levi decides not to return to Sugar Creek and the*

Plain life? Hannah banished the thought from her mind. All she could do was trust that Levi would return to her after he'd had his fill of the English world . . . whenever that might be.

~

Hannah took one last look at her favorite photo of Levi, the one of him in front of a baseball stadium, and sighed. And then her mother's voice interrupted her thoughts.

"Hannah? What are you doing still up?" Eunice asked, startling Hannah so much that she sent the album flying several inches into the air.

Quickly Hannah retrieved the album and tucked it under the quilt then sheepishly stepped out of her closet, closing the door behind her. Her mother stood in her bedroom doorway, waiting for an answer.

"Uh, nothing, Mother," Hannah said. She knew immediately it wasn't the most truthful answer. One doesn't do "nothing" in the shadows of a lantern in your closet in the middle of the night. Hannah was caught red-handed.

"What were you doing?" her mother asked again, opening the closet door to check for herself. Hannah looked down and saw a portion of the red album peeking out from under the quilt.

"What's that?" Eunice asked.

"Oh, that? It's just that old quilt I tried to make. Remember? And I know it's way past my bedtime, and I'm sorry, Mother." Hannah pushed the quilt back a bit farther on the shelf, making sure the album was safely tucked underneath. "I was cold, so I was just getting an extra quilt. But now I don't think I need it after all. I'll just be going back to bed now."

Hannah's mother knew better. She held out her hand without saying a word. Hannah handed over the album.

"It's not what you think, Mother," Hannah said, dreading whatever punishment was about to be handed down.

"Oh?" Mrs. Weaver flipped through the pages. "Because I'm thinking you've been collecting a lot of pictures and news stories about Levi Troyer."

"Well, then, I guess it *is* what you think," Hannah admitted. "But I'm doing it for a perfectly good reason." Hannah knew she should stop talking right about then. Their bishop had said in so many sermons, "When you find yourself in a hole, stop digging." But whenever Hannah got nervous, her tongue seemed to have a mind of its own, and no matter how hard she tried to keep them in, the words just kept falling out of her mouth as that hole got deeper and deeper.

"The bishop asked me collect them," Hannah said. "It's for a sermon he's working on about pride."

"Hmm," was all Hannah's mother said as she continued thumbing through the album. "So the bishop's been working on this sermon for well over two years now, has he?"

Hannah thought quickly. "He wants to be thorough. He needs a lot of examples to make his points."

"Well, then, I'll look forward to that sermon." She held up the album. "And I'll run this over to him first thing in the morning. I'm sure you've collected much more than he ever expected."

Hannah wiped the beads of sweat from her brow with her night shirt, wishing she'd bit her tongue before giving such a ridiculous excuse about the album, one that wouldn't hold up for a minute in the light of day. "Uh, well . . . okay. I hope he'll be pleased."

Mrs. Weaver waited for a moment then said, "Now, do you want to tell me the truth, Hannah?"

Hannah knew the tone of her mother's voice all too well. There would be no getting around the matter any longer. "I'm sorry, Mother. Please don't tell Father. Or the bishop."

"You know I *have* to tell your father, Hannah. I'll discuss it with him in the morning. We'll decide then how you should be punished, and whether or not we should discuss this with the bishop."

"Yes, ma'am."

Before leaving Hannah's room, Mrs. Weaver turned back to Hannah, once again holding up the album. "Do you love him, Hannah? Or do you love all *this?*"

"I love *him,* Mother."

Eunice sighed. "You know the world he's chosen is no life for an Amish girl who wants to be faithful to her faith."

"Or an Amish boy who's drifted from his, I would imagine." Hannah took a shaky breath. "I pray every day that he'll come home."

"You know, Hannah, when and if he ever does, he won't be the same Levi Troyer who left."

"I would still love him."

"It may not be that easy," Mrs. Weaver said. Then she turned out the light and walked out of the room.

CHAPTER FIFTY-FIVE

"S teeee-rike!" yelled the umpire as Levi's fast ball zoomed over home plate and slammed into the catcher's mitt.

With the count at O and one, the batter got into position again.

Levi pulled his mitt and ball up close to his chest and stared down the strike line. He was focused and determined. That batter wasn't going to get on base if Levi Troyer had anything to say about it.

Straight down the line he threw it—another perfect delivery.

"Steeee-rike two!" the umpire shouted. You could feel the tension in the stadium. Levi was one strike away from his third major league no-hitter.

Levi stood up on the mound and wiped the sweat off his brow. A hush fell over the stadium. With baseball in hand, Levi drew back his arm, nodded to Marco, and released the fury of the dreaded Troyer Tornado.

"Steeee-rike three!" the ump hollered.

The crowd erupted in cheers so loud Levi figured they could've been heard all the way to Sugar Creek. It was a game for the record books. Levi Troyer, the Amish pitcher who learned to play baseball on a leveled-out Ohio cornfield, the boy some had called a slacker and destined for no good thing, had just pitched his third no-hitter in his first season of pro-ball. If he never did another thing in his life, he'd carved out his name in baseball history. No family member was there to cheer for him, but that didn't matter. He didn't need anyone. Levi Troyer had fulfilled his dream, and he'd done every bit of it on his own. That's what he told himself anyway.

❧

Fans and players gathered later at the Dugout Bar to revel in the record-making achievement. "The drinks are on me," Levi told everyone gathered there. It was a moment to celebrate. Even with his occasional mess-ups, the hangovers, and the rebel in him, Levi Troyer was still a phenomenal ballplayer who could pull off an astonishing game when he wanted to.

But inside, trouble was brewing.

CHAPTER FIFTY-SIX

"Thank you for seeing us on such short notice, Bishop," Eli said when he and Eunice stepped into his home the morning after Eunice found the album.

"Well, it sounded serious when I ran into you at the general store." He led them to the kitchen. "Happy to help. Please, sit down."

Eli and Eunice took seats at the table, with the bishop sitting across from them.

"Now then, what seems to be the trouble?"

"It's Hannah," Eli said.

"Oh, no. I was afraid of this."

"You were?" Eunice asked.

"What hospital did they take them to?" Bishop Gingrich said. "Was it tourists or locals? Don't worry. I'll certainly vouch for her. It wasn't intentional. And I'm sure it's not serious. We haven't lost anyone yet on account of her cooking."

"No," Eli said. "Nobody went to the hospital. Her food may make you ill, but it's never been toxic."

Eunice slid the album across the table.

"What's this?" the bishop asked.

"Look inside," Eli said then he watched as the bishop looked through the album, page by page.

"She was hiding it in her closet," Eunice added.

The bishop continued to turn the pages, nodding uncomfortably at each one.

"Oh, my," the bishop murmured. "My, my, my."

"We were quite surprised, as well," Eli said, scooting his chair in a little closer so he could see which page Bishop Gingrich was looking at.

"Levi's pitched three no-hitters already?" the bishop said.

"Well, yes. But, Bishop Gingrich, we don't know what to do. Our Hannah has been sneaking around behind our back and saving every article and magazine cover about that Troyer boy. Obviously, he's all she's been thinking about ever since he left."

"Levi pitched *three* no-hitters in *one* season?" Then, regaining his proper composure, the bishop closed the album.

"It's serious, isn't it?" Eunice asked.

Eli took Eunice's hand, as they waited to receive the bishop's perceptive wisdom. "What should we do, bishop?"

"Well, she hasn't joined the church yet," the bishop said. Then he added, "By the way, is she planning on doing that soon?"

Eli nodded. "Oh, yah. Hannah has made her decision to do so."

"But she wants to wait and do it with Levi Troyer," Eunice said.

"But as you can see from the album," Eli said, "that day could be a long way off."

"I see. Well, then, let me ask you this. Does she love him?"

"Oh, yes, she loves him very much," Eunice said.

"Whether he is the right man for her," Eli said, "I don't know."

The bishop nodded understandingly. "Well, I like Levi. He's still finding his way, but when he does, I believe he'll return to us. Then, with God first in his life, he could become the very man you'd want for your daughter."

"With all due respect, Bishop Gingrich," Eli said, "God would have to do a miracle on the boy for that to be the case."

"You don't believe He can, Eli?"

"Oh, I believe God can," Eli said. "I'm just not so sure the boy will let Him."

CHAPTER FIFTY-SEVEN

John Troyer stopped by the Walmart to pick up more paper. He enjoyed dropping off newsy letters at *The Budget*, letting their friends and family from Pennsylvania and other areas, including Sugar Creek, keep up with the goings on in the David Troyer family. John would write about his father and their farm. He'd tell everyone which vegetables were ready for harvesting, and he'd share the news of any upcoming social events. But he seldom wrote about Levi. Even when Levi lived at home, nothing he did seemed particularly noteworthy to John. Beyond the family, that is. John thought it was a helpful gesture to raise the bar for his brother, trying to help snap him out of his idle ways and actually accomplish something in life that others would deem worthy of attention. Now that he actually had, at least according to the English, John still couldn't bring himself to mention it. *If I brag on his worldly success, wouldn't that tempt others to be just like him?*

There was, however, one incident that occurred before Levi left that John did think was worth mentioning in the community news. Levi had hit a baseball into the hind-quarter of a bull, making that critter so angry he broke through the fence and chased Levi and the whole Amish ball team around the field. *That deserves a special mention*, John figured. But that was one of the rare times John wrote of Levi, and it was the only time he could remember ever wishing the Amish allowed the taking of photographs.

So that night in Walmart, when John happened to pass by the magazine aisle again and saw Levi's picture on the cover of *Sports Time* magazine, he did a double-take.

John read the headline out loud, right there in the aisle: "Troyer Pitches Record-Making Third No-Hitter in First Season!"

"Well, look at that," John said to himself. One more accolade for his overly applauded brother. But there was something else in the photograph that caught John's attention. It was the look in Levi's eyes. It was a look he'd seen before. Behind the barn. And all those other times. A look that told him that all was not what it seemed.

Yet John had his own problems to deal with. He had a farm to run and a father to take care of. He wasn't the one who'd taken off to seek fame and fortune. He wasn't the one continually making bad decisions in his life.

John walked on, putting the image of his brother out of his mind. Whatever trouble Levi was in, he was going to have to reach out to someone if he wanted help. He was too far away now for David and John to monitor his actions—or to save him from himself. He'd made it quite clear that he was making his own choices now, and with that came the freedom to live with them too.

It grieved John to know their mother had lost her life bringing the two of them into this world, and that from all appearances, Levi didn't seem to appreciate her sacrifice.

"Couldn't *I* have had a choice in the matter?" John said under his breath as he pushed his cart up the next aisle.

The man grabbing the can of Miller's baked beans from the shelf turned and looked at him. "Why, sure, buddy," he said. "Go ahead and get you some. I wasn't gonna take 'em all."

Realizing the man had heard him talking to himself, John simply nodded, grabbed a can of hickory smoked beans, which he didn't really need, and walked on to the checkout counter. A friendly clerk, as well as another full rack of *Sports Time* magazines with Levi on the cover, were there to greet him. Poor

John. No matter how hard he tried, he never could get away from that brother of his.

CHAPTER FIFTY-EIGHT

Hannah tried her best not to listen as she wiped down the tables at the Battered Donut. But she couldn't help it. She worked her way toward Table #2 since it was directly across from Table #7, where two tourists sat with their cellphone playing the Vipers' game against the Los Angeles Dodgers.

As Hannah scrubbed, the sportscaster called the plays.

"It's the bottom of the ninth, sports fans," he said. "Vipers are down by one. They've got a man on base, and Number 17 is up at bat. If Troyer knocks him in, the Vipers tie the game. If he hits a homerun, they'll take the win. Can he do it?"

Just then Hannah decided Table #2 could use a little extra cleaning. She scrubbed it over and over, leaning in just a bit toward the cellphone on the ladies' table.

"And Troyer hits it into the stands! It's gone, ladies and gentlemen. Levi Troyer has won the game for the Vipers."

Hannah let out a squeal of delight, which she quickly covered up by transforming it into a cough. "Excuse me," she said, moving on to the next table. "I've got a tickle in my throat."

The ladies nodded sympathetically. "I'm just getting over a virus myself," one lady said.

"Well, this is sure a nasty one that's been going around," Hannah said. "It starts with a scratchy throat then moves into your chest."

"And it seems to hit during professional baseball games," Mrs. Weaver said as she walked by the table.

Hannah smiled at her mother. "I'm wiping down the tables, Mother."

"Yes, well . . . you might want to clean one of the other ones now."

"Go easy on her, ma'am. We're Viper fans too," one of the ladies explained. "They just won."

Eunice raised her eyebrows. "Oh? Is that so?"

"Their pitcher was raised on an Amish farm, you know. Somewhere around here. Levi Troyer. Do you know him?" the other lady asked.

Hannah started to answer, but her mother jumped in first.

"Oh, everyone around here knows Levi."

"Well, then, you all must be very proud of his success."

"Sure, we've always admired his talent. But success to us is a whole lot more than playing ball," Eunice said. Then she walked to the back to get some more baked goods.

The ladies called Hannah over.

"So? Are you going to tell us?" one of them asked.

"Tell you what?"

"Oh, sweetie," the other lady said, "I'm sure you get asked all the time—about that handsome Amish pitcher."

"Well, what would you like to know about him?"

"What else? Is he taken?"

"You mean, is he courting someone?"

The women nodded excitedly.

"Well, I understand he *has* asked someone to wait for him," Hannah said.

"And what'd she say?" the first lady asked.

"Well, of course she said yes," said the second one. "Who wouldn't wait for Levi Troyer?"

Hannah put the mystery to rest. "Yes, she's waiting for him."

"Oh, that's so romantic!" the women cooed in tandem.

Eunice Weaver stepped back into the room. "Hannah, the other tables need cleaning."

"Yes, Mother." Hannah nodded to the ladies then walked over to another section of tables.

For the rest of the night Hannah wondered about Levi's request for her to wait for him. Was it even what he wanted anymore? *Maybe he's forgotten all about me by now.*

It was easy to see why she'd think that, too. No recent letters, no official announcement of engagement, nothing. Maybe Levi Troyer wasn't taken after all.

CHAPTER FIFTY-NINE

When Levi showed up to the game the next day, Marco took him aside.

"You okay, man?"

"Sure," Levi said. "Why?"

"I saw the coach talking to you again."

"Oh, that. He was just pumping me up to win it today. You know how it goes."

Marco could tell Levi was covering something. But he didn't want to push it any further, telling himself that Levi's private life was none of his business. Besides, there was something about his Amish friend that made Marco trust his word. If he said he had everything under control, then it must be true. So Marco backed off and gave his friend space.

Out on the field, though, Levi's condition was getting harder and harder to cover up.

His first pitch was low and outside. Still, the batter took it for a single. The next player stepped up to home plate. Levi threw the pitch, but it didn't pass anywhere near home plate. Levi felt a bit woozy but managed to shake it off before Coach Brenner noticed. His third pitch was a wild one that would've hit the batter had he not jumped out of the way.

"What's he doing?" Phil said to whoever was within earshot.

Levi tried to control whatever was going on inside of him. But after Levi walked the next two players, Coach Brenner was steamed. The fickle fans cheered when Brenner stepped in and took him off the mound. But the Vipers were too far behind to make it up, and in the end, they lost.

I need a drink, Levi told himself on his way out of the locker room after the game. *That'll fix everything.*

But Coach Brenner walked in and caught up with him before he could slip out.

"What were you doing out there, Troyer? Bowling?"

"It won't happen again, sir. I promise."

"No more promises, Troyer. Just do your blasted job!"

"I'll do better next time, sir."

Coach Brenner got right in his face. "What's going on with you, man? Or do I give you a drug test right here and now?"

"Go ahead," Levi challenged. "I'm clean. I'm just coming down with something, I guess."

"That's why your breath reeks of booze?"

Levi didn't answer. Like Hannah, he remembered the bishop's sermon about when you find yourself in a hole, stop digging. But Coach Brenner wanted an answer.

"Troyer, you'd better pray this is the flu because if I find out you're hungover—again—you'll be riding the pine for the rest of the season. You hear me? We've got too much riding on this to have our best pitcher start walking every player who comes up to bat. Now we've got another game tomorrow. You sure as anything better be ready for it!"

Levi nodded. He'd let the coach win this one, he figured. After Brenner left, though, Levi headed straight downtown.

"A round of drinks for everyone in the house," he shouted as he walked in. The place erupted in cheers and hollow praise for an Amish ballplayer who was throwing around his money like it didn't mean a thing to him. And maybe it didn't anymore.

As the bartender handed out the free drinks, Levi greeted his bought and paid for friends of the moment. He knew most of their names but not much else about them. And none of them knew him, not the real Levi Troyer. They only knew what they'd read about him in the papers or saw him do on the field. But that wasn't who he really was, or all that he was.

Still, to Levi, it was some measure of acceptance, and it felt good.

CHAPTER SIXTY

Clouds billowed from Hannah Weaver's house once again, and some in the community showed up to help douse the flames. They passed the buckets of water between them with the precision of an Olympic relay team. Hannah didn't want to be known as the worst cook in all of Sugar Creek, she really didn't, but with so many eyewitnesses to her kitchen disasters, the title was getting hard to shake.

Quickly Hannah ran through all the safety drills. No one else was home at the time—she was sure of that—so she wasn't worried that a family member was trapped inside. She could also see her horse, Dreamer, grazing in the field at a comfortable distance from all the commotion and smoke. Her only concern was making sure the fire was out and finding out what caused it in the first place. She did seem to recall that she was in the middle of melting chocolate pieces for a batch of brownies. She hoped that hadn't been the cause of the fire. She also hoped that, if it had been, both the kitchen and the chocolate would still be salvageable. *Nothing is more depressing than a perfectly good batch of chocolate pieces going up in smoke!*

Whatever caused the fire, it didn't seem too serious, thanks to the volunteers who showed up. It'd be doused and all cleaned up in no time. Hannah watched the water brigade, wishing Levi could be there in the line. He'd been a part of it many times in the past, and she always enjoyed watching the muscles on his toned and tanned arms tighten as he passed the buckets down the line. She especially liked how he'd slip in an understanding glance or two in her direction, his eyes telling her that no matter what, everything was going to be all right.

Hannah didn't know exactly where Levi was on this very day when she longed to see him. All she knew was he was out there somewhere, far beyond their Amish community. He could have been in any number of cities, playing ball in any number of stadiums. Wherever he was, though, Hannah hoped he was well and happy, and still enjoying his dream.

$\approx$

As if her week couldn't get any worse, the next morning Hannah stopped off at the market and noticed the headline on one of the tabloids: "Baseball Star Levi Troyer to Marry Socialite."

Her breath caught in her throat. She didn't understand the world of tabloid journalism and therefore took the headline as the gospel truth. Her arm seemed to involuntarily thrust forward to grab a copy and read it. But she stopped herself. Looking at sports magazines and history books was as far as her conscience would allow her to go.

But the longer she stood there in the check-out line, the harder and harder it was to ignore the headline. The words, in the biggest and boldest font possible, were almost shouting at her, mocking her in a way.

Hannah felt as though everyone in the store was watching her at that very moment. Being publicly jilted—even though she and Levi were not officially engaged and hadn't even really dated for that matter—still called for her to take a higher path.

What Hannah didn't realize, though, was that some of these tabloid stories aren't even true. In some situations, the reporter simply takes a photograph of a perfectly harmless encounter between two people—usually a celebrity, politician, or sports figure—and edits it so it appears to be something other than what it actually is. Most people in the English world read such stories with that in mind.

But Hannah didn't know that. All she knew was that she'd always loved Levi and was fully convinced he loved her, too.

She'd faithfully waited for him to get over this professional baseball phase of his life and return to her. But now it appeared Levi had more on his mind than baseball. The photo on the cover of that tabloid clearly showed Levi Troyer and a lady walking arm-in-arm into a restaurant.

That night Hannah cried herself to sleep, vowing never again to look at those tabloids. She even decided to stop buying the sports magazines too. *Those magazines and photographs get thoughts into your head and start making you think all sorts of crazy things,* Hannah told herself. In one brief moment, while innocently standing in line at the check-out counter, her otherwise peaceful heart had been assaulted, and her mind was now racing and chasing all kinds of ridiculous notions.

Levi doesn't love me anymore.

Levi never loved me.

Levi loves her now.

Would he like me better if I dressed like that?

How could I have been so stupid?

That night Hannah's mind was going everywhere but where it should have gone, which was to the truth that she knew, despite what the tabloid said. But it didn't. Hannah tossed and turned and couldn't sleep a wink. Had she been wasting her time waiting on Levi? Had she risked her relationship with her parents by keeping an album for a man who was in love with someone else? Had she gotten herself into a bit of trouble with the bishop for keeping that album, full of photographs of Levi Troyer? A man who didn't even care enough to write more often? Finally she climbed out of bed and stepped over to her closet to do what she should have done with that album long ago.

Just one last look, she promised herself. Then she'd throw it away.

This time, though, every picture in that album looked completely different. Expressions that used to melt her heart now only brought sadness. Hannah knew she shouldn't give the tabloid headline the power to rob her of her joy or change her opinion of someone she knew and loved, but that was easier said than done. The proof was right there in the photo of Levi with that lady. Hannah's hope was sinking fast. *Levi's never coming home!*

Brokenhearted, Hannah closed the album, blew out the kerosene lamp, and went to bed. She'd dispose of the album tomorrow. If Levi Troyer had found love in the arms of another woman, Hannah was going to have to accept it. There was nothing she could do about it except pray that if it was God's will, Levi would change his mind. *You can't hogtie a man and drag him kicking and screaming to his own wedding,* she told herself. Well, maybe you could, but it would cause quite a ruckus. God had someone for Hannah Weaver, and she was confident that one day she'd know who that was. And if He didn't, well, she'd learn to be content and happy being single. She believed that down deep in her heart, and no tabloid in the world could change her mind on that.

CHAPTER SIXTY-ONE

Well, there's always John," Hannah joked to herself. Then she quickly pushed that thought out of her mind as quickly as it had entered. She'd never been interested in John, not in the slightest. She and John were complete opposites. *It would never work out. Ruth is more his type. And I don't love him. Not as in a "hanging out with him" kind of love. Not in a committed, nobody-else, courting-kind of love either. And especially not in a happily-ever-after kind of love. Maybe in a brother-in-law kind of love, but that's it.*

Ruth on the other hand, was a different matter. Ruth and John had plenty of things in common. They were both home-oriented, industrious, dedicated, and near-perfect. He was a farmer, so he could grow the food, and she could cook it. And they each had taken their baptismal vows, so they were committed to remaining Amish.

There was just one problem. Hannah wasn't sure Ruth and John cared for each other that way. But why was Hannah matchmaking Ruth and John when she couldn't even get that socialite off Levi's arm?

Hannah wasn't sure who she could talk to about what she'd seen in the tabloid. She wished she could have talked to her mother, but she was afraid she'd say Levi Troyer wasn't worth the bother, and she should move on with her life. The same was true of her father. And she certainly couldn't talk to John about it. Even though he was Levi's brother, Hannah didn't think it was proper to go stirring up more trouble in the Troyer household. So she chose the one she usually chose in matters of the heart—her big sister.

"Oh, Ruth, do you think it's true?" she asked, pointing the tabloid out to her on their next trip to the store.

"Well, it certainly looks like it, huh?"

"I know. That's what I thought too. What should I do?"

"Write to him and ask. Go right to the source. You can't always believe what you read, Hannah."

"But she's holding his arm."

"Maybe she almost tripped in the street just before someone took that picture. Would you have wanted her to fall flat on her face?"

Hannah hesitated.

"Hannah! That is not the Amish way to act."

"Sorry." Hannah sighed. "No, I wouldn't have wanted that. But he's *my* boyfriend!"

"So see what the truth is before you react. Unless . . . "

"Unless what?"

"Unless you're afraid to know the truth."

CHAPTER SIXTY-TWO

Have you thought of working at the library, Hannah?" Eli asked one evening. The supper dishes were done and put away, and everyone had settled in for an evening in front of the fireplace on this early fall night.

"The library? Well, I do love to read. And I'm good at filing, too."

"Sounds like the perfect job for you," Eli said.

Hannah agreed. She made plans to apply there next. Old news, such as what's written in history books, would be easier to work with than current news, she figured. *You can't mess up history, right?* Besides, working at the library would fit in quite nicely with another plan she had.

༄

Come to find out, the library was in need of help, so Hannah was immediately hired. Even though it was an English library, it catered to the Amish community as well. Hannah appreciated that. Many books that would be of interest to her Amish friends were stocked there, as well as more mainstream titles. And the head librarian couldn't have been nicer.

It was Hannah's job to keep the shelves neat and orderly. She actually enjoyed dusting and restocking the shelves, and her efforts afforded her the opportunity to see all the different books that were available. It wasn't long before Hannah found herself lingering around the "B" titles a little more than the rest of the alphabet. "B" as in "Baseball." Whenever she could, Hannah borrowed a book on professional baseball and read it at her desk in between waiting on customers. Sometimes she'd get so engrossed in a particular professional baseball-related book that she'd check it out and sneak it home to finish. Her covert operation would involve wrapping the English book under the cover of a "bishop-approved book," just to avoid any situation at home. It wasn't that baseball was wrong. It certainly wasn't. After all, the Amish played and loved the sport too. But it was all those other trappings that tended to come along with the professional sports world.

And there was one other thing. Hannah knew her parents wanted her to forget all about "that Troyer boy" and his dreams that had led him away from his Amish faith. Having professional baseball books around would give evidence that she surely hadn't forgotten about Levi Troyer at all.

But Hannah wanted to read as much as she could about Levi's new world, memorize the names and batting averages of all the players, and study the history of the teams, especially the Las Vegas Vipers. That way, when and if Levi ever returned to Sugar Creek, she could impress him with her vast knowledge. After that a marriage proposal would be imminent; Hannah was certain of it. A man like Levi Troyer couldn't resist a girl who knew so much about the sport he loved. What man could? So that's what Hannah did. Every free moment at the library, she read about Willie Mays, Mickey Mantle, Sandy Koufax, Babe Ruth, and all the other greats. She even memorized dozens of Yogi Berra quotes and laughed to herself over them.

Levi had been gone two and a half years now. But socialite on his arm or not, Hannah was still determined to wait for him. *People break off engagements all the time,* Hannah told herself. *Mr. Berra was right. It ain't over 'til it's over!*

CHAPTER SIXTY-THREE

So do you miss your home in Cuba?" Levi asked Marco one night in the locker room when it was just the two of them left gathering up their gear after a game.

"Parts of it," Marco admitted.

"So tell me, what was it like?"

"Our family was poor, so I remember the hunger most. I sure don't miss that. But I learned to fool my stomach by thinking about things I liked more than food. Like baseball. Eventually the hunger gave up and went away. For a while, anyway."

"I miss my home," Levi said. "The green rolling hills of Sugar Creek . . . . They call it the Little Switzerland of Ohio."

"Why's that?"

Levi shrugged. "I think it reminded some of the early settlers of their homeland. It's beautiful—this time of year especially. So many colors everywhere, all over the hillsides."

Marco nodded. "I miss the beaches and fields of sugar cane as far as you can see. And my family. I miss them a lot. But I like it here. My mother believed with all her heart that baseball would be my ticket to success. She was right, but I still miss her."

"I didn't think I would, but I miss my family too," Levi said. "Man, before I left I couldn't get away fast enough. There were so many rules! Why, do you know the first time I stole second base, I felt guilty?"

Marco chuckled. "There are rules in baseball too, my friend."

"That's different." Levi laughed. "And I sure can't identify with you about going to bed hungry. I don't think I've ever heard my stomach growl. I was surrounded by a whole community of great cooks. Well, except for this one girl. Hannah's her name. Her family owns a bakery, and people didn't take to her cooking, but I sure liked it."

"She's pretty?"

"Prettier than anyone I've seen in Vegas. And natural too. Not a speck of make-up."

"So . . . you dating?"

"The Amish call it courting. But no, not officially. Although I did ask her to wait for me."

"Wait? How long have you been gone?"

"Two and a half years," Levi said.

"Two and a half years? That's a long time, bro."

"Not where I come from. And not if you love each other." Then he added in his own defense, "Hey, I'm waiting for her too."

Marco shook his head. "To each his own, I guess."

"I still remember the first and only time I ever kissed Hannah. On the cheek. It tasted sweeter than sugar."

"Didn't you say she works in a bakery? It probably *was* sugar."

Levi laughed, and Marco continued. "I don't know, man, you're waiting two and a half years for someone you've only kissed on the cheek. Are you sure you're in professional sports?"

"You don't know Hannah. Believe me, she's worth the wait."

"Well, all I can say is, she sure must love you a lot."

"I hope."

"Sounds like you've got some doubts."

Levi took a deep breath. "My brother wrote and told me she's moving on with her life."

"You believe him?"

"I don't know."

"Well, you can't really blame her, huh?"

Levi sighed. "No, I guess not. I probably shouldn't expect her to ever give up her world for me."

"Would you give up yours for her?"

"I'd like to say yes. But right now, my life's going exactly how I planned it."

"This is how you planned it? Sitting in a sweaty locker room talking with me on a Friday night, with nowhere to go but the Dugout Bar, and you won't remember any of it tomorrow?"

"Glamourous, huh?"

Just then a desert storm announced its arrival with a flash of lightning and a loud rumble of thunder.

"Finally some rain, huh? Maybe this'll finally cool things off," Levi said.

"Hope so," Marco said, as the wind began to kick up and the rain started pounding on the ceiling. "But I'll tell you that's something else I sure don't miss about Cuba. The hurricanes."

"Bad, huh?"

"Oh, yeah. Floodwaters washing your whole house away. Hard to come back from that."

"In Ohio we had thunderstorms," Levi said. "They'd roll in over the cornfields and light up the whole sky."

"Like the fireworks after one of our games, huh?"

"Fireworks don't even come close to the show an Ohio lightning storm can put on."

"Thanks, but I'll take the sunshine any day."

"I love the sun," Levi said. "But I love a good storm, too. And the best part is those last few rumbles of thunder, the ones you hear off in the distance, letting you know that no matter how rough things had gotten, the storm had finally moved on and God was still in charge."

"So you believe in God?"

"Well, yeah, sure. Don't you?"

"Guess I'm still asking questions."

"Like?"

"Well, *why* for starters."

"Why what?"

"Why didn't He stop my father from being killed?" This was the first time Marco had opened up about his father, and Levi leaned in with interest as Marco continued.

"I'd run home from school every day. My father would be there waiting to play catch with me. *Every* day. He never missed. Except this one day, he didn't show up. I waited and waited, but he never came." Marco dropped his gaze for a moment, then looked back up, sadness and tears filling his dark brown eyes. "They killed him. The drug lords. All because they wanted our land. That'd be my first why. If God is God, why didn't He stop them from killing my dad?"

Levi wasn't sure what to say. He couldn't condemn Marco for wondering why God hadn't saved his father. Levi had plenty of questions himself.

"I've got a 'why,'" Levi said. "Why couldn't my brother and I ever get to know our mother? Our father told us what she looked like, but it's not the same as hearing the sound of her laughter. Or knowing the touch of her hand."

Marco nodded. "Guess we both have our questions, huh?"

"My father says God's big enough to handle our questions . . . even the hard ones."

"But what if you've asked and asked, and He still doesn't answer?"

"It doesn't make Him any less real or less able to hear us. We're both here, aren't we? That was two prayers answered, right?"

"*Si.*" Marcos smiled. "*Dos milagros.*"

"Milagros?"

"Two miracles. You and me—*dos milagros.*"

Levi nodded. "Dos milagros indeed."

"So does your brother know you made it to the pros?"

"John? He's never been very interested in seeing me succeed . . . if he'd even call this success." Levi pulled a towel out of his sports bag. Marco couldn't help but notice the flask that almost fell out. Levi quickly tucked it back into the bag.

"Look . . . " Marco hesitated before plunging ahead. "I don't mean to be getting into your business, but . . . well, is everything okay? You were late to practice twice last week. And your pitching's been off."

"Nothing I can't handle."

"Just don't want you taking on the 'wrath of Brenner.'"

"Don't worry. Everything's fine," Levi assured him.

"Listen," Marco said, "I haven't told the other players this, but I've beat 'em."

"Beat who?"

"Alcohol. Gambling. Habits that were starting to call the shots in my life."

"Hey, I can hold my liquor. And as for the tables . . . I'm just having a little fun, that's all."

"Saw you lose at poker the other night. Forty grand is more than a little fun."

"It's my money to lose."

"Just trying to be a friend," Marco said.

"Yeah? Well, don't you worry any about ol' Number 17," Levi said. "I've got everything under control."

❧

The conversation was lasting longer than either Levi or Marco had anticipated. But neither seemed in any hurry to end it.

"So when did you know you wanted to play baseball?" Marco asked.

"From the first time I held a fencepost in my hand and took a swing."

"A fencepost?"

"That's how I learned to hit." Levi laughed. "And why I bought some new bats and mailed 'em home for the Sugar Creek team. I still prefer a fencepost myself. All in all, though, I guess it worked out, especially for my brother and me. He has his farming, and I have baseball."

"You're each doing your own thing, huh?"

Levi nodded. "My brother and I may be twins, but about the only thing we share is a birthday."

CHAPTER SIXTY-FOUR

Charley Miller stopped by the library to check out a book. Being a blacksmith, he enjoyed reading about blacksmithing in the old west.

When he entered the free-standing building, he gave a friendly nod to Hannah then made his way back to the "B" section. He glanced through a shelf of books and made some selections. But as he was about to leave that aisle, his eyes zeroed in on something sticking out of one of the books. He pulled the book off the shelf and read the title: *The Encyclopedia of Baseball Legends.*

Charley opened the book at the place where a crocheted bookmark stuck out. Upon closer inspection, he could see the initials "HW" prominently crocheted into it. He closed the book and made his way to the checkout counter where Hannah Weaver sat waiting.

"Did you find some good books today, Charley?" she asked.

"I did. Always enjoy reading about blacksmithing. What kinds of books do you like to read, Hannah?"

"Oh, I enjoy lots of different topics," Hannah offered with her sweet smile. "I mostly read inspirational books and Amish fiction. I like to get lost in a good story. Oh, and cookbooks too. Still trying!" She laughed.

"You read much about sports?"

"Sports?" Hannah cleared her throat. "You mean, like . . . fishing and such?"

"Yes. Or professional baseball."

Hannah's mind raced through the possibilities of how Charley could have discovered her secret. Charley looked around to make sure no one could hear him then he held up the book-mark.

"Any particular reason this might've been sticking up out of one of the professional baseball books?" he asked with a friendly wink. "You studying the stats?"

Hannah's eyes widened. "Uh, well, that's where I stopped dusting. It's my marker, you see. Tomorrow I'll dust the 'Cs.'" Hannah knew what she was saying wasn't exactly the way it was. And she felt terrible about it, quickly asking God's for-giveness, and keeping the inner repentance going even as they continued.

"One letter a day, huh, Hannah?" Charley said, playing along. "Gonna take you a while to get through the whole alphabet that way, don't you think?"

By now Hannah figured Charley knew the real reason her crocheted bookmark was sticking up out of that book on base-ball and its legends. She might as well go ahead and tell him the whole truth. But at that moment she saw Bishop Gingrich talk-ing to the librarian, and Hannah had to measure her words carefully. Charley caught on and changed the subject. Then af-ter the bishop left, Charley leaned in. "So what have you learned so far, Hannah?" he asked, politely keeping his voice down. Even so, the librarian looked up and gave Hannah an inquisitive look. Hannah spoke in a near-whisper now.

"About professional baseball? Charley, you know we don't read about such things that can lead to pride and such."

"That's why I'm Mennonite," Charley said with a chuckle. "I love everything about professional baseball."

Hannah finished stamping Charley's three books on black-smithing and slid them back to him.

"You've got two weeks to finish them," she said.

"I'm a fast reader. But you still haven't told me what you've learned."

Hannah looked around cautiously. The librarian was nowhere in sight. "Well, did you know a player by the name of Willie Mays, Number 24, hit 650 career homeruns and once hit four in one game?"

"The 'Say Hey Kid,'" Charley said. "That was his nickname."

"So you *have* heard of him?"

Charley grinned. "Oh, yeah. He's pretty famous."

"Elected to the Baseball Hall of Fame in 1979. Also known for the catch he made in the 1954 World Series," Hannah said with all the confidence of a sports reporter.

Charley smiled. "Listen to you. I'm impressed."

"Thanks. You'd be surprised what you can learn while dusting."

"I'm sure Levi will be impressed too."

Hannah sighed deeply. "If he ever comes home. Not that I'm doing any of this for him, you understand. The way I figure it, when people ask us questions, as a clerk here I should know certain things about the English world, don't you think?"

Charley wasn't going to let her off the hook that easily. "Do you love him, Hannah?"

Hannah blushed. "Oh, Charley, Levi Troyer is the only boy I've ever loved. It's my dream to take our baptismal vows together one day and get married. But people tell me I'm wasting my life to wait for him."

"Do *you* think you're wasting your life, Hannah?"

Hannah shook her head.

"Then, wait for him. Don't worry about what anyone else says. You wait for him. When he's ready, he'll come home."

Hannah smiled. "Oh, I'm counting on it, Charley."

CHAPTER SIXTY-FIVE

You missed home plate! How do you miss home plate?" Coach Brenner barked at Levi after the game—a game they lost twelve to four to the Dodgers. *Lost!* It was dismal. And even though the last play wouldn't have given them the win anyway, Levi had a shot at a face-saving homerun but got tagged out after failing to touch home plate.

"You can do a lot of careless things, Troyer," Coach Brenner yelled, "but you *don't miss home plate!*"

"I know, Coach. I don't know how it happened. I'm sorry." And for once, he seemed to really mean it, though the coach wasn't ready to let it go.

"Sorry's not enough, Troyer. You've been making a lot more of these blunders lately. What's going on?"

"Nothing I can't handle, Coach."

"Well, you'd better get it under control. Whatever it is, whatever demons you're fighting, you conquer 'em or you're outta here. You hear me, Troyer? You're not messing up our chance at the World Series."

"It won't happen again. I give you my word."

Brenner shook his head. "Your word means nothing, Troyer. All I care about is what you do out there on the field. You cost us a pretty penny, but if things don't change, I'll let you ride the pine 'til your contract runs out."

"The fans would never let you do that. I'm the one selling the tickets."

"The fans want to win, Troyer," Coach Brenner snapped. "If you're a drag on the team, they'll be the first ones demanding we cut you loose. Don't think they won't! Despite what your ego has told you, one player doesn't make this team, and I'm not about to let one player take it down. Straighten up your act, or you're gone."

"You wouldn't do that," Levi challenged. "Not this close to the Series."

"Watch me!"

Levi wanted to say more, but he figured it wasn't going to help his situation any, so he held his tongue. He knew the coach was right. It was obvious to anyone watching that his game had been slipping. It had become increasingly more difficult for this farm boy from Amish country to hide his addiction and his anxiety over his mounting gambling debts. That's why he seldom socialized with the other players anymore, other than Marco, and even their friendship seemed to be waning at times. Levi was becoming more and more of a recluse, pushing everyone away, even Phil to some extent. He didn't write to Hannah anymore, not since John's letter to him in which he'd been brutally honest about Hannah wanting to move on with her life, and also about how the doctor had given orders for Levi not to write to David anymore because of the stress it put on his weakened heart. Levi was on a downward spiral with no bottom in sight.

And the World Series was just around the corner. But first they had to clinch the playoffs.

CHAPTER SIXTY-SIX

The Vipers' next game was against the Brewers in Milwaukee. Levi hadn't had a drink in over a week, and there, in the mecca of breweries, he was feeling it. But the coach's warning of "Straighten up or you're out!" was set on "replay" in his head. He knew he needed to get sober, and he believed he had the willpower to do it. If a professional baseball player knows anything, it's willpower. *I* will *do this!* Levi pledged to himself.

Easier said than done.

It was the top of the third, and Levi was up at bat. His head was a bit woozy, so he decided to play it safe and bunt the ball. He fouled it instead. Levi positioned himself for the next pitch. But that ball didn't want to be bunted either. It was as though it knew what this batter was capable of, and it was going to force him to swing for the fences, whether Levi felt like it or not.

"Steeee-rike!" the umpire yelled.

The next pitch rocketed down the line, setting Levi up perfectly. He waited until it got closer. Then, when it was in range, he pounced on it, smacking it so hard the wood of the bat split in two. As for the ball? It was long gone, deep into right field.

"Well, the Amish Sensation is back, folks. Chalk up another homerun for Number 17," the sportscaster said, as the right fielder ran after the ball, albeit in vain. Levi was already rounding for third and waving to his cheering fans. By the time the right fielder caught up to the ball, Levi was heading in to home plate. And this time he made a great show of touching it—not once, but twice. And one more time just to make a point to Coach Brenner.

When they got to the bottom of the eighth, the Vipers had the game all but sewn up. Twenty to three. "There's no catching the Vipers tonight," the sportscaster said. "Load up the kids, Grandma. We can all go home. The Vipers have made their comeback."

❧

The next game in the playoffs was the Vipers versus the Chicago Cubs. If the stadium noise from the Viper fans was any indication, they were beyond confident that their team was going to pull this off.

It was a hard-fought game, and by the ninth inning, the Vipers were taking it ten to six. But it was the Cubs at the top of the ninth, and the bases were loaded with no outs in sight. A homerun hit would tie up the game and force it into overtime, giving the Cubs a chance at the win. The pressure was on, and sportscaster Will Grayson loved every minute of it.

The next batter was determined to make Troyer earn his press. Levi choked on the next two pitches, sending them down the pike low and outside. Then he threw a strike next, right in the strike zone. It still didn't suit the batter, and he let it go by.

"Steeee-rike!" the ump shouted.

Levi readied himself on the mound, hoping for a repeat. He nodded to the catcher, and then, with everything he had, he hurled that ball dead center, another perfect pitch, his fastest yet. The batter had no choice but to swing at it or be knocked aside by the wind of that sphere flying by at 103 mph.

"Steeee-rike two!"

"I won't even ask if you saw that thing, sports fans," Grayson said. "Nobody did."

It wasn't a record-breaker, but it was close. Levi watched as the batter tapped home plate with the end of his bat and took position again. This time he was ready for whatever Levi threw at him. And Levi threw his best—the Troyer Tornado. It flew by the batter before he could bring the bat around. The crowd didn't even wait for the umpire's call. They were already on their feet cheering.

"Strike three!" the umpire yelled to the ecstasy of the fans.

This time the pitch was clocked at 104 mph! The Vipers ended up holding the score at ten to six.

The whole team erupted in cheers. One year on a professional baseball team, and Levi Troyer could end up heading to the World Series. It really could happen! They were getting closer and closer.

❦

Back in the locker room, the celebration continued. The players were pumped and couldn't wait to make it all official. But they weren't there yet. They still had to win the playoffs. Amidst the exuberance, Marco couldn't help but notice that Levi was being unusually quiet. "What's the problem, *mi amigo*? We won another one! You do know that, *si*? We've almost locked up the playoffs."

"I know," Levi said.

Marco was perplexed. "Isn't this what all our hard work has been about? For this very moment? We're all heading down to the Dugout to celebrate. You're coming, right?"

Levi shook his head. "I don't think so. Just not feeling it tonight."

Marco realized his friend might be making the right decision, so he let up. "Want me to stay with you? We can do something else if you want."

"Thanks, but you go on. Don't worry about me."

Marco didn't want to leave, but Levi insisted.

"Hey, you're doing the right thing, man," Marco said.

Levi nodded. "I know."

❧

Marco left the locker room that night feeling proud of his friend. But Levi hadn't passed on going to the bar for sobriety reasons. It was so he could drink in the privacy of his own home, outside the scrutiny of anyone who might put a limit on him or get word back to Brenner. But it wouldn't have mattered. Because as hard as Coach Brenner rode him or the fans jeered him when he blew it, no one was tougher on Levi Troyer than Levi himself. The voices trapped inside his head continued to replay his failures, and Levi was convinced that what they were saying was the truth. In spite of making it to a pro-team, being close to winning the playoffs, and possibly cinching a spot in the World Series, Levi was convinced that ol' Number 17 couldn't do *anything* right.

CHAPTER SIXTY-SEVEN

David found Joseph at the fishing hole, just as he figured he would. This time David brought his own gear, and he was planning on going home with a bucket-load of fish *and* good advice.

Once they cast out their lines, David explained what was going on with Levi.

"I'm concerned," David said. "I hardly hear from him anymore, and Hannah Weaver says his letters to her have tapered off too. The longer he's in that world, the less likely it is he'll ever come home."

Joseph listened without commenting. He let David get everything off his chest before saying a word. David had always appreciated that about Joseph. He saved his advice until he'd gotten all the pieces of the puzzle in place. Only then would he offer his counsel.

Knowing this, David continued laying out each piece of his fatherly concern. "As you know, Levi's always been my one to push the limits. He's nothing like his brother."

"You have two sons, David," Joseph reminded him. "They may be twins, but they each have their own heart and mind. They'll make their own choices, right or wrong. I know it's not easy to stand by and watch it all play out, but Levi's an adult. Sometimes the best lessons people learn in life are from the mistakes they make."

"I know." David sighed. "And who knows? He may not be making any mistakes at all. It's just this feeling I have in my heart."

"Well, I'm sure your father didn't understand some of your behavior when you were his age, yah?"

David smiled at the memories. "I suppose you're right. So you think I should leave Levi in God's hands and trust that it'll all work out?"

"Trust that God loves him even more than you do, my friend."

David knew Joseph was right, but the heartache he was feeling was unbearable. "It's getting harder and harder to do that," he said. "Levi may not make the best choices, but he's still my son. Sometimes you just want to suffer the pain for them."

"I know exactly what you mean."

"So how did you get your children to grow up into such good and godly people?"

"Well, I did the best I could, and then I leaned on God for the rest. Oh, and I double-locked all the doors so they couldn't sneak out at night."

They both laughed, a hearty kind of laugh that only comes from those who've known real pain in life and have somehow survived it.

"Don't worry, David. God gave you two strong, healthy boys to love and nurture, and you've done that. Levi will return to his roots someday, and he'll be the man God created him to be."

"I hope and pray you're right, Joseph."

"Just think about your horses. Some were harder to break than others. But you still knew they were good horses. They just needed a little taming. Levi will get broken, one way or the other."

"Perhaps that's what I'm afraid of," David admitted.

CHAPTER SIXTY-EIGHT

Levi stepped up to the cashier's booth in the middle of the casino and handed the lady behind the counter Vinny's metal card. "Five thousand, please."

The cashier read the name on the card. "Ah, of course. Another guest of Mr. Delmonico's. I'll run it right now for you, sir."

Levi waited and watched the people as they tried their best to win against the odds. It didn't matter what they were playing; it seemed the outcome was always the same—winners were going home with the money and losers weren't. And in most cases, Levi figured that winner was the casinos. Still, he told himself he was only one jackpot away from winning back all of his loses. And he was feeling lucky tonight.

The cashier frowned and handed Vinny's card back to him. "Sorry," she said. "It seems Mr. Delmonico's put a stop on it."

"You serious?" Levi asked.

"I can try it again if you like."

"Would you mind? I'm sure it's a mistake."

The cashier tried it again. "Sorry, sir. It still won't go through. Would you like me to see if I can reach Mr. Delmonico for you?"

"No, no. I'll call him myself. I've got his number. I'm sure it's an oversight."

Levi stepped away from the booth and made the call.

"Yeah, what can I do for you, Levi?" Vinny asked.

"Well, I'm downtown, Vinny, and feeling a bit lucky tonight, so I tried to get another five grand. But the cashier said you'd put a stop on my account. Can you get that lifted for me? There must be some mistake."

"No mistake, kid," Vinny said, the icy words hanging in the air. "You're already in for a sweet chunk of change, my man. And the interest keeps mounting up."

"You know I'm good for it, Vinny."

"I know you are, kid. It's my accountants that get a little nervous. You know what I mean? Especially since you missed your last two payments."

"I know, and I was going to talk to you about that."

"I know you were, kid. But you're up to sixty grand now. Just didn't want to see you getting in over your head. I take care of my friends, am I right, Tornado? But I gotta keep the lights on, know what I mean?"

"Sure, sure. But like I said, I'm feeling lucky tonight. If you'd just front me the five grand, I know I could win it all back for you."

"I wish I could help you out, kid. I really do. But your account's frozen." He paused. "Have my money by one o'clock tomorrow."

"All sixty grand?"

"I'll take cash."

"I don't know if I can do that, Vinny."

"Oh, I think you can."

"I wouldn't be asking you for a loan if I had it."

"You're not going to disappoint me, are you, Troyer?"

"No, Vinny. I'll do my best, but—"

"I know you will. In fact, I'd bet your pitching arm on it. One o'clock, Troyer."

Vinny hung up and Levi immediately called Phil Watson to try to talk him into another loan. Phil bought Levi's story about being behind on his rent and needing to catch up. The five grand wasn't enough to square him with Vinny, but he figured if he could parlay it into some casino poker wins, that might do it.

If all goes according to plan, I'll win enough to pay Vinny, Phil, and everyone else back, Levi told himself.

But Levi soon found out that everything doesn't always go according to plan. Especially when you owe Vinny Delmonico sixty grand.

CHAPTER SIXTY-NINE

The next morning Levi ordered a drink to help him calm his nerves while he concentrated on winning at the tables. But that drink did nothing to stop the hands of time from ticking their way toward Vinny's arrival at one o'clock. Levi didn't have all the money yet, and he was even down a grand from the five Phil had loaned him.

At a quarter past one, Levi decided to go for broke at the roulette table. It was his best shot at winning anything significant. But he was risking losing it all too. The clock ticked on. Levi knew it was just a matter of time before Vinny came looking for him.

The roulette wheel hadn't even come to a stop when two of Vinny's goons showed up. Levi watched the ball spin and roll, completely missing the number he'd called. The two goons approached Levi and told him that Mr. Delmonico wanted to see him outside.

Levi's better sense told him to stay put, but he'd stopped listening to his better sense years ago. So he went along with the brawny bullies.

Once outside in the shadows of the alleyway, Vinny called to him from the back seat of his limo. Levi walked over and talked to him through the lowered car window.

"How ya been, kid?" Vinny asked, as one of the goons punched Levi in the stomach.

Levi, doubled over in pain, gathered his breath. "I've been better."

"Yeah, me, too. I don't like it when someone owes me money and doesn't pay."

"I know, Vinny, but I told you, I'm good for it."

The other goon clipped Levi with a right hook to the chin. Vinny didn't flinch. "I know you are, kid. And I really like doing business with you. In fact, you're one of my best customers."

Another hit to the chin left Levi wiping blood from his lip.

"I just need a little insurance, you know? That's all," Vinny said.

Levi expected another punch, but the goons backed off when Vinny raised his hand.

"So, tell me, kid, how have your games been going?"

Levi held his gut and tried to catch his breath. "Good."

"Yeah. Saw you pitched another no-hitter. What does that make now? Three?"

Levi didn't answer quickly enough for Vinny, so the first goon punched him in the gut again. Levi may have been his favorite customer, but Vinny's preferential treatment stunk.

"You know, kid, it sure would be a shame to have something happen to that golden arm of yours. Know what I mean?"

Levi knew good and well what Vinny meant. "I'll get it for you, Vinny. I promise."

The goons gave him one more punch to the gut then climbed back into the black limousine and left.

Sixty thousand dollars. Where was Levi going to get that kind of cash that fast? Everything he owned was already heavily indebted. Lucky for him, Phil Watson's phone number was on speed dial.

CHAPTER SEVENTY

John headed out to Waneta Swartzentruber's place again. It was time for another delivery of fresh vegetables, flour, and her beloved chocolate donuts. But this time he didn't find her waiting at the door. He knocked for quite a while before turning to head back to his buggy. It concerned him that she hadn't answered, but just as he took the first step off the rickety porch, he heard the creak of the door and a familiar voice behind him.

"Where do you think you're going with them donuts, boy?"

John turned around and saw Waneta, looking frailer than usual, standing in the doorway. He was glad nothing had happened to his friend.

"Not going anywhere, Waneta. Not until we have a donut together."

"Well, come on in. I've got the coffee ready."

Waneta asked John about all the goings-on in the community, how his father and brother were doing, and other such news. But then she moved on to talking about more serious matters. "I don't know how much time I've got left in this world, but if I leave outta here tomorrow, I won't have any regrets."

"That's good, but I'm counting on you being around for more years to come."

"Just getting prepared. No regrets—it's the only way to live your life."

John knew she was right, but his situation was complicated. Surely he was doing the right thing by helping his father with the farm. No regrets there. And as far as marrying and raising a family, he was still young. He did, in his own way, regret the way things turned out with Levi. But leaving had been his brother's choice. What responsibility did John bear for that decision?

Waneta's discussion of death got John to thinking about David and what would happen to the farm if anything happened to him. Would Levi want to sell it and divide up the money? That farm was all John knew. It was his home. He wasn't about to sell it. His father wouldn't want him to either. But John was certain Levi wouldn't want any part of it.

"Whatcha thinking about so intently?" Waneta asked.

"Oh, sorry," John said, bringing his thoughts back around to the moment. "Nothing important." He took another bite of Ruth's delicious donut.

"Well, when you get right down to it, that's the biggest regret for all of us, huh?" Waneta said.

"What's that?"

"Wasting all our time thinking on things that in the long run just aren't that important."

CHAPTER SEVENTY-ONE

It was the last game of the playoffs. Levi shook off Marco's first two signals. If the Vipers took this, they'd secure their place in the World Series. But something was wrong. Levi seemed unusually distracted as he stood on the bump that night. His mind wasn't on the game. It was on the train wreck that his life had become. Vinny Delmonico had made his demands clearly known. He wanted his money, all of it, with interest. But Levi had already mortgaged his house and car, tapped out Phil with loans to pay off past gambling debts, and run out of options. Vinny had given him a short extension, and increased the amount with more interest. No one on the team knew how deeply Troyer was indebted to the mob boss—not the coach, and not even Marco. But matters were taking a turn for the worse.

Levi shifted his neck to the left, and then to the right, as if the movement would snap everything in his life back into place. It didn't. It couldn't.

Sensing the shakes returning, Levi glanced in Coach Brenner's direction, trying to read the man's expression. Had he noticed Levi's tremors? He didn't think so. He shifted his head a few more times then took his pitching position.

The pitch looked good all the way down the line, but at the last second it dropped out of the zone.

"Ball!" the umpire called out.

Coach Brenner paced. There was a lot riding on his pitcher. The Vipers had done remarkably well so far. Now this was it. All they had to do was get this last win under their belt, and they'd be the ones representing the National League in the

World Series. The score was already twelve to seven, Vipers. It was the top of the ninth, and it was all over but the shouting. The shouting came soon enough. Even under the pressure of the playoffs and his personal problems, Levi Troyer pitched a ninth-inning shut-out, sealing the deal. The World Series would now be a match-up between the National League champions, the Las Vegas Vipers, and the American League Champions, the New York Yankees, who had beat out the Kansas City Royals. Again, the team was heading over to the Dugout to celebrate.

Levi took Marco aside. "I think I'm going on home."

Marco was surprised. "Home? We've made it to the World Series, man! You're not going to go with us?"

If there was any cause for celebration in Levi Troyer's life, this was it. It had been a dream of his ever since he pitched his first no-hitter back on that dusty field in Sugar Creek, Ohio. But Levi also knew, if there was any cause for caution, this was it.

But the team eventually talked him into it. *I'll go, but I'll use my head,* Levi vowed to himself. *I'm not about to mess this up! Not this time. I'm going to prove I can do this—to John, to father, and to Coach Brenner!* He was still ticking off names in his head when he ordered his first drink. His second wasn't very far behind. After that, he lost count. That's because it wasn't Coach Brenner, David, or even John that he was trying to prove anything to. It was Levi Troyer.

CHAPTER SEVENTY-TWO

Levi thought it was the sun shining on his face that woke him up. But it wasn't. It wasn't even dawn yet. The light he felt was coming from a flashlight being held by the man in a suit standing over him.

"Hey," the man said, "you've got to find someplace else to sleep it off. We're going to be opening up soon, and we can't have you passed out here."

Levi wasn't sure where "here" was. He couldn't even recall having walked out of the bar the night before. Quickly he ran through all of the possibilities. Had the bouncers carried him out? Had he stumbled out on his own and collapsed onto the pavement to sleep it off? Had he been mugged and left for dead? His mind was too fuzzy to pull up an accurate recollection. All he knew was that somehow he wound up on the outside steps of a large and respectable building. Levi's head throbbed, he was a mess, and he was ashamed. He certainly didn't blame the man with the flashlight for wanting him to "move along."

"Come on, I'll help you up," the man said, aiding Levi to his feet. Levi wasn't sure if the man recognized him or not, but he didn't seem to. When Levi was standing, he nodded a thank you to the man then walked back toward the bar where he figured his car was waiting for him. All he wanted to do was get in it, turn the heater on, and sleep the rest of the night away.

Levi felt in his pockets. *Where are my keys?* He still had his money and his wallet with his driver's license. His car was even there, ruling out the possibility of any mugging or carjacking. The obvious scenario was that Marco, or some other teammate, had taken away his keys so he wouldn't try to drive himself home. Levi figured it wouldn't have been Coach Brenner because he probably would have driven him straight over to rehab. Or the unemployment office.

He took out his cellphone and gave Marco a call.

"Hey . . . sorry to wake you, man, but I'm downtown. Please tell me you've got my keys."

"I've got 'em."

Levi breathed a sigh of relief. "Can you bring them to me?"

"Sure, after you've slept it all off."

"By the time you get here, I'll be fine. I've already been shooed away once, okay? So will you bring them?"

"They're under your car. By the left front tire."

"What? What were you thinking, man? What if it had gotten stolen?"

"You're welcome for saving your life." Marco changed the subject. "You do remember there's a practice today, right?"

"Yeah," Levi said. "Do I have to bring my head?"

"Listen, *amigo*, you've got to get yourself together. You're playing with fire, man. Don't blow this for all of us."

"I won't. Right after the World Series, I'll get help. I promise."

CHAPTER SEVENTY-THREE

"Were you sleeping?" Hannah asked Ruth as she stood over her bed. Ruth's eyes were closed, so Hannah figured she probably was, but she desperately needed to talk to her sister.

Ruth opened one eye and groaned.

"Hi," Hannah said.

Ruth furrowed her brow and stared at her sister, who was more than ready to talk.

"Do you think I should give up?"

"Trying to wake me? Yes!" Ruth turned over and pressed the pillow over her head.

"I mean with Levi," Hannah clarified. "I've been waiting a long time. But am I holding onto an impossible dream?"

Ruth turned back to look up at Hannah. "Well, you've already waited almost three years."

"Not quite three. Not yet anyway. Two and a half."

"Two and three-quarters."

"You always were better than me at fractions. So should I keep waiting?"

"Well, according to that magazine, he's engaged."

"If that's even true."

"What if it is? You've got to think about it. And there's also the real possibility that Levi has no intention of leaving professional baseball and coming back here."

"Well, yah, that could happen."

"So given all of that, do you still feel like waiting?"

Hannah thought about it. "As much as ever. I know he'll come home one day." She leaned down and gave Ruth a big hug, told her she was the best sister ever, and went back to bed.

Ruth, on the other hand, was now wide awake, wondering what she could do to save her sister from imminent heartbreak.

CHAPTER SEVENTY-FOUR

In Amish country, good food and honest conversation are a staple. And since John had prepared an exceptional meatloaf for dinner that day, he figured it'd be a good time to get a few questions answered.

"How come you never remarried, Father?" he asked.

David shrugged. "Oh, I don't know. Guess I never found anyone as special as your mother."

"But didn't you ever get lonely?"

"Oh, I'll admit it would be nice to have someone to hold onto on a cold winter's night, or to share my heart with. But she'd have to be exceptional. Your mother set the standard pretty high."

"Tell me more about her."

"What do you want to know, John?"

"Well, you've told me she was young and beautiful and had the color of Levi's hair and eyes. But tell me more."

"Well, did I ever tell you that you have her smile?"

"Really?" John said, quite pleased.

"I'm sure I've told you that already, while you were growing up. Maybe you've forgotten."

"Maybe you did, but it means more to me now. What else?"

"Well, she had a good business mind, just like you."

"I wish I could have known her."

"And I'll tell you something else—she wanted you boys more than anything. Even if she'd known it meant her life, she wouldn't have thought twice about it."

John let that reality sink in then asked, "If she hadn't died, do you think she'd be proud of me, Father?"

"I do, John," David said. "I think she'd be very proud of you."

$$\sim$$

After dinner John returned to the fields to work, and David went out to the stables to brush down the horses. There was another auction coming up, and he needed to get a few of them ready for John to sell. But David's mind wasn't on the horses that day. It was on his beautiful wife, Tess, and all the tender moments they'd shared together. The Amish, who take no photographs of themselves or their loved ones, have to guard their memories just a little more tightly than the rest of us. David kept his locked deep inside his heart.

CHAPTER SEVENTY-FIVE

Ruth Troyer decided if she could teach her sister to make at least a few simple Amish meals like chicken and dumplings, meatloaf, and fried chicken, Hannah would feel better about her future. Even if she never married, she still had to cook. Not that meal duties fell only to Amish wives. Many Amish men were quite comfortable in the kitchen. David Troyer had been preparing meals for his boys all of their lives.

Ruth knew Hannah was getting along just fine working at the library. She also knew her sister was able to sound off baseball statistics better than a lot of sportscasters in the English world, but improving Hannah's culinary talents had always been an enticing challenge for Ruth.

One afternoon she approached Hannah and invited her to lesson number one. "Come with me into the kitchen," Ruth said.

"Why?" Hannah frowned. "We've already done all the dishes."

"I'm going to give you a cooking lesson."

"Another one? Oh, Ruth, you've tried that so many times before. Cooking just isn't my gift. I've accepted it, and I've moved on."

"I promise, Hannah—*this time* I won't let anything go wrong. You have my word. I've been reading up on which kitchen ingredients could possibly have explosive reactions when combined with others. I don't know them all yet, but I'll watch out for you."

But the real reason behind Ruth's offer was to lift Hannah's spirits. She'd seemed to be down lately, and Ruth wanted to renew her hope in the future.

"Maybe someday Levi will come to his senses and come back and marry you," she said. "And if he doesn't, you'll meet someone else. Either way, you're going to need to know how to cook at least two or three good Amish recipes. You could get by on just one, but your husband would likely tire of it eventually. Three is a good number. By the time you get to that third meal, he'll have forgotten all about the first one, and you can start over again."

"The memory of my cooking tends to last longer than three days, Ruth."

"And that's what we're going to work on." Ruth took her sister's hand and practically dragged her into the kitchen. "It's nothing to feel bad about, Hannah. Growing up in a bakery doesn't automatically make you a good cook, any more than growing up in a farmer's home makes you a farmer. Just look at Levi."

"Now then," Ruth said, commencing with her lesson, "when you're preparing a full meal, you must always focus on the task at hand. Don't allow yourself to become distracted."

"What?" Hannah said.

"Pay attention, Hannah."

"Sorry."

"Now, stay with me. We're going to begin with dumplings. Over the years there have been a wide variety of doughy items that have passed themselves off as dumplings. First, there are the light, airy biscuits you'll often see sitting on top of a pond of chicken stew. These are not true dumplings."

"They're not?"

"No," Ruth said firmly. "They're cousins. Now, a second cousin to those dumplings, but still not a true dumpling, is the *ooey*, gooey biscuit. These have been dunked and rolled over several times in the sauce. They can no longer pass for biscuits because they're wet. But they're still not true dumplings."

"So what is a true dumpling then?"

"True dumplings," Ruth said, lifting one off the dough board in front of her, "are ribbons or squares of dough that have never even thought about being a biscuit. They're content being exactly who they are—a hidden treasure buried in the depths of a bowl of stew or soup, waiting to be discovered by the skilled spoon diver."

Hannah was mesmerized with Ruth's description. "Ruth, you *are* the dough whisperer."

"I know," Ruth said, smiling proudly. "If you can master the dumpling, you can make just about anything. So are you ready to give it a try?"

Hannah shrugged. "You really think I can do this?"

"Hannah," Ruth said, "you can do anything you set your mind to."

$$\approx$$

What Hannah ended up creating that day didn't look like any of the three dumplings Ruth had described. Hannah didn't figure it was anywhere in the dumpling family at all. She resisted the temptation to compare them to baseballs—out loud anyway. But they did look a bit like baseballs, without the stitching, of course. And they didn't bounce.

"I'm not giving up on you, Hannah," Ruth vowed. "Before Levi comes back, you're going to know how to cook."

Hannah sighed. "Yeah, well, whenever *that* is."

"Don't give up, Sis. I've been at this a lot of years. There's only one secret to good cooking. No matter how hopeless things look, you never, ever, *ever* give up."

"Then I shouldn't give up on Levi either, right? Even if he's not writing to me. I should never give up on him . . . unless he tells me in his very own words not to wait for him, yah?"

Ruth didn't want to agree. She didn't want her sister wasting her life waiting on a boy who might never return. But she could see where Hannah was coming from. "You're right, Hannah. If you love him, you never give up hope."

CHAPTER SEVENTY-SIX

Well, Coach Brenner," Will Grayson said as he wrapped up the television interview, "how do you think your team is going to do in the World Series? Are you predicting a win for the Vipers?"

"I'll tell you, Will, we've worked hard for this moment. Real hard," Coach Brenner said. "So yeah, I'm confident we're gonna win."

"Are you counting on any particular player ending up the MVP?"

Coach Brenner knew exactly who the reporter was hinting at. Levi Troyer was the darling of the sports press. The interviewer wanted a good quote to wrap up the piece, and if he could capture Brenner praising Troyer, he'd have it. But Brenner had an aversion to setting up any one of his players on the press's pedestal—especially a player who took the position so casually.

"We're a team," Coach Brenner said forcefully. "Not one of us can win this thing alone."

No, Brenner didn't mention Levi by name, but it was obvious to anyone watching who he was cautioning. He was also scolding himself for having helped turn Levi into his star pitcher, the talk of the league, the irreplaceable one who would take them all the way to the World Series. The team had paid big bucks for his talent. But now their chances of winning it all rested in the hands of this same talented but unpredictable and troubled player who could just as easily take the whole team down with him.

Coach Brenner had absorbed the heat of Levi's volatile temper on too many occasions to count, and he'd done little to stop its damage to himself and those around him. He'd seen the shakes too. But the Vipers had too much invested in Number 17 to cut him loose or even get him help. *What if the press gets hold of this? Besides, the fans love him. If he can just hold it together for a few more days,* Brenner told himself, *that's all we need. Just a few more days. We'll get the series behind us, and then we'll see what we can do to help him.*

That was the gallant plan, anyway. Now if only self-confident pitchers and controlling habits would cooperate.

෪

Levi called Marco and asked him to meet him at the Dugout. Marco was set to turn in early for the night, but he figured he'd better keep an eye on the lead pitcher, especially on the night before the World Series was to start.

When Marco arrived, he found Levi sitting at the bar alone. There were already several empty glasses in front of him.

"You should've called me earlier, man," Marco said. "How many have you had? The Series starts tomorrow, you know."

"You telling me how to live my life now?" Levi snapped.

"Just looking out for a friend. And the team," Marco explained. "We've all put a lot of hope in you, *mi amigo.*"

A man at the end of the bar overheard their private conversation and apparently couldn't resist the temptation to chime in. "Doesn't matter a hill of beans what you Vipers do tonight 'cause the Yankees are gonna whoop your sorry tails tomorrow."

Levi considered it an invitation to put that Yankees fan in his place. "Oh, yeah? We'll see if your Yankees even get one hit off of me tomorrow!"

"Oh, the whole world's gonna see the Yankees tomorrow," the stranger said. "They're gonna see them crush you Vipers and skin you alive."

Levi stood to his feet and challenged the man, who'd no doubt had as many drinks as Levi.

"Don't, Levi," Marco intervened. "Don't do anything stupid, man."

"He already did," the Yankees fan said. "He picked a losing team."

"Just one hit," Levi pleaded with Marco. "That's all I'm asking for."

"Let him say what he wants," Marco said, trying to calm his friend. "He's just messing with your head."

Levi settled back onto his barstool. "Yeah, you're right. He's just a loser rooting for a losing team."

Levi and the stranger continued to exchange hostile glances while Marco continued trying to talk some sense into Levi.

"What's happened to you, man? When I first met you, all you wanted to do was play baseball. Now you're going to let some drunk Yankees fan rob you of everything you've worked so hard for? Look, I don't wanna tell you how to live your life, but . . . I think you should go back home."

"I'll leave this bar when I'm good and ready," Levi snapped.

"I'm talking about going *home*. Back to Sugar Creek. After the World Series, pack up and get back to your life. This isn't your dream—in over your head, drunk, and with a chip on your shoulder the size of a backstop. You're better than this. Go home to your family. Marry that girl from the bakery. You don't need this."

"My family? *What* family? My father doesn't want me back. And I'm sure John's doing just fine now that I'm not around. And Hannah? She's moved on. Either place, I come up empty. So, yeah, I'm gonna stay right here and win the Series tomorrow, and it'll be no thanks to anyone but myself."

"You really believe that? That you're the one who got us to the Series? You did it by yourself?"

"Hey, you've read the press. They're the ones saying it, not me. All the pressure's on *me* this week."

"The last time I checked the rules, all the positions have to be covered in the game."

"Yeah, well, all my life I've only been able to count on myself. So if we win the series, I'm thanking *me*."

"Will it even feel like winning if you don't have anyone to share it with?" Marco shook his head. "Come on, I'll drive you home."

"Thanks, but I'm going to hang out here a little longer. Don't worry, I'll be fine. Arm for baseball, brains for everything else. See, I remember."

"I don't know. I think you should come with me."

"I'll be fine. Four games up, four games down?"

"A Viper Wiper."

"You know it. I'm going to make those Yankees regret passing me over."

"Oh, yeah?" the stranger said, obviously still listening in on the conversation. "Well, maybe they didn't want to get their pitcher from a cow pasture."

Levi jumped up and got in the man's face. "What's that supposed to mean?"

"It means you can't hold a candle to the Yankees. And you do know about candles, don't you, Amish boy?"

Something in Levi told him he should let the comment go, told him that thin skin and shots don't mix, but he couldn't resist coming back just one more time.

"Look, buddy, what I know is, I'm pitching another no-hitter tomorrow. And the Yankees are going to have no doubt that the Tornado has blown into town."

The man begged to differ. "In your dreams, hay-baler!" he shouted. Then he pushed Levi, sending him stumbling back a few feet. Levi steadied himself.

"Yeah? Well, I think your mouth is one fist past closing time," Levi said, rearing his arm back and tightening his fist in preparation of whatever came next.

"Not if I let you have it first," the stranger said just before tossing a chair in Levi's direction. It missed, but Levi's punch to the man's mouth sure didn't. A wild-west bar-room brawl broke out right there in the Dugout Bar. The stranger got in some good hits, as did Levi. But it was Levi's final punch that sent the man to the ground, knocking him out cold.

"Come on, Levi, let's go," Marco said. "Now!"

"We can't go now. We've got to see if he's okay."

Marco grabbed his arm. "You can't get yourself arrested the night before the World Series begins."

"Why would I get arrested? He started it all. He threw a chair at me."

"And you punched him in the mouth and knocked him out," Marco said. "Besides, you're Levi Troyer."

"I know. That's why I can't leave."

"And if they arrest you?"

"The coach'll bail me out. He's done it before."

"I wouldn't bank on it this time, *amigo.*"

❧

Within minutes a siren could be heard in the distance.

"This is your last chance, Levi, before the press starts swarming this place," Marco said, grabbing his arm again. "Let's go! You can make some calls. Talk to Phil, the coach, your attorney. You need advice, man, before you say anything to the cops."

Levi pulled away from Marco's grip with a yank. "I'm not leaving the scene," Levi told Marco emphatically. "For once in my life, I'm not going to run when the fire gets too hot."

CHAPTER SEVENTY-SEVEN

"We interrupt our program to bring you the following breaking news bulletin," the newscaster said. "Tonight, on the eve of the first game of the World Series, Levi Troyer, celebrated pitcher of the Las Vegas Vipers, has been arrested on assault and battery charges stemming from an altercation that took place at the Dugout Bar. So far we don't know the condition of the victim or what this will mean for the Vipers. But it looks like this is one night the Amish pitcher should have gone for another no-hitter, huh, folks? Stay tuned for more details as they develop."

Charley couldn't believe it when he heard the television report. All sorts of questions ran through his head. What exactly had happened, and how in the world did Levi Troyer get himself into such a mess? That night he lay in bed, wondering if he should drive over to the Troyers' home and tell David about it. They couldn't have known the news already, Charley figured. The Troyers didn't have a television or the internet in their home. But if he did go over there, what would he tell them? He didn't have that many details himself. And what about Hannah? How was she going to take the news when she heard about it from the tourists the next morning?

Charley turned up the volume on his TV and settled in for a night of watching the twenty-four-hour news programs for any updates. He also said a prayer for his friend. He didn't know what had taken place at the Dugout Bar that night, but he was sure Levi had to be feeling pretty low right about then. All alone in that jail cell. Broken dreams, broken promises . . . broken man.

❧

Hannah was scheduled to help out at the bakery the following morning. As she wiped down the tables, she couldn't help but overhear the news streaming through a tourist's cellphone. "Vipers' pitcher Levi Troyer has been arrested for assault and battery," the reporter said. "The victim, who was unconscious at the scene, has been taken to an area hospital. Team owner Hector Gonzalez and Coach Larry Brenner apologized to the Viper fans and announced that Troyer will not be playing in the World Series. Our sources also tell us that discussions are underway to drop the troubled pitcher from the team altogether. We'll keep you posted as more developments unfold. This is a major blow to the Vipers' hopes of a World Series victory."

There was a stunned hush around the bakery. Some had already heard the news and began to fill in the missing pieces for the other patrons. Many of the residents and tourists had been following Levi's career and were huge fans. But now? Things were starting to take a turn for this Amish hero from the Little Switzerland of Ohio.

"I bet he wasn't even really Amish," one lady said.

"I always thought there was something about that boy," an older man added.

"He's a disgrace," a tourist commented. "What kind of a player lets his team down just before the World Series?"

Hannah wanted to tell them all they were wrong to judge Levi before all the details of the incident were made known. No one was hearing his side of the story. But instead of speaking up, Hannah simply scrubbed the tables that much harder, so hard she almost took off a whole layer of varnish.

"Who knows what else he's done?" someone said.

Hannah bit down hard on her tongue. *Oh, how quickly fans and acquaintances can turn on you!* She continued to hold her peace, wiping down the rest of the tables as quickly as she could. Then she told her parents she was going home to finish her chores there.

"Are you okay, Hannah?" Eunice Weaver asked.

"I'll be all right." But she wasn't sure herself if that was true. *How can all those people judge Levi like that? One day they love you, and the next day they want to toss you aside like yesterday's knackwurst. Fickle people!*

That night Hannah went to bed early. She felt sad for Levi, and for herself too. She figured a good sleep might be the only thing capable of turning off her surge of thoughts. She knew the Levi Troyer they were talking about wasn't the Levi Troyer she knew and loved. What had happened? From everything she'd been hearing and reading, he'd gone straight to the top, fulfilled his dream, and made a name for himself. So none of this made any sense. If Hannah Weaver knew anything, she knew Levi's heart. *Fighting in a bar?* That wasn't who he was. Yet there he was—sitting in jail now. It wasn't going to be easy for Levi to get through this inning of his life, but Hannah knew beyond any doubt that people weren't considering the real Levi. And she could only imagine how hard it must be to prove to the world who you really are when you're looking through the bars of a jail cell.

CHAPTER SEVENTY-EIGHT

"Maybe it's all just a misunderstanding," Ruth said when she finally got a chance to talk to Hannah alone.

"Oh, Ruth, I don't know what to think anymore. I knew something was wrong. I just knew it! This must be why he stopped writing to me."

"They say sometimes a person has to hit bottom before they'll ask for anyone's help. Even God's."

"Do you think this is the bottom?" Hannah asked.

"I don't know, but if he doesn't get to play in any of the World Series this week, I'd say it's pretty close to it."

"Oh, Ruth, I feel so bad for him."

Ruth laid her hand on her sister's arm. "These are choices he's made. You know that."

Hannah nodded. "But we all make mistakes."

"Yah, but if you've got people's attention like Levi has, you're going to get judged a lot harder."

"It's not fair. All he wanted to do was play baseball. That's all. He was no match for that world."

"He should have asked for help," Ruth said.

"You still believe there's good in him, don't you?"

"Of course I do."

Hannah smiled, comforted by her sister's words.

"And so does God," Ruth continued. "For you both to believe in him like you do, Levi must have a side to him not everyone sees."

"I think most folks see in others whatever they're looking for, good or bad. And when I look at Levi Troyer, I see one of the kindest boys I've ever known."

"Well, I shouldn't be surprised. You've always had a heart for lost and injured animals."

"People get lost and injured too," Hannah said.

CHAPTER SEVENTY-NINE

Phil sat down in front of the glass partition in the visitation area of the jail. He picked up the phone that connected him to inmate #46537, who sat across from him, on the other side of the glass partition, wearing jailhouse orange. It was a much different look than the Amish clothes Levi had been wearing when Phil Watson first met him.

"How are you doing, kid?" Phil asked.

"I've been better."

"They treating you good?"

"Haven't given me my own house key yet, if that's what you mean."

Phil gave an understanding nod. "How's the food?"

"Not as good as Hannah's, I'll guarantee you that. Did Coach Brenner make the call?"

"For bail? Not yet."

"But he *is* going to do it, right?"

Phil hesitated. He didn't want to answer, didn't want to tell Levi the truth that Coach Brenner had reached the end of his patience with him.

"The Series starts tonight, Phil. I can't pitch it from in here. One of you has got to get this cleared up."

Phil decided to shoot straight with him. "This may be one you're gonna have to face, kid. The victim's pressing charges."

"*What?!* He started it all. But he's gonna be okay, right?"

"Yeah, yeah, I think so. He woke up in the ambulance. But I'm sure he thinks you've got deep pockets. Injuries tend to get a whole lot worse once the victim and his attorney get that into their heads. He already gave one press conference this morning in a neck brace. It'll be a body cast next."

"Gimme a break! He was itching for a fight."

"We'll see what the judge says. It's been my experience as far as barroom brawls go, it's a short trip from being in the right to being in the wrong. But you're lucky. Right now it's a misdemeanor. But if he racks up enough medical bills . . . "

"But you're going to take care of it all, right? Keep it all from getting out of hand."

"I wish I could, kid, but you knocked this one outta my reach. The press has gotten hold of it, and these kinds of things are hard to pull back. Fans have turned on a player for a lot less."

"My fans won't turn on me," Levi said confidently. "They'll give me another chance. And anyway, Brenner wouldn't go into a World Series without me."

"Brenner's a team man. And right now he doesn't see you playing for the team. You and I both know this wasn't your first fight. Brenner's gotten wind of it too. Says you've become a liability." He paused before continuing. "He's . . . cutting his losses, kid."

"Come on! How many times do I have to tell everybody I've quit? I'm not touching another drop."

"I'm glad for you, kid. But like they say, it's easy to say that in here."

"I mean it this time. It'll be different. I promise! I've gotta be on that mound tonight. Come on, Phil. Do whatever you've got to do. Get me outta here!"

"Listen, kid, do the time, get yourself into rehab, then let's see how things go."

"*Rehab?* I don't need rehab. That's for drunks. Call my attorney. He'll post my bail."

"I already did. He says you're broke. And you've tapped me out."

Levi saw his lifelong dream slipping away from him. "So that's it?"

"You need help, kid."

"Coach Brenner can't do this to me! This is the World Series. The team needs me."

"You're right. They *did* need you. But you've let us all down. I warned you about getting a handle on this." Phil shook his head. "I don't know what else to tell you, kid. Maybe the warden will let you watch the games from in here."

"Come on, Phil, help me out. I'm Levi Troyer! You can't walk out on the Tornado. No more hangovers or fights, I promise."

"Like I said, kid, we've heard it all before. And frankly, that's not the rallying cry Brenner wants to hear going into a World Series."

"Then call my father. He'll post my bail."

"Tried that too. Your brother said he's not taking your calls."

The shock registered on Levi's face. "So that's it?" Levi repeated. "Everyone's turning their back on me? Well, go on and go then. Get out of here!"

"Like I said, get all this behind you and we'll talk. Maybe Brenner will give you another chance someday."

"Another chance? You listen here, Phil. If I don't play in this series, it's over. I'm telling you, I'm walking. Do you hear me, Phil? It's over!"

"It already is, son."

"Son? *Son?!*" Levi tried his best to keep his voice down so he wouldn't attract the attention of the guards, but he was livid. "You are *not* my father," he said. Levi ran his fingers through his hair, pulling at clumps of it in frustration. "So was this your plan, huh? To bring me here, ride my talent all the way to the Series, then cut me loose? That's it?"

"*This* is the game you have to win, Levi. Not the World Series. It's *this* one. This is one opponent you have to beat. For your sake."

"I said *go*! Get outta here! I'll get through this on my own. Like I've always done. I don't need any of you!"

It was obvious to Phil that Levi was done with the conversation. But Phil wasn't. "You know, Levi, it's not home plate that's moved. It's right where it's always been. You just need to find it again."

Phil started to hang up the phone that connected him to Levi and then leave, but before he could do it, Levi called out to him.

"Phil . . . wait!"

Phil put the phone to his ear again. He noticed tears welling up in Levi's eyes.

"What if . . . what if I . . . can't? What if John's right? What if I'm nothing but a mess-up who's sabotaged every good thing that's ever come my way? What if this time I've gone too far?"

"Too far?" Phil said, shaking his head. "You're never too far as long as you're heading toward home."

CHAPTER EIGHTY

It was the last thing David wanted to see that morning, but John dropped it on the table as soon as they sat down to eat. The front page of the English newspaper was hard to ignore. It featured a familiar face, and there was no escaping the headline: "Vipers' Pitcher Levi Troyer Arrested."

David felt his breath catch in his throat. He couldn't bear to pick up the paper and read the details for himself, but John was more than willing to oblige.

"Levi Troyer, pitcher for the National League's World Series contenders, the Las Vegas Vipers, hand-picked from the middle of Amish country, has been arrested on assault-and-battery charges. The victim, James Rawlings of nearby Boulder City, was taken away by ambulance to Desert Springs Medical Center."

John closed the paper and waited for David to speak.

"Bring the buggy around, will you, John?"

"Where are you going?"

"To the bishop's."

David could tell John was chomping at the bit to discuss the matter further, perhaps even gloat a bit on his brother's predicament, but David was in no mood to hear it.

"I'll ride with you over there, Father. You don't need to be alone."

"No, John," David said. "I think I do."

☙

David saw that John was clearly disappointed not to be included. After all, isn't that what a family does in a time of crisis—

close in ranks and stand together? But David also knew his sons had not stood together in years. Why would he expect them to do it now? David needed someone around him who'd be able to point him to whatever possible good could be found in this latest turn of events. And for now, that someone wasn't John. A situation as troubling as this was going to require the advice and consolation of the bishop.

When David pulled up to the bishop's house, he wasn't quite sure how he was going to bring up the matter. But by the time he reached the front door and knocked on it, his words had taken shape.

"Bishop Gingrich," David said as the door opened, "Levi's running has finally come to an end."

CHAPTER EIGHTY-ONE

As it turned out, the warden did allow the World Series to play in the recreation area of the jail. Levi could sense the inmates staring at him all through the first inning. He wasn't sure if it was because he was the new kid on the cellblock, or because they recognized him from all the sports coverage in the news. He wondered if they were aware of the details of his fall from grace—the true story, apart from the sports news hype.

He figured most of the prisoners and guards indeed knew who he was. The English world was well-practiced in turning celebrities into household names then eagerly watching their fall. But he certainly didn't enjoy being the latest sports figure to end up in their midst.

For the most part, it seemed to Levi that the guards and prisoners felt some degree of empathy for him. They too had lost possessions, careers, relationships, and a good degree of self-respect on their own downward spiral. In there, the whys didn't really matter anymore.

Watching his team play in the World Series without him was the last thing Levi Troyer expected to be doing that night, particularly in jail. But there he was.

"Welcome back to the World Series," the sports announcer said. "We're in the top of the second inning. Score is four to two. Vipers are trailing."

If only I were there . . . Levi told himself that if only he were pitching, it'd be another no-hitter for sure. Whether or not that would have happened with the pressure of the World Series on his shoulders was something he could only speculate about. It

was a moot point anyway. This time his team would have to go
it alone.

◈

The team did exactly that, and they did it well. Exceptionally
well. They ended up winning that game and two more. The
Yankees took the next one. Now they were in the fifth game in
the series. If the Vipers could take this one, they'd be the World
Series champions. But it wasn't looking like that was going to
happen. Not yet anyway. Not at the bottom of the ninth inning,
when the Vipers found themselves down by three. But the bases
were loaded, and Mark Johnson was up at bat.

"Come on, Johnson," Levi said under his breath. "You can
do this!"

Levi watched as Johnson tapped home plate with his bat.
The Yankees pitcher pounded the baseball into his mitt a few
times, then reared his arm back and released that ball straight
down the strike corridor. Johnson swung at it with everything
he had in him.

And he missed.

"Steeee-rike!" the umpire called out.

Johnson took his stance again. This time the pitcher threw
a fast ball, and Johnson took it with gusto, sending it right back
out and deep into left field. The left fielder reached for it, but
that ball just kept right on sailing above him. Johnson was already on second base before the ball even thought about dropping back down to earth. And in the Vipers came—one run, two
runs, three runs, and four. Johnson had hit a home run, scoring
four big ones, upsetting the ten-to-seven score and pulling the
Vipers into the lead for an eleven-to-ten victory. The Las Vegas
Vipers had done it!

"Sealed and delivered! The Vipers are the new World Series
Champions!" The network sportscaster shouted over the air-
waves.

The inmates erupted in cheers—all but the die-hard Yankee fans, anyway.

The sportscaster continued. "They pulled it off, folks. The Vipers have taken their first World Series win. Guess they didn't need that Amish pitcher after all."

The inmates looked at Levi to see how he was going to react, but Levi let it go.

"Don't let 'em get you down, kid," an older inmate they called "Pops" told Levi. "They're just reporters. It's their job to fill the dead air."

Levi nodded. Then Pops asked a question Levi had been asking himself ever since the incident first happened and he was being booked into jail.

"Troyer, what in the world were you thinking?"

CHAPTER EIGHTY-TWO

Ruth's heart broke for her sister. News of Levi's situation had spread throughout their Amish community, and while most of their close friends were reserved in their judgement against the "troubled" Troyer twin and his latest antics, some had a field day, adding even more chapters to the story. They didn't want to wait around for the facts. They were filling in whatever puzzle pieces needed filling in, and a lot of them weren't anywhere close to the truth. Ruth didn't want to tell Hannah all she'd heard. She figured her sister was depressed enough with the pieces that were true without piling on the speculations of the shadow-talkers, too.

Still, Ruth couldn't stand by and watch her sister in such a state. She thought about inviting her to go out to the field and pick blackberries together, like they did when they were young. But the blackberries were beyond the ballfield, and Ruth figured that passing through there would have brought up too many sad memories for Hannah. Ruth also thought about asking her sister to go into town and do some shopping. But she nixed that idea too. To go into town they would have to pass the Troyer farm, so that wasn't going to work either. Ruth would have to find another way to lift her sister's spirits.

Hannah's downcast mood had been concerning Ruth for months now. She often heard Hannah crying in her bed at night. At mealtimes she picked at her food, hardly eating anything. And now, with this new turn of events, Ruth wondered how her sister was ever going to get through it all. Ruth wondered something else too, something that many in Hannah's life were wondering now. Should Hannah Weaver continue to waste so much of her life waiting for someone like Levi Troyer?

CHAPTER EIGHTY-THREE

Levi was sentenced to six months—four months in jail and two months in lockdown supervised rehab. It was clear the judge was making an example out of the latest sports hero to have a run-in with the law.

During the trial, though, it was discovered that the victim had a lengthy history of these types of altercations and cashing in afterwards. Apparently it had turned into a bit of a part-time job for him, and a very lucrative one for his ambulance-chasing attorney. The judge didn't lighten Levi's sentence any, but the man got some charges thrown at him too, so that made the sentence a little easier to take.

Levi Troyer was finally in a place to work on his disease and himself. Beneath all that bravado was a scared little boy, crying out for help and love, while pushing everyone away. Including God.

But there on his cot, in an open room shared with twenty or so other men, Levi closed his eyes and prayed quietly to himself. He was tired of chasing after dreams that took him away from the people he loved. Marco was right. This wasn't his world. He loved baseball, but he promised himself that when this stint was over, he was going to make amends to the man he'd hurt, then go home and try to restore his relationship with his family and Hannah—whatever it took.

CHAPTER EIGHTY-FOUR

The two ladies standing in line in front of David at the local Walmart were commenting about the headlines in the tabloids. Shoppers could hardly miss these papers, with their intriguing and attention-getting headlines. On this particular day there was yet another one—this time about Levi Troyer, and David couldn't avoid reading it. The two ladies standing in line in front of him couldn't either.

"Can you believe that kid?" the first lady said. "To have everything and then throw it all away. Young people today don't have a lick of sense."

The other woman agreed. "The Amish must be so embarrassed. They're such good, upstanding people, and that kid's done just about everything they're against. He may have been a good ballplayer, but he sure struck out in life."

The first lady nodded in agreement. "Why, if he were my kid . . ."

Their conversation continued, blaming Levi's mother, father, and even the bishop's sermons. That made no sense at all to David. The bishop's sermons were full of warnings about choosing the wrong path, and Levi had heard them all.

The ladies never mentioned the fact that Levi was a grown man and had been making his own decisions for quite a while now. Or that he'd been raised Amish but had never committed himself to the Amish church. Or that maybe this had been an answer to a father's desperate prayer, and now that his son had hit bottom he'd finally turn his life around. None of that entered their conversation because they didn't know any of it. They didn't even know that Levi's mother had passed away in child-birth, so why were they blaming her? All they'd read was a headline, and that's all they knew about this family that had already seen more than their share of heartache and strife.

David patiently listened to all he could stand before finally interrupting the women. And then he didn't hold back.

"Ladies, I don't know what your faith is; maybe you aren't even religious at all. But I am Amish. And we believe in forgiveness. So if that young man has the good sense to pick himself up after falling, then it's clear to me that anyone with a shred of human decency and grace would be cheering that fact, instead of saying such discouraging things about the poor fellow. Turning one's life around . . . Is that not the best homerun of all?"

David waited for the ladies to respond, but it was obvious they didn't quite know what to say. So he helped them by continuing.

"Now I hope I didn't make you feel uncomfortable, but I felt I had to speak up because that young man's *past* is in his *past*. I have a feeling his father is probably rejoicing right now, looking forward to embracing his son one day. And as for God, he's waiting to welcome him home too, don't you think?"

The women stared at David, dumbfounded. Then they smiled awkwardly and released a nervous laugh. Without saying another word to the Amish man who'd interrupted them, they paid for their purchases and hurried out to the parking lot. David probably should have left the matter at that. But he decided to follow them all the way to their fifteen-passenger van that was parked at the left side of the lot, over by Walmart's buggy-hitching post. He even walked over to the driver and had a little chat with him while the women loaded up. David didn't say anything to the driver about the ladies' critical attitude, especially considering the name of their church that was printed on the side of the van—Heart of Grace Fellowship. David simply talked with the driver about superficial matters, such as the best places to eat in town and whether or not it was fixing to rain. He didn't even have any eye contact with the women who were now sitting in the back, looking casually out the side window. But he had a hunch his presence was making them feel rather uncomfortable. In fact, they seemed to be sweating quite a bit. Maybe it was because the driver didn't have the air conditioner running. Or maybe it was because, as David noted on the driver's name tag, Reverend Philip Moore was their pastor, and David was enjoying a good discussion on the meaning of grace.

"Well, very nice meeting you, pastor," David said. "Now you all have a blessed day!" He gave a big smile and a friendly wave to the ladies before he turned away and walked on to his buggy.

CHAPTER EIGHTY-FIVE

The four months of jail time went surprisingly fast. But it was the two months in mandatory rehab that gave Levi the tools to live a sober life. When he first walked through the doors of the rehab center, he wasn't sure what to expect. But he quickly acclimated to the regime there. He was used to group gatherings because he'd grown up attending Amish church services, which were always held in one of the member's homes. So gathering together to listen to other people share what was on their hearts wasn't foreign to him in the least.

Delving that deeply into old hurts and pains, however, was. Levi didn't realize how many emotional injuries he'd buried over the years. Many of them had been simple misunderstandings, a child's interpretation of situations he couldn't comprehend at the time. But some of the injuries had been intentional, especially where John's resentment toward him was concerned. Levi had dealt with those things in the only ways he knew how—denial, burying the pain, and ultimately, numbing the hurts and losses with alcohol. Now it was time to find a new way.

Rehab hadn't been his choice. The decision had been forced upon him by the court. But the counseling was clearing up his head, and he was thankful for it. The reality of his torpedoed career had sunk in, and Levi was ready for a change.

"I had a dream last night," he shared with the group one day.

"I dreamed I hit the ball all the way across the field and into the stands. The whole stadium was on their feet cheering me on, except for two people on the front row—my brother and my father. The odd thing was, as soon as I saw them, I could no longer hear the cheers of the crowd. Their silence drowned out everything else."

"So what did you do?" the counselor asked.

"I dropped the bat and ran to first base anyway."

"And then?"

"I ran on to second."

"Did you keep on going?"

Levi lowered his head. "No. As I rounded third base, I looked back up to the stands and they were gone."

"So what did you do then?"

"Nothing. I stopped. I didn't care anymore, and I just stopped. I could've made it home, but what was the use of a stadium full of fans if I couldn't get those two to care?"

Another man, who appeared to be in his forties, spoke up next. "My mother was a judge. Every punishment she handed down felt like a life sentence. You think the parole board here is tough, try living with a judge."

"How'd you get sent up the river if your mother was a judge?" someone asked.

"Tough love, I guess. Sure didn't feel like love, though."

"For a lot of us, this is where it stops," another man said. "My addiction took everything. My wife left me. My kids won't talk to me. I lost my job and wore out all my friends."

Almost everyone in the room nodded understandingly.

"Our bishop always told us that God will restore the years the locusts have eaten," Levi said.

"Locusts? They got those here too?" one of the other men asked. "I was just getting used to the roaches."

The inmates laughed.

"The locusts mean whatever comes into your life and steals away what's dear to you," the counselor said. "Could be alcohol, drugs, gambling, fear—anything that's controlling your life."

One of the inmates asked, "And what if you didn't realize how much the locusts were eating?"

The counselor nodded. "Well, that's one thing about locusts. They always eat more than you figured on."

CHAPTER EIGHTY-SIX

So have you asked Him yet?" Marco inquired the next time he visited Levi in rehab.

"Ask who what?"

"You said you can ask God anything. So have you asked Him where He was when your mom died?"

"Yeah, I've asked him that plenty of times," Levi admitted.

"And what'd He say?"

"He always says the same thing. That He was right there with me—and my brother and Mother."

"Out loud? You hear him?"

"No. Not out loud. But I hear him."

"And you believe Him? That He was there?"

"My father does. And I guess I do too. We got through it, didn't we? So He must have been with us."

Marco gave a slight shrug. "When I was hungry in Cuba, I asked God where He was, but He never answered me. So when my father got killed, I didn't bother asking where God was. All I knew was, He wasn't with my dad. Otherwise He would have stopped it."

"The Amish believe that nothing happens outside of God's knowledge and, ultimately, His will."

"Are you saying it was God's will for my father to be killed?"

"No, that was the will of the drug lords. But for whatever reason, God allowed it. But He was with you through it all. And look, you're still here. In spite of it all, you made it. Just like I did."

"Dos milagros?" Marco said.

"Dos milagros," Levi repeated.

∾

In the group discussion the next day, Levi listened as one by one the others talked of being kicked out of their homes, being in and out of jail, or how their parents had written them off because of their addictions. Levi couldn't relate. His father loved him. If Levi knew anything, he knew that. It was Levi who'd done the leaving. And if he ever decided to leave Las Vegas and return home, he was certain his father would at least give him a job working on the family farm. Even John would be open to that, he figured. *I may have written myself off as a son,* Levi thought, *but my father would never turn his back on me.* He was sure of that.

But then again, he'd never gone down this road before . . .

CHAPTER EIGHTY-SEVEN

The embers on Charley's fire pit were about to burn out. He figured he'd hammered enough horseshoes and fused enough tools back together to call it a day.

John stopped in just as Charley was tallying up his receipts.

"I was hoping you'd still be here," John said.

"Another five minutes and you'd have missed me. What do you need, John?"

"Just wanted to talk to you for a minute. Friend to friend?"

"Well, sure," Charley said, sitting down on a wrought iron stool and offering John another one. "What's on your mind?"

"I'm sure you heard about my brother's situation."

Charley nodded. "I did. Was sure sorry to hear it too."

"His manager left a message for us on the community phone. When I called back, you know what he wanted? He wanted to know if my father could bail Levi out. Mortgage the farm for his folly. Can you imagine that?"

"He couldn't meet his bail?"

"He's broke, Charley. Gambled it all away. Everything, that's what his manager told me. His house, his fancy car, he's losing all of it. And I'm afraid now that's he's gone through his money, he's going to try to go through Father's next."

"You really think that would happen?"

"If Levi's lost millions, he won't think twice about risking one farm in Sugar Creek. But that farm is all Father has. If he borrows against it to clean up another one of my brother's messes, we could end up losing it. And Levi wouldn't care. The farm means nothing to him. But it's our home, Charley. It's our life."

"Well, if you really believe Levi wants no part of it, why don't you offer to buy him out? Sounds like he could use the money."

John shook his head. "Father would never do that. Shoot, I'd buy him out myself, but all my money is tied up in the farm."

"Well, you can get yourself a side job, I suppose."

"I thought of that too, but the farm takes most of the day—every day except Sundays, of course."

"Well, I do see your predicament. You're just gonna have to find some way to get some extra cash. Wish I could help you out."

"It's okay, Charley," John said, deep in thought. "I think you just did."

CHAPTER EIGHTY-EIGHT

The men at the rehab center had the option to attend regular chapel services, and one night Levi decided he'd go see what it was all about. The services were nothing like the Amish services he remembered. No one was singing from the *Ausbund*, the traditional Amish hymnal handed down through the centuries, which he'd grown up with. But Levi recognized many of songs, including one of his favorites, "Amazing Grace."

Levi found himself enjoying the entire experience. He was astounded at how these men, locked up and monitored, could sing their songs with such freedom and gratitude.

On this particular evening, with the *amens* flying freely, the preacher stepped to the center of the room and began to speak. There were about thirty men gathered there—some young, some old, some bitter, some angry, some searching, some lost—all broken.

Levi was especially open to hearing what the minister had to say.

"I know what you're feeling right now because I've been there myself. The mistakes, the baggage, the habits may differ. It doesn't matter. All that matters is this—it's time to lay it all down."

The men responded with nods of agreement.

❧

That night something clicked within Levi. How many times had he told himself he wouldn't touch another drop, all the while convincing himself that he could still handle just *one*. But this night it was different. Levi had finally gotten to the place where he realized it really did hurt more to be drunk than to be sober. So much had changed. Pitching a no-hitter back on the Amish farm used to give him such a rush, but the thrill of a no-hitter hadn't fazed him for months now, maybe even years.

He longed to go back to that dusty diamond in a leveled-out cornfield, using a fencepost for a bat and shoes for bases. He longed to taste another one of Hannah Weaver's deep-fried pies. He longed to see his father. And yes, even John.

But going home was no longer his choice. Not until he was done with rehab. And then the real fight for his sobriety would begin.

On the night before his release, one of the other inmates tried to pick a fight with him, a mind game often played to sabotage a rival's discharge. But word of the plan reached Levi, and he was ready for it and didn't take the bait. One more battle won. And so it would go. Day by day, battle by battle, victory to victory.

~

When Phil showed up to pick Levi up on the morning of his release, he found a different Levi Troyer. He couldn't have been more proud of his friend.

"You've got a lot of courage, kid," Phil said. "Do you know how many people never face their addictions? I'm proud of you."

"Thanks."

"I'm thinking of tackling a few of mine too," Phil added.

Levi nodded understandingly. "It's worth it."

As they walked to Phil's car, Levi stopped a minute to breathe in the air and take in the moment. Even though Las Vegas looked nothing like Sugar Creek, in his mind he saw green, rolling hills stretching on for miles before him.

"By the way," Phil said, "we got a good price on your car. And it looks like the sale of your house is going through. That means you can pay off Vinny once and for all."

Levi nodded. As much as he'd loved buying that fancy car and huge house, they no longer meant anything to him. "Thanks. That's good to know."

"So what do you want to do now?" Phil asked. "You name it, and I'll make it happen. You just say the word. Anything—*anything* at all."

Levi didn't have to think about that question for very long.

"I want to go home," he said.

CHAPTER EIGHTY-NINE

Phil purchased a plane ticket for Levi to fly to Akron, and he arranged for a driver to pick him up at the airport and drive him wherever he needed to go in the Sugar Creek area. Levi thanked Phil for sticking with him through thick and thin, and he apologized again for the way things had turned out.

"Hey, you fell down, but you got back up," Phil said. "That's the important thing. That's all any of us can do, huh, kid? Get back up, brush ourselves off, and go on."

"Yah," Levi agreed. "But I'll tell you this. It sure makes it a lot easier when someone's there, offering you a hand."

～

Levi's plane descended into the Akron-Canton airport. As arranged, the driver met him and drove him to Sugar Creek. Levi couldn't believe he was finally going home. It had been too long. As much as he yearned to see his father, he had no idea what kind of welcome, if any, he'd receive from either John or David. He needed something to boost his courage. A stop in at the Battered Donut was just the remedy.

"Well, well, looky who's here!" Eunice Weaver exclaimed when Levi walked into the bakery.

"Hello, Mrs. Weaver. Is . . . is Hannah around?"

"Oh, I'm so sorry, Levi. She's not. She works over at the library now."

"Really? She doesn't work here anymore?"

"Oh, she still helps out some, but today she's over there. You can stop in and see her if you like."

"Uh, yeah, maybe I will. I really just came in for a couple of her donuts. Sure have been missing those. Are there any left?"

"Well, now, let me see . . ." Eunice walked over to a full tray of glazed donuts. "I do believe Hannah made these before she left this morning."

"And you still have some left?"

"Yah, imagine that," Eunice said.

"I'll take two and a carton of milk."

Eunice bagged up his order. "So how long are you going to be in town, Levi?"

"Not sure. Just taking things a day at a time, you know."

"That's the best way, yah? Levi . . ." Eunice said, hesitantly. "I was sure sorry to hear about everything."

"It was for the best. I've learned a lot through it all."

Eunice nodded, and Levi thanked her for the good service and delicious food, as usual. Then he walked back outside and got into the waiting car. Levi had the driver take him over to the Sugar Creek library, but when they pulled up in front, he talked himself out of going in. After all, John *had* told him in that letter that Hannah had moved on with her life. And although John didn't say, Levi assumed that meant she was being courted by someone else. Perhaps he should leave well enough alone and not interfere.

What he didn't realize, of course, was that Hannah had been following his career and life, and wanted just as much to see him. In fact, she'd been looking out the window wondering who it was in that big black car that had pulled up in front of the library and then drove off.

"Tourists," she said under her breath. "Some of them think every building around here is a restaurant."

She'd have left it at that too, had Ruth not come rushing into the library, ignoring all the rules about keeping quiet.

"Hannah!" she said. "Hannah, you will never guess who's back in town!"

"Levi?" Hannah said hopefully.

Ruth nodded excitedly. "He stopped by the bakery not ten minutes ago. He asked about you, and Mother said you were here."

"Then that must have been him," Hannah exclaimed. "A black car just pulled up out front, but then it left."

"Why didn't he come in?"

Hannah shrugged. "I don't know."

"Well, I'm sure he'll be back."

"Oh, I hope so," Hannah said, looking longingly out the window for a shiny black car that was already long gone.

∽

Word had gotten to Charley that Levi was back in town and visiting some of his old friends. He hoped his blacksmith shop was on that "old friends" list.

Hannah hoped the same thing and ran over to Charley's to ask him to deliver a message for her if Levi did show up there.

"Please, Charley," she said, out of breath. "If Levi stops by, would you ask him to meet me at the ballfield at four o'clock today?"

Charley wondered why Levi hadn't already seen Hannah, or why Hannah wouldn't just go over to the Troyer home and see him there. Surely that's where he must be headed by now. But Charley assured her he would go along with her plan, even though Hannah ended up changing that plan several times before it was set.

"No, wait. Don't say that *I* want to meet him there. Just tell him that's where I'll be at four o'clock. Then, if he wants to see me, he'll come. Now remember, don't say *I* want to see him. Just say I'll be there. It's important, Charley."

"But you *do* want to see him, right?"

"Of course I want to see him."

"You just don't want him to know that you do?"

"Right."

"You want me to tell him you'll be there and then suggest he should go on over there too?"

"Exactly. I only want him to show up if he *wants* to see me." She paused and then frowned. "No, wait. What if he doesn't show up for some other reason? I won't know whether he's not showing up because he doesn't want to see me, or if he just didn't get the message, or . . . Oh, never mind. Just give him the message. You *will* give him the message, won't you, Charley?"

"Yes, but if you don't mind my saying so, I think I can see where this plan of yours could go terribly wrong."

"Yah, you're right," Hannah admitted. "So maybe you should go ahead and tell him that I *do* want to see him. Yes, yes, that's better. Tell him the truth. That's always the best way. Tell him I would very much like to meet him at the ballfield. No, no . . . that's not going to work. Just say I'm there. That's the truth too. But I *must* know he's going there because he *wants* to see me, not because I've asked him to meet me there. You understand, don't you, Charley?"

Charley didn't, but he was certainly trying. "I'll tell him," he promised, "but I can't guarantee he'll show up."

"I know. But if he does show up, at least I'll know it's because he *wants* to see me. But then again . . . "

Charley stopped Hannah before she rearranged the instructions yet again. He figured he had a good enough handle on what she wanted. What happened after that was up to Levi and Hannah.

～

Levi was on his way to the family farm, but when he passed the auction barn, he decided to stop in and see some of his old friends first. It would take only a moment, and Mel Byler, the auctioneer, had always been a good friend to Levi.

"Levi, welcome home!" Mel said when he saw Levi walking through the auction door.

"Thanks, Mel. It's good to be home."

Several others gathered around to greet Levi. It seemed they picked up right where they'd left off, as though nothing else had happened in the years that Levi had been gone.

"You gonna stay and watch some of the auction?" Mel asked.

"Nah, I'm headed over to Father's right now. Hope he's home."

"Should be," Mel told him. "John was in earlier. He auctioned off Double Trouble. Got fifteen hundred for her."

"Fifteen hundred? That's a good price for a horse of her age. John's better at these auctions than I ever was."

"We all have our own gifts, yah?" Mel said. "Well, tell David I said hi," Mel added when he noticed how anxious Levi was getting to get on home.

"I will, Mel," he said.

Levi had wanted to honor the doctor's request and not do anything to cause his father any stress and worsen his heart condition. But he really wanted to see him. He needed his father. He may have been coming home with a record now, and he was broke, so his departing promise of paying off the family farm upon his return now rang hollow. But he still longed to see his father. David would be welcoming a broken man, if he welcomed him at all. Levi wasn't sure if his father was up for that challenge.

But he still had the driver take him home—to the Troyer family farm. He had to know for himself where things stood.

&

David was sweeping off the front porch when he noticed the black car pull into the driveway. He wasn't sure what to think, but it certainly looked official—like one of those black government cars he'd seen on occasion driving through Akron when he'd visited there. He held his breath, wondering if he was about to receive news that something else had happened to his wayward son.

David watched and waited. But the driver didn't move. Then, suddenly, the rear passenger door opened and out stepped Levi. David's heart raced as Levi waited for a moment, looking at his father, hoping and praying he wouldn't turn around and go back into the house.

But David didn't turn away. "Levi!" he called out, dropping his broom and running to him. "Levi! Levi, you've come home!"

Levi was overcome as David threw his arms around him, embracing him so tightly that Levi could hardly breathe. But it felt oh, so good.

"I'm sorry, Father . . . " Levi said, choking back his tears. "Sorry for letting you down. Sorry for everything. I love you, and if you'll have me, I would very much like to come back . . . even as a hired farmhand."

"I'm sorry. I can't do that."

"I understand," Levi said, his heart sinking.

"You are my son, Levi," David said, overcome with emotion. "You will always be my son. Welcome home."

CHAPTER NINETY

John had witnessed the whole loving reunion from the window. He'd always figured this day would come, but still, he was a little taken aback by his father's blanket forgiveness. Had he forgotten everything Levi had done?

When David and Levi stepped into the house, embracing his brother was the last thing on John's mind. He greeted him, reservedly, and then as soon as he could, he took David aside.

"How could you forgive him so easily, Father?"

"John, I forgive your brother because he is my son. He was lost, but now he's found. Come, give him a proper welcome home."

"Levi was never *lost,*" John said. "His face was all over the place. Magazine covers, billboards, newspapers. He's only home now because he had nowhere else to go. You realize that, don't you?"

"He's here because he picked himself up and remembered where his family was," David countered.

John wasn't getting anywhere. When a man has forgiveness on his mind, it's hard to reason with him. *Why can't he see it?* John thought. *All the trouble Levi has brought into our lives?* But David didn't seem to care a lick about the troubles, the hurts, or even all the wasted years. It had all been erased, as far as David was concerned. That old barn had been swept clean.

After David left the room, John confronted Levi. "So how does it feel?"

Levi could tell John was itching for another argument, and he wasn't in the mood for it. "Not now, John."

But John pressed on anyway. "It's a simple question, Levi. How does it feel to have had it all—and then lost it? This was your big plan, right? You'd make your fortune, blow through it, and then come crawling back home. You didn't have to worry about anything, did you?"

"Are you done?"

"Done? I'm just getting started. So tell me, who's coming over to help us celebrate your homecoming? Did Father invite the bishop? Hannah? The whole community? Perhaps we should tell the English tourists too. You're such a big name now. That string of bad choices didn't hurt you at all. How do you do it? Nothing ever touches you. Everyone just looks the other way. So I guess your coach will be sending a plane ticket for you soon. Take up right where you left off, huh?"

"They let me go, John."

"How many no-hitters are you going to pitch this year? You going to break your own record?"

"John, the coach doesn't want me back."

"Of course he does. You're their best player. The only reason you didn't play in the World Series was because you were in jail. They're not going to let you go."

"John . . . they did. I'm off the team. They let me out of my contract. I've lost everything."

John wasn't sure how he was supposed to feel. It may not have seemed like it on occasion, but he truly did love his brother. He just wanted him to grow up, consider others, and act responsibly. It also appalled him to know that all the money he'd earned playing ball was now gone, gambled away, according to the newspapers. His house, his Lamborghini, his fortune—gone. And what John feared most was that Levi would now want to burn through David's money just as quickly.

CHAPTER NINETY-ONE

As promised, when Levi stopped by Charley's shop a little later that day, Charley told him Hannah Weaver would be down at the ballfield at four o'clock that afternoon, and he suggested Levi might want to go over there to see her. Levi told him he wanted to, but he had his doubts as to whether or not she'd want to see him.

"Don't get me wrong, Charley. I'd love to see Hannah again. But her heart belongs to someone else now. I have to respect that."

Charley was quite surprised to hear that, but he continued to listen as Levi talked.

"It's my own fault, I suppose," Levi said. "I've stayed away too long."

Charley shook his head, bewildered. "Someone else? Levi, no one's courting Hannah Weaver, if that's what you're saying."

"But I was told—"

"Go see her. Ask her for yourself. If you don't, you'll always regret it."

Levi gave a slight nod but didn't actually say if he would go. "You know she hasn't written to me in over six months," he said.

"Is that so?" Charley shrugged. "Have you written to her?"

Levi shook his head. "Like I said, I didn't want to interfere."

"Well, I'd still go see her. Four o'clock. At the ballfield. I'm sure she'll be there. You should be too."

☙

At three-thirty Hannah started making her way down to the
baseball field. She could feel her heart pounding in her chest.
She had no intention whatsoever of disrupting Levi's marriage
plans. If that socialite was the one he wanted to marry, then
she'd try her best to be happy for him. No matter where their
paths had taken them, she'd always considered Levi Troyer a
dear friend.

At least, that's how she explained it to herself. She was
simply going down to the ballfield to welcome him home, bring
him up to date on everything he'd missed out on in the community while he was gone, and find out how long he planned
on staying. Her original plans, of course, had they gone her way,
were to welcome Levi home with their long awaited first real
kiss, if he offered, of course; and then impress him with her
newfound baseball knowledge. *Why, he'd have been so astounded,
he would have asked me to marry him right then and there!* But now,
in light of his engagement to someone else, learning all those
statistics and keeping that secret album seemed to have been a
big waste of Hannah's time.

CHAPTER NINETY-TWO

At a quarter to four, Hannah looked up from the tree stump where she was sitting and saw Levi walking across the ballfield toward her. He looked as handsome as ever. She raised her arm and waved to him, and he returned the gesture. *A good sign,* Hannah thought.

When he got close enough, he called to her. "Hello, Hannah!"

Hannah resisted the temptation to run into his arms. "Hello, Levi," was all she said.

"How have you been?" he asked, resisting the same urge to embrace her.

"Oh, busy. You know how it is. Always something to do around here. I thought I'd come down to the ballfield and clean it up a bit after that rainstorm last night."

"A storm came through last night?"

"A little one," Hannah said, trying her best to support her alibi.

"Oh?" Levi looked puzzled. "I didn't notice the ground being wet this morning."

"It was a dry storm. Wind mostly."

"Well, the field doesn't look too bad," he said, glancing around.

"I've already picked up most of it," Hannah explained, realizing she was just digging her hole deeper. "Branches mainly. Gathered up a big pile of them already."

Levi looked around and pointed to two small branches that lay side by side next to home plate. "You mean those two over there?"

Hannah shot a quick prayer for forgiveness then quickly changed the subject. "So how does it feel to be home?"

Levi sat down on the tree stump next to her.

"Oh, wonderful! I've missed everybody, Hannah . . . especially you. You've always been such a good friend."

"And you as well."

He took a deep breath. "I want you to know that I always used to look forward to receiving your letters."

Used to enjoy? Hannah thought to herself. *Yah, before you went and got yourself engaged!*

But she didn't say that. Instead she went with, "And I used to enjoy your letters too, Levi."

Levi wondered why Hannah didn't go on to explain why her own letters had suddenly stopped. But he didn't go there.

"How are things going at the Battered Donut?"

"Well, Ruth and my parents still run it. And I still work there part-time, but I've been trying other jobs. Most didn't work out. But then I got a job at the library, and I love it."

"Yah, your mother told me about that."

"Oh, Levi, I've learned so much already."

"Like what?"

"Oh, I plan to tell you all about it someday . . . when the time is right."

"I've got time now."

"But I'm afraid I don't. I have to get back to work."

Oh, no, there it was again. Another one of those not-quite-true statements that she was going to have to repent of. They sure were piling up. Hannah didn't really have to leave. She'd already clocked out of the library for the day. But Levi hadn't said a word so far about his fiancé back in Las Vegas, and the continuing mystery was breaking her heart. And making her feel quite guilty for being so hopelessly in love with someone else's fiancé.

༺

After Hannah left, Levi began walking back home. It hurt him
to realize that Hannah had indeed moved on with her life. But
it was another painful fact that he was going to have to accept.
On his way he passed John, who was out working in the field.
Levi was still trying to make amends to his brother, to talk
through their hurts and get past them. But John hadn't been interested in hearing anything Levi had to say. Still, Levi was determined to make things right, so when he got close enough, he
waved John down.

"Ah, you've come to help?" John asked. "The sun will be setting soon. Perfect timing . . . as usual."

"I'll help you tomorrow," Levi said. "First thing in the morning. You have my word."

"Yah. We'll see if you show up," John said, continuing on
with his work.

"John!" Levi called.

John stopped again.

"What?" he asked, bothered at the interruption.

"Couldn't you have been proud of me just once?"

John dropped the reins and left the horses then walked toward Levi. "Proud? Proud of *what*? That you always leave your
messes for others to clean up? Do something I can be proud of,
and I'll heap all the praise on you that you'd like."

"When have I ever *asked* you to clean up one of my messes,
John? You just stepped in and did it. But there was always a
price to be paid for your help."

"You still don't get it, do you? We have *all* paid for your self-
ish actions. Especially Father. I care about you, Levi, I really do,
but get thee over thyself, brother!"

"Do you wish I'd never come home? Then you'd have the
farm, the house and Father—all to yourself. Is that it? I came
along and ruined everything for you, didn't I?"

"If you're going back to Mother's death, I never blamed you for that."

"Oh, I'm sure the thought has crossed your mind. But you're not the only one who grew up without a mother, John. We *both* did."

"Are you quite done? I need to get back to work."

"No. I'm not done," Levi said. "You're not going to go on with your 'perfect' schedule as if everything was fine—no harm, no foul. We're going to talk this through once and for all."

"What's talking going to do?"

"Clear the air, for one. That's how things heal. And then we should talk about the future of this farm."

There it was—the real reason for the visit. "Don't you even go there, Levi." John clenched his fists. "If you try to take this farm, you'll have to go through me to do it."

Levi frowned, truly puzzled. "What are you talking about?"

"You know good and well what I'm talking about. And we can settle that discussion right here and now."

"Are you threatening to fight me, John?"

"It's how you like to settle things, isn't it?"

Levi was dumbfounded. "John, I'm not your enemy. I'm your brother. I came home to make peace. I just thought we could talk about the farm and my part in it."

In a flash, John's fist flew toward Levi's face. *Smack!* A left hook right across the chin sent Levi backwards onto the ground. He picked himself up. He didn't want to do it, but John's fist was coming at him again, so he blocked it and planted one of his own across John's face, just clipping him at the corner of his cheekbone. Neither one cared that they were breaking several rules of their Amish *Ordnung*. They also knew their father would have plenty to say if word of the brawl ever reached his ears. At the moment, though, they didn't care about any of that. The brothers were venting two decades' worth of bitterness and blame, and neither one was about to stop until the pressure valve on their emotions had gained some release.

Or until they saw their father walking toward them across the field, just as he was at that very moment. Quickly they got to their feet and brushed themselves off.

"Not a word of this, you hear?" John said.

Levi wiped blood off his lip. "I don't have to say anything. That shiner of yours will do all the talking."

John pressed at the flesh beneath his eye. It was already puffy and swollen. "This isn't over," he warned.

"So tell me the part again where you care about me," Levi said. "Because I think I missed it."

John didn't answer. He took off in another direction before their father could reach them.

When David got close enough to Levi, he asked sternly, "What was going on out here?"

"This is between John and me, Father."

"It looked like you were fighting."

"It was long overdue."

"When will you two ever act like brothers?"

"I moved out, Father. Out of our home and across the country. I started a new life. And yet I still wasn't far enough away to please him."

"Your brother has a hard time forgiving your failures. Give him time."

"Is it my failures that trouble him, Father? Or was it my success?"

CHAPTER NINETY-THREE

John and Levi never talked about the scuffle. What happens in a cornfield between brothers when resentment and tensions are allowed to boil over stays in the cornfield, they figured. Other than the shiner John was sporting, no one had a clue that anything so non-Amish-like had ever taken place. Whenever anyone asked about the extra color around John's eye, he merely blamed it on an unexpected encounter with some farm equipment.

The brawl had settled nothing, of course. Conversations spoken with fists profit little. But it let off an ample amount of steam that had been waiting to bubble to the surface for years now.

❧

John needed somewhere to vent his raging emotions, and he hoped he'd find a sympathetic ear with Charley. Charley already knew of Levi's troubles; John had kept him abreast of every detail as they developed over the years. Charley also knew how much John had been put upon in Levi's absence. He'd seen it firsthand. Most importantly, his advice had always been fair. John might not have liked it at times, but he couldn't deny that it had indeed been fair.

Charley listened to John talk about David's blind forgiveness of his brother and how he doubted he could ever do the same. When Charley was sure John was done, he spoke.

"You know, John, there was a time when I had to forgive some people. For what, it doesn't really matter. But I knew I had to do it. Now I don't know if the Amish struggle with it as much as we English do, but I sure didn't want to forgive them. Guess that's because I thought forgiveness was forgetting. But those are two completely different words. Still, I knew God was working on my heart, so I finally got into my car and went for a little drive."

"Over to their house?"

"No. I did like Jonah in the Bible and took off in the opposite direction. I rode around for a while just thinking about all the reasons those people didn't deserve my forgiveness. Then I finally pulled off the road and sat there talking it over with God."

"So who won?"

"Well, now, that's the interesting thing," Charley said. "I thought I had . . . until I started to turn around and head back home and forget the whole thing. That's when I looked up and saw it. Proof positive that God had gotten in the last word after all."

"What was it?"

"Oh, just a giant billboard with only two words written on it. It said, 'Forgive them.' And it was signed, 'God.' Now, I'm smart enough to know God didn't write that on that billboard Himself, or even sign it, but He did say it, and there it was, as big as you please. So this time I headed straight over to their house and took care of the matter."

"So you think I should forgive Levi?"

Charley nodded. "A billboard's kind of hard to ignore."

CHAPTER NINETY-FOUR

Later that night Levi walked down the hallway and over-heard John talking to David about Double Trouble, the horse John had sold at the auction earlier that day. Levi moved in closer and pressed his ear against the door.

"He went for a good price then?" David asked.

"A thousand dollars is a good price, yah?"

"Well, he should have brought a bit more. He was a good horse. But with the economy being what it is, I suppose we'll have to live with it."

It was obvious to Levi that John was cheating their father out of five hundred dollars. But why? Levi thought about stepping into the room and telling his father the truth—that the horse had actually sold for fifteen hundred. But he decided he was going to let this one play itself out. More walls being erected between him and his brother was the last thing Levi Troyer needed.

CHAPTER NINETY-FIVE

Phil had given Levi a little money to help him get started in his new life. Levi didn't want to take it, but Phil had insisted. And so Levi was able to take Hannah to dinner the following afternoon.

Hannah had a feeling that something was up because her family kept trying to get her to get going.

"Levi's waiting for you. Hurry up, Hannah," Eunice said.

Even her father seemed eager.

"Go on now," Eli said. "Have yourself a nice time."

"You approve of Levi Troyer now?" Hannah asked.

"The bishop said he's talked to him," Eli said. "He said he's made a lot of positive changes in his life. And then the bishop had a good talk with your mother and me."

"So you forgive him of his past?"

Eunice smiled and nodded. "Just doing what God already did."

∂⌒

After dinner at a local restaurant, Hannah and Levi took a stroll down the street. They talked about their hopes and their friendship, and then Levi stopped and turned to her.

"Hannah Weaver, I'm going to ask you something I should have asked you a long time ago."

"Oh, you are, huh? And what's that?"

"Hannah Weaver, will you marry me?"

Hannah was beyond surprised. "But what about . . . I mean, don't you have a—"

"Oh, don't worry. I'm gonna give you the biggest diamond you've ever seen."

Hannah laughed. "Levi, you know the Amish don't wear wedding rings. But what I was going to say was . . . I thought you already had a fiancé. I read that in a headline once."

Levi laughed. "Oh, Hannah, you can't believe everything you read. Especially in those tabloids. Some of them just take a photograph then rig it to look like something it's not. That lady was my accountant's wife. We'd all gone out to dinner together, but the photographer cut him out of the shot."

"What?" Hannah was genuinely shocked—and ecstatic. "So it isn't true?"

"No. And the diamond I was talking about is a new baseball diamond. Bigger and better. With real bleachers and everything. I've got it all figured out. We'll coach the teams together. I'll coach the men's team, and you coach the women's."

Hannah smiled, her heart warming with his every word.

"And I will promise you this—I won't be spending all my time on the baseball field either. I've got a house to build, a barn to raise, and a farm to tend to. So what do you think?"

"You really want to marry the only Amish girl who can't cook?"

"I do."

Levi took Hannah's hand in his. "So . . . what's your answer, Hannah? Will you do me the honor of being a farmer's wife?"

"Oh, Levi, yes. Yes, I will marry you."

Levi took his sweet Hannah in his arms and at long last kissed her. A real kiss. Right on the lips.

Babe Ruth's best day couldn't have felt any better than this!

CHAPTER NINETY-SIX

I came to one of your games," David told Levi as the three Troyer men sat on the front porch together the next morning.

"So that *was* you!" Levi said. "In Cincinnati?"

David nodded. "John and I went."

"I saw you. Up in the stands, above the dugout. Why didn't you stay?"

"John was right. We would have embarrassed you."

"*Embarrassed* me? You said that, John?"

"It's all right, Levi. I understand," David said.

"No, it's *not* all right, Father. John, did you tell him that?"

"We weren't a part of your world, Levi," John said.

Levi turned to David. "Father, do you have any idea how many times I looked up into those stands, hoping to see you there? Just once. It would have meant the world to me . . . to know you cared. Embarrass me? John, how could you say such a thing?"

"Your brother was only trying to protect you, Levi," David said. "Besides, I'd seen what I'd gone there to see—that you were doing well, that you were healthy and safe . . . and not ready to come home."

"But I *might've* come home had you stayed and talked to me. Who knows? Maybe I could've saved myself a lot of trouble."

"I wish you'd told me what was going on," David said. "You should have written and told me, son."

"I *did*," Levi said. "But you never answered my letters. I didn't know what to think until John wrote and told me about your situation. You didn't need my problems giving you more stress."

"You wrote to me?" David asked.

"Dozens of letters, Father. Didn't you get them?"

"Don't listen to him," John interjected. "He was too busy living it up to write to us."

Levi looked at John and started adding things up. "How long have you been keeping my letters from Father, John?"

"Levi," David said, "why would your brother do such a thing? You're talking nonsense."

"This is why I couldn't get away from here fast enough," Levi said. "I'd rather take on the whole world than my adversary here at home."

It was John's turn to be angry now. "Me? Your *adversary*? You're the one who always put baseball ahead of us. That's why we didn't stay at your precious ballgame. You know good and well you wouldn't have given us the time of day. Well, I don't have to stay and listen to this." John moved toward the steps of the porch. "I've got work to do."

"Of course you do," Levi said. "That's what you do best, isn't it, John? Work. Out in the fields so everyone can see and admire you."

John turned back around, and looked his brother in the eye. "Or I could do it in a stadium like you."

"I was foolish to think anything had changed," Levi snapped. "Go on, go! Get back to your plowing."

"Somebody has to! Father sure can't count on you to do it, can he? No one's ever been able to count on you, Levi. Not even your ball team!"

"John," David pleaded, "that's enough."

"No, Father. Why did he really come home? Ask him. His heart has never been here."

"I came home to make amends. Or try to, anyway."

"Too little and far too late," John said.

"It's never too late for old wounds to heal," David argued.

"Please, Father. This is between John and me," Levi said.

"Think of your heart."

"My heart?"

"It's okay. John told me about it . . . how your doctor didn't want me writing to you anymore because it would cause too much stress on your heart. That's why I stopped writing and how I finally knew why you weren't writing to me. I was glad John told me. It hurt, but if you can't be honest with your brother, who can you be honest with?"

David turned to John. "Did you write and tell him that, John?"

"Who are you going to believe, Father? Levi, or your son who has served you faithfully every day of his life?"

"I'm going to believe the truth," David said.

"He's the cause of all our problems," John continued. "It's always been him. He wouldn't be here right now if he hadn't fallen flat on his face . . . again. I'm the one who's kept this farm going and fed you when you've been hungry. And where has my brother been? Living it up in Vegas!"

"Living it up? I had bills coming out of my ears from gambling debts and habits that took more than I ever bargained for."

"And now you come home groveling and expecting to find us all waiting with open arms. Well, not me, brother. And you're not going to lose our farm too, if I have anything to say about it!"

"You know what's sad, John? We've been together since the womb, but you've never even taken the time to get to know me."

"I know you're a prideful son and brother who needs an endless supply of praise to face another day."

"Is that me, John . . . or is it you?"

John's cheeks flamed, but he didn't answer.

"In all my stumbling," Levi said, "did you pray for me, even once?"

"Of course," John said. "I prayed that you'd at long last be brought to your knees."

"Then your prayers were answered. Or were you also praying that I wouldn't get back up?"

"Of course he wanted you to get up," David assured him. "Tell him, John."

David waited for John to speak up in his own defense, but he didn't.

"John," Levi said, "I'm sorry. Sorry that I haven't helped you more with the work around here. It wasn't fair to you. But I'm here now, asking what I should have asked you a long time ago. John . . . will you forgive me?"

David waited, but John still didn't speak.

"John, your brother has asked you a question."

"Father, I'm the one who has done everything you've ever asked me to do," John said.

"Except forgive your brother. You're good at putting up fences, John. Maybe it's time to tear this one down."

But John's heart wouldn't soften.

"The Scriptures tell us we're to offer our brother forgiveness seven times seventy," David said. "That's not how many times he should have to ask for it."

"But you *always* forgive him! No matter what he does, you forgive him," John lamented. "How far will a father's love go for such a wayward son?"

"As far as he runs from it," David said. "Either one of my sons." He took a deep breath before continuing. "John . . . I know. About the horses. Charley told me. I was going to talk to you privately about it, but we might as well talk now. John, why have you been stealing from me in the auctions?"

"Stealing from you? Father, I don't know what Charley told you, but you know the kind of records I keep. Charley must have misheard the auctioneer. Sometimes his cadence makes it hard to make out the winning bid."

"Tell me the truth, John," David demanded.

John was indignant. "I'll stop by the auction tomorrow and verify the figures. Even get a signed receipt, if you want."

"There's no need for that," David said. "I went by there yesterday and verified the figures myself. Now tell me the truth, John. My patience is wearing thin."

John knew his father deserved the truth, but it was doubly hard to own up to it in front of Levi. At last he opened up. "I was trying to save enough money to buy Levi out . . . before he gambled our farm away next. But whatever I did, Father, it was to protect you."

"Protect me? By stealing from me? If I'd wanted to buy him out, I could have done it myself. And what of the letters, John? Did you do what Levi said?"

"It's not what you think, Father."

"I think you kept me from my son even when you knew how I longed to hear from him."

"You have two sons," John said.

The conversation seemed to be causing more pain that it was healing.

"John, I wouldn't do anything to lose this farm," Levi said. "In jail I finally realized what all I'd walked away from. I never knew how blessed I was. John, I would've given up everything to have had what you have here."

"What did I have here that you possibly could have wanted?" John asked.

"Father's respect. But now I fear we've both lost that."

David shook his head, his face drawn. "What pain have you wrought on our family, John? I am so very disappointed in you."

Regret washed over John, and he fell to his knees. "Father, I'm sorry. Forgive me, please. I was only trying to save the farm. That's why I did it. I'm so sorry, Father."

"John . . . I do forgive you, just as I've forgiven your brother," David said as he reached out and placed his hand on John's shoulder. "And now that life has brought you both to your knees, maybe you'll finally see eye to eye."

Before John knew it, Levi had come to stand in front of him too.

"John, will you forgive me now?"

As John rose to his feet, Levi opened his arms and embraced his brother. It wasn't like any embrace Levi had ever given John before. Their childhood hugs, when ordered to do so, barely held any emotion. But not tonight. This clasp was so very different.

"Levi, I'm the one who's sorry," John said, stepping back to look Levi in the eyes. "I've lied to you and about you. I was wrong. Now I'm asking—can you forgive me?"

Levi smiled. "I already have."

John gave a heartfelt nod. "You know, ever since we were kids, all I ever wanted was your admiration."

"And all I ever wanted was your respect."

David shook his head. "Well, you surely are twins," he said with a smile.

John nodded. "And at long last . . . brothers."

CHAPTER NINETY-SEVEN

The mail came," David announced when he walked back into the house several weeks later. Then, thumbing through the envelopes, he handed one to Levi, who was finishing up his breakfast. "This one's for you."

"I got a letter? Here?" Levi was surprised. Then, noting the return address, he said, "It's from my coach. He must be letting me know if he can come to the wedding."

"It was good of you to invite him," David said.

"In the spirit of reconciliation, yah?" Levi said. Then he quickly ripped open the envelope and read the letter. "What? I don't believe this!"

"What did he say?" David asked, curious.

"He's inviting me back to the team. Says the board met, and they decided they want to put the matter behind us all and move on."

"Is that so?" David said, wondering if they were going to have to go down the same painful path all over again. But he decided to leave the future in God's hands. "Well, we've all needed a second chance at some point in our lives. It feels good, huh, son?"

"It feels *very* good, Father. And I know exactly what I'm going to tell him."

"Tell who what?" John asked as he stepped into the room.

"Levi's coach has invited him back," David explained.

"Why am I not surprised?" John said, genuinely trying to be happy for him.

"And neither one of you can talk me out of my decision," Levi said.

David nodded. "You make your own decisions as always, son."

"Well . . . so what are you going to do?" John asked.

"I'm turning him down," Levi said decisively.

John nearly dropped his glass of lemonade. "What?"

"That's not the life for me. I know that now. Besides, I figure you could both use some help around here running this farm. That's what I meant when I said I wanted to talk about my part in the farm, John. This time I want to do my share of the work."

John was impressed. Maybe his little brother had finally grown up after all.

"But now, I won't be giving up baseball totally," Levi said. "I'll be playing it here. I'm going to coach our Amish and Mennonite teams for the boys, and Hannah's going to coach for the girls. Who knows? Maybe we'll make such a name for ourselves that we can get them to bring the World Series to Sugar Creek someday."

"Well, if they do, I promise I'll go to all the games and stay until the very last inning," David said, smiling.

"I'm going to hold you to that, Father," Levi said, putting the letter back into the envelope. But something blocked it from sliding all the way in. Levi reached his fingers inside and pulled out an old newspaper article.

"What's that?" John asked.

"I don't know." Levi unfolded the old clipping and started reading it.

"Well? What's it about?" David asked.

"The Yankees."

"The Yankees want you now? Will it ever stop?" John said, teasing.

Levi laughed. "It's not about me. It's about some guy who used to play for the Yankees years ago, and no one's heard from him since."

John raised an eyebrow. "Yah?"

"Says he quit to marry an Amish girl and become a farmer."

"Well, I can't say as I blame him," David said. "It's a good life."

"And for some reason," Levi said, handing him the clipping, "the fella in this photograph looks a lot like you, Father. Something you want to tell us?"

David looked at the article. It was clear he recognized the man in the photograph. Clear too that he'd seen that article before. And quite clear that he had a lot of explaining to do.

John took the article from David. His eyes widened when he saw it. "Well, Father?" John pressed.

David took a deep breath. "You boys got the rest of the afternoon?"

"So it's true?" John asked.

"Yes. It's all true."

"Why didn't you ever tell us about this before?" Levi asked.

"Well, I wanted to. But it always seemed too prideful to bring it up. And after we moved to Ohio, your mother asked me not to talk about that part of my life anymore. It was in the past."

"So you're telling us you played professional baseball?" Levi asked. "For the *Yankees?*"

"Well, I was on the team. Don't know how good I was," David said.

"You were good enough to be on the team and good enough to be written about when you left it. I'd say you were plenty good!" Levi said.

"Well, I was so impressive that most people have forgotten all about me. But I guess I earned my pay at the time."

"But then, how'd you meet Mom?" John asked.

"Well, the team was headed to a game in Cincinnati when our bus broke down in Akron. So while the bus was getting fixed, we all walked over to a nearby Amish restaurant."

"And she was there?"

"She was our waitress. I thought she was so beautiful. And she had the sweetest smile I'd ever seen. My grandfather was Mennonite, so I was already familiar with the Mennonite and Amish lifestyles. So when we fell in love, I was willing to give it a try."

David continued to answer John and Levi's bevy of questions for the rest of the afternoon, filling in the blanks on a family secret that had been hidden for decades.

"So the Yankees didn't pass on us Troyers after all?" Levi said.

David laughed. "No, they sure didn't. Baseball's in your blood, son. And it just goes to show you—in God's plans *anything* can happen."

"So who's your favorite player?" Levi asked.

"That's an easy one. Mickey Mantle. Got to meet him once . . ." David then proceeded to tell his sons all about his chance encounter with The Mick. Levi and John hung on every word. In fact, the three of them stayed out on that porch long after the sun went down. Just talking. There wasn't a question John and Levi didn't ask and that David didn't answer. Levi had never felt closer to his father than he did that night. John either. Sharing life stories has a funny way of accomplishing that.

CHAPTER NINETY-EIGHT

Hannah packed a picnic lunch in case Levi was down at the ballfield. If he wasn't there, she figured she could sit and read a book or something. But if he did happen to be there, they could eat lunch together and continue discussing their wedding plans. But when Hannah reached the field, what was waiting for her there was more than she ever expected.

Can it be? Hannah thought to herself when she reached the clearing. *Can it really be? David? And John—and Levi? All playing baseball—together?*

"Come on, Hannah," Levi called out as soon as he saw her approaching. "We need you in left field."

I'm sleepwalking. That's what I'm doing. The Troyer men all playing baseball together. This can't be real! But it was broad daylight, and Hannah Weaver was wide awake.

Levi called out to her again. "Come on, Hannah!"

Hannah looked down at the Amish dress she was wearing. She'd just washed and pressed it with her old fashioned iron. But the team *did* need her help. Surely it would be a good thing to help out the Troyer family in their time of need, wouldn't it? Before Hannah could think any more about it, she grabbed a mitt and ran toward the outfield position.

"Okay, I'm ready," she said, as she bent her knees just a bit to steady herself.

David was at bat now, and Levi covered first base. John was pitching.

"Alright, John, give me one this old man can hit," David called.

"*You* old, Father?" Levi laughed. "Never!"

John threw the ball, and David knocked it straight to Hannah. She tried catching it, but it rolled off her mitt and onto the ground. Quick as a flash, she picked it up and threw it to Levi. David slid into first base, but he wasn't quick enough.

"Out!" Levi called.

"Hey, at my age, sliding should count for something," David said, laughing as he got back up on his feet and brushed himself off.

It was John's turn at bat next, with David pitching now. Levi remained at first.

"Alright, John, give us one of your homeruns," Levi called out.

"I've never hit a homerun in my life, you know that," John objected, though good-naturedly.

"Don't sell yourself short," Levi said. "You can do this!"

Hannah cocked her head to the side. She looked at Levi, then over to John, then back to Levi again. *What's going on?* she asked herself. As far as she could see, there wasn't a hint of jealousy or resentment between them. And David? She couldn't recall the last time she'd seen David Troyer laughing this much.

John took a few practice swings and positioned himself for the pitch. David threw a fast ball right into the strike zone. John swung and connected with a *whack!* That ball went sailing high over first base, too high for Levi to catch. When it finally landed, it bounced a few times then rolled along the foul line but never rolled out. John took full advantage of the solid hit and ran to first, then on to second, and he was rounding to third when Levi reached that ball, picked it up, and threw it to Hannah, who was now covering third base. Hannah made a worthy catch, but it was too late to stop John. He'd already touched third and was heading for home, with Hannah racing right behind him. She ran her fastest, but she couldn't reach him.

Levi, who now covered home plate, shouted to her. "Throw it, Hannah!"

Hannah threw the ball straight to Levi, but John slid under him, touching home plate with his hand.

"Safe!" David shouted.

"Homerun!" they all cheered.

"You did it, John!" Levi said, high-fiving his brother.

Hannah congratulated John too. She and Levi were only engaged, but Hannah was already feeling very much a part of the Troyer family.

CHAPTER NINETY-NINE

Levi met Hannah at the library at the end of her shift. She wasn't quite done with her work, so he watched as she put some of the returned books back on their proper shelves.

"You've loved to read for as long as I've known you, Hannah Weaver. This must be your dream job."

She smiled and nodded. "I love it here. I can visit every city and state where you've been, and never even leave Sugar Creek."

"There are a lot of good adventures in books."

"And you can read about people's lives too. That's my favorite kind of book—biographies," she said.

"Read about anyone interesting?"

"Oh, yes, a lot of different people."

Hannah had to file a book over in the "C" section, and Levi followed. When she was done, she stopped off at the "B" section.

"See? Look here," she said, taking a book off the shelf and showing him. "This is one of the books I read while you were gone."

Levi read the title of the book: *The Biography of Babe Ruth.*

"Seven-hundred-fourteen career homeruns," Hannah said. "They called him 'The Great Bambino,' and he held the record for decades until Hank Aaron finally broke it."

"Hmm . . . Not bad. And what team was Hank on?"

"Hank was right fielder for the Milwaukee Braves, which later became the Atlanta Braves. He was known as Hammerin' Hank. Number 44."

"And who did Ruth play for?"

"Started out as the pitcher for the Boston Red Sox then played right field for the Yankees. Inducted into the Hall of Fame in 1936. And did you know the bat Babe Ruth used when he hit his first home run at Yankee Stadium sold for over one million dollars? And that both his parents were German?"

"I didn't know that."

"Shh . . . " the head librarian hissed to whoever was talking in the "B" section.

Levi pulled out the next book. It was the biography of Mickey Mantle.

"Ah, yes . . . 'The Mick,'" Hannah said, keeping her voice down. "He played for the New York Yankees too."

"You learned all that from working here?"

"To be of help to our customers," Hannah said.

Levi began picking out books at random and quizzing Hannah about the different players. She nailed every answer. Levi laughed, amazed that she'd taken such an interest in something so close to his heart. "I had no idea they had all these books here."

Levi read off a few more titles: *The Biography of Willie Mays, The Biography of Sandy Koufax.* Then he reached for the last one on the shelf, but it wasn't a book at all. It was Hannah's photo album with a handwritten title, *The Biography of Levi Troyer.*

"Hey, what's this?" Levi asked, surprised.

"Open it."

Levi opened the album and began to turn the pages, one by one. He couldn't believe that someone had taken the time to collect so many articles and photos of him. It even included his baseball card!

By the time he reached the final page, he had tears in his eyes.

"Who did this?" he asked.

Hannah didn't answer. She just smiled.

Levi took her by the hand. "Hannah Weaver, this is the nicest thing anyone's ever done for me."

"You probably have all of those things already, yah?"

"To tell you the truth, I don't. I saved a few for a while, but then I lost interest. Success doesn't mean much when you don't have someone to share it with."

The librarian hushed them again, so they quieted their voices almost to a whisper.

"You're a part of history now, Levi," Hannah said, remembering how relieved she'd been at the bishop's decision not to punish her for putting together the album but rather to place it in the library where everyone could see it. "I talked to my parents and the bishop, and my boss, of course. They all agree. It needed to be here. You're a local hero."

"I'm no hero," Levi protested.

"Your story will inspire a lot of people, Levi. People who need to be given hope for a second chance and be reminded of God's grace."

Levi tenderly gripped her arms and looked into her eyes. "Hannah, I love you. You and my family and everything I want in life is all right here in Sugar Creek. But you're going to have to take me as I am. I'm not that guy in this album anymore. Or the same boy I was when I left. I'm just me."

Hannah gazed back into his eyes. "You're the Levi Troyer I've been waiting for my whole life."

CHAPTER ONE HUNDRED

For a long time many of the guests avoided the wedding cake table, walking a good distance out of their way so they wouldn't be called over and offered a slice. Word had spread that Hannah herself had made it, so some would say it was wisdom that was causing the hesitation to sample it.

But those brave enough to partake were pleasantly surprised.

"Oh, my, this is delicious, Hannah," the bishop said. "Looks like you're going to make Levi a mighty fine wife after all."

"It's amazing what you can accomplish when someone believes in you," she said. "But Levi has promised to cook too."

The wedding guests gathered outside the building to give their blessings to Levi and Hannah as they passed by them. The ceremony had been beautiful. Friends from Pennsylvania, as well as the professional baseball community, had come to celebrate the union of Levi Troyer and Hannah Weaver. The newlyweds waved to their guests, hundreds of them, and then climbed into their shiny new buggy, a gift from David and John.

"Come on," Levi said, giving the reins a snap. Hannah's horse Dreamer raised his head, snorted a time or two, and then took off like he could sense the joyful occasion. Someone had even tied baseballs to the back of the buggy, and they bounced up and down behind it as it made its way down onto the road and through town. Everyone chanced a guess as to who had done it, naming all the likely suspects. Charley the blacksmith was at the top of the list.

Baseball meant something different to the Troyer family now. It wasn't a source of contention or jealousy. It wasn't a way to prove one's worth in playing it or one's piety in resisting it. It was just baseball—a sport most Americans loved more than any other. Even the Amish.

৵

Within their first year of marriage, Levi accomplished all he'd promised. He made a new baseball field, and he and Hannah coached the local Amish and Mennonite baseball teams together, winning all the local tournaments. As the years continued to pass, Levi and Hannah also fulfilled that other promise to David—the one about having a whole baseball team of grandchildren. They almost accomplished it on their own with five—the infield positions anyway. But then John and Ruth married too, and filled in the outfield positions and the shortstop with their four.

Leaving behind whatever fouls or strike-outs, wins or losses they each had suffered, the Troyers faced the future with hope. They'd all made it through their season of testing and fiery trials. And they were better for it. Closer for it. And in the end, it was the whole Troyer family that had finally made it home.

EPILOGUE

Some years later, while Levi and Hannah were shopping at Walmart, they walked by the magazine aisle. Levi had trained himself to avert his eyes from the sports magazines, just to avoid any temptation. But neither could avert their ears from overhearing the conversation between two men who were thumbing through the periodicals while no doubt taking a break from their wives' shopping.

"Hey, Hank, did you see this?" the first man said.

"What's that, George?"

"Well, I guess they opened an exhibit at the Baseball Hall of Fame for that Amish pitcher."

"Is that so?"

"That's what it says. Looky here . . ."

George handed the magazine over for Hank to take a look.

"That might be worth seeing some time," George said.

The men didn't recognize Levi, who'd grown a full beard now and was toting three impeccably dressed Amish children in the basket—his three youngest. If the men had recognized him, they might have gotten up the nerve to ask him to autograph the magazine for them, right then and there. Or to get their picture taken with him, which he would have to decline due to his Amish rules, now that he'd joined the church. But they didn't ask for any of that. They simply talked until their wives appeared at the end of the aisle to retrieve them, and then the two men left.

When they'd turned the corner, Hannah reached for the magazine herself and opened it to the same article the men had been reading. It wasn't a long piece, so it didn't take long to read. When she was done, she handed it to Levi. This is what it said:

"The Baseball Hall of Fame is proud to announce the opening of the Levi Troyer Exhibit to celebrate the Amish ballplayer's outstanding contribution to the world of baseball and his record-making no-hitter games and fast pitch. Troyer left baseball to return to his Amish community, but his time in our world and his comeback in life has been an inspiration to all of us, both on and off the field. Picking yourself up and finding your way back—now *that* is a real hero."

Levi was too moved to speak.

"Did you read it to the end?" Hannah asked.

"Not yet."

"You need to read it all."

Levi read about the hours of operation, the cost of entrance, and a brief accounting of his baseball stats. Then he got to the last sentence.

"The exhibit is being funded by a private donor who wishes to remain anonymous. But reliable sources tell us that it was Levi's twin brother, John Troyer."

ACKNOWLEDGMENTS

Portions of THE HOME GAME were written in each location where THE HOME GAME musical will be playing:
The Blue Gate Garden Inn, Shipshewana, Indiana
The Carlisle Inn in Sugar Creek, Ohio
The Bird in Hand Family Inn, Bird in Hand, Pennsylvania

Thanks to Mel and June Riegsecker of The Blue Gate Theater, whose vision to produce faith-based Broadway-style musicals in Amish country, has been beyond amazing, fun, and has touched so many lives.

Thanks to Dan Posthuma (Producer) and Wally Nason (Composer/Director), my partners on the creative team of Blue Gate Musicals. The Home Game is our fifth hit musical. We are each so thankful for God's blessings and to all of you who have supported our efforts and encouraged us along the way. And thanks to Russ, Sara, and Lori, our spouses, who have stood by our sides and shared our calendars. A special thanks to Jaime Janiszewski for her help in staging the production of The Home Game, Russell Mauldin for his incredible arrangements and orchestrations, and to Robert Dragotta for his endless encouragement.

Thanks to Sylvia Shayler, Andy Rohrer, and all the staff at the Blue Gate Restaurant and Theater, hotel and shops.

Thanks to the Smucker Family of the Bird in Hand Family Inn, Restaurant and Theater.

And also to the Dutchman Hospitality Group and everyone at the Ohio Star Theater and the Carlisle Inn and shops.

Thanks to all the actors who have done a phenomenal job bringing the stories and characters to life on these stages.

Thanks to Greg Johnson and Keely Boeving for their faith in this book, and to Kathi Mills, my longtime friend, for her editorial services.

Thanks to everyone who has ever said an encouraging word to me throughout my writing career and life journey.

Thanks to those faithful friends and family members who have been there through it all. I appreciate you so much!

And with a heart full of gratitude in memory of my sister Melva, who always believed I could do this.

ABOUT THE PUBLISHER

FH Publishers is a division of FaithHappenings.com

FaithHappenings.com is the premier, first-of-its kind, online Christian resource that contains an array of valuable local and national faith-based information all in one place. Our mission is "to inform, enrich, inspire and mobilize Christians and churches while enhancing the unity of the local Christian community so they can better serve the needs of the people around them." FaithHappenings.com will be the primary i-Phone, Droid App/Site and website that people with a traditional Trinitarian theology will turn to for national and local information to impact virtually every area of life.

The vision of FaithHappenings.com is to build the vibrancy of the local church with a true "one-stop-resource" of information and events that will enrich the soul, marriage, family, and church life for people of faith. We want people to be touched by God's Kingdom, so they can touch others FOR the Kingdom.

Find out more at www.faithhappenings.com.

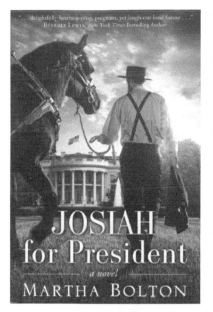

When former Congressman Mark Stedman throws in the towel on his presidential campaign, his only choice is to return to his home state and decide how to spend the rest of his life ... until he meets Josiah Stoltzfus, an Amish farmer from Pennsylvania.

Stedman learns more from Josiah in a few hours than in his many years in office. He comes to the conclusion that someone like Josiah should be running the country. Not a career politician, but someone with a little old-fashioned common sense, someone who's not afraid of rolling up his sleeves and getting his hands dirty. Someone like Josiah Stoltzfus.

Using his old campaign headquarters for a base, Mark Stedman determines to introduce a new candidate to America. He pledges to do everything in his power to make sure Josiah gets elected. But can a plain man of faith turn the tide of politics and become the leader of America, and what will he have to risk to do it?